The approaching sound flooded Germanicus's head. The fingers of his right hand fumbled for his sword. Then, it was on him. A screech from the thing made Germanicus reel backward and totter on his heels. Two ruby eyes, round and huge with cruel wisdom, bored through him. He felt sharp, broken teeth rake across his forehead. Drops of blood collected in his eyelashes and trickled down the bridge of his nose. For the first time in a thousand combats Germanicus feared he might petrify with terror . . .

KIRK MITCHELL

Procurator

ACE BOOKS, NEW YORK

This is a work of fiction. Names, characters, places, and incidents are either the product of the author's imagination or are used fictitiously, and any resemblance to actual persons, living or dead, business establishments, events, or locales is entirely coincidental.

PROCURATOR

An Ace Book / published by arrangement with
the author

PRINTING HISTORY
Ace Original / April 1984

All rights reserved.
Copyright © 1984 by Kirk Mitchell
Cover art by Jim Gurney
This book may not be reproduced in whole or in part,
by mimeograph or any other means, without permission.
For information address: The Berkley Publishing Group,
a division of Penguin Putnam Inc.,
375 Hudson Street, New York, New York 10014.

ISBN: 0-441-68029-1

Ace Books are published by The Berkley Publishing Group,
a division of Penguin Putnam Inc.,
375 Hudson Street, New York, New York 10014.

PRINTED IN THE UNITED STATES OF AMERICA

10 9 8 7 6 5 4 3 2

CHAPTER I

WHEN LAST SEEN alive, the sentry had been pacing up and down the Firat Station platform. The February chill sucked the steam out of his mouth. He looked over his shoulder from time to time, watching for the Bosporus–Parthia rail-galley to slip past in pneumatic silence.

Perhaps he had been dreaming of leaving this place. Duty in the east of Anatolia was not good. All the action was in the Novo Provinces against the newly discovered barbarians. And the girls here were too hobbled by their strange religion to be any fun.

When the rail-galley was gone in a blur of green, red, and white lights, the sentry was found face down on the ice. He was as dead as carrion. But there were no marks on his body.

Within the hour the rumor scampered through the Firat garrison that the soldier had bled to death through the tips of his hair and that his eyeballs had burst in their sockets like overripe pomegranates. Within two hours it was alleged that one of the barbarian *zaims,* or holy men, had *massed* against the legionary.

And *massing* was what the Romans at those snow-blasted

1

outposts along the Great Artery feared most that winter.

As chance would have it, Germanicus Julius Agricola, the military governor of Anatolia, was two hours out from Nova Antiochia when his rail-galley squealed into Firat Station for refueling. This did much for the morale of the men, who thought Germanicus had come on account of the *massing*. Actually, he was beginning a month-long inspection tour.

Germanicus stepped out onto the platform to stretch his legs and was met by a frantic "Hail, Procurator!" from a large number of soldiers clustered around the station.

Germanicus turned to his adjutant, the Parthian Marcellus. "Colonel, find out what stirs here."

"Aye, Procurator."

Then Germanicus began pacing back and forth—just as the now dead legionary had been doing a few hours before. The procurator was a stocky man of fifty years. He had always been solid-looking, and his childhood friends had nicknamed him Taurus, the bull. He had frank hazel eyes that made men immediately wish they had done better for him—even if they had given their best.

Yet for all the authority he exuded, there was wry humor, even a little self-effacing sadness to his mouth.

Colonel Marcellus came racing back from garrison headquarters, ten steps ahead of his breath, which hung in the air.

"Well?" Germanicus asked.

"A *massing*. The men think one of the local *zaims* killed a legionary."

"What *zaim* is suspected?"

"The eldest holy man of Firat village," Marcellus said. "Shall I order his crucifixion?"

"No, wait. Summon my surgeon. Let's see the body."

A few minutes later Germanicus, Marcellus, and the procurator's Greek physician, Epizelus, were slogging through knee-high snow toward the legionaries' bath, where the body was being kept until a priest of Isis could arrive from the provincial capital. Yellow steam roiled along the ceiling. The deceased was laid out on a bench beside the soaking pool. One eye was a quarter open.

"Is it a bona fide case?" Germanicus asked in a whisper, because five or six legionaries milling around the place were hanging on every word he said.

The doctor frowned. "Intent cannot be deduced from human

tissue, Procurator. Can rape be proved from traces of semen?"

"I'm not a jurist. I asked for an answer—yes or no."

"Patience, sir." Epizelus turned to a German centurion who was pouring water on hot stones. "Who is the deceased?"

"He be Gaius Paulus, sir."

"His age?"

"Twenty-four."

"Any diseases you know of?"

"Aye, syphilis in Ephesus this summer."

Epizelus shook his bald head and said to Germanicus, "How many times must I ask you to close down those damned places on the coast?"

"And have rape against the Anatolians increase tenfold?" Germanicus silently watched the doctor prop open the eyes of the dead man, thump his white chest, lift his genitals with frank fingers. "What else can you tell, Epizelus?"

"This is a Roman adult of twenty-four or -five years, approximately one hundred and eighty pounds, six feet," he answered.

"Is that all? I can see that much for myself."

"I will need permission for a dissection."

"You have it."

"And some privacy in which to work."

"Everyone out!" Germanicus barked.

"Including you, Procurator," the doctor said. "Colonel Marcellus may remain to record my observations—with your consent, of course."

Outside, the winter night stinging his nostrils, Germanicus studied the centurion. Hot mist rose off the man's uniform. It looked as if he were smoldering under his clothes. "What is your name, centurion?"

"Rolf, sir."

"A good name. Are you a good soldier?"

"Aye," he answered gravely.

"Come show me where this happened."

Near the station a group of soldiers stood off by themselves, smoking lungweed. They were veterans, by the looks of them. A raw voice asked, "Procurator, what struck down the lad?"

Germanicus smiled. "Flatulence."

"Sir?"

"Wind. I will reprimand the cooks."

Their laughter still had worry in it. But Germanicus knew

he had started a counterrumor. How could it be an authentic *massing* if the procurator himself was joking about it?

A spot of light arced up into the sky and exploded into a shower of sparks. "Flares already tonight?" Germanicus asked.

"Aye, sir," Rolf said. "All night, every night now—to keep the wrapheads from sneaking up to the Artery. We never know when the next attack be coming."

Germanicus carried vinegar in his canteen. It was the soldier's drink of three thousand years of campaigns and occupations. Nothing slaked the thirst like it. He offered some to Rolf, who drained half the vessel.

The German spit most of what he had drunk into the snow. "Not wine. If I be procurator, it would be Gaul wine."

Germanicus laughed. As supreme commander of Anatolia, he governed three hundred thousand square miles. His jurisdiction incorporated the ancient provinces of Galatia and Cappadocia, plus the defunct kingdom of Armenia. Had the Emperor not abolished the office long ago in the bloody wake of the Proconsular Conspiracy, Germanicus would have been the foremost proconsul in the Empire. But he still had vinegar in his canteen.

"What kind of legionary was this fellow Paulus?" Germanicus asked.

The German shrugged before speaking—which indicated some kind of problem he did not wish to name. "He be all right. Good with both the *pilum* and the blade."

"Did he like women?"

"No women here, sir, what be willing."

"Was it boys, centurion?"

The man said nothing.

Germanicus frowned. "So that's what got the *zaim* after him."

They bounded up the steps to the platform. In the station light, Germanicus got a better look at the centurion.

Here was a scrapper, to be sure. Well over six feet tall, the German was stoutly built without packing a dram of fat on his ribs. The backs of his ruddy hands were freckled with gold, like salmon skin, and he had full, blond mustaches. The veteran knew just how to stand in the presence of a superior without surrendering an inch of his own calm dignity.

"How long in service, centurion?" Germanicus asked.

"Twenty years, sir."

"Where have you served the Emperor?"

"First, four years with the guard in Rome."

"Aye." Germanicus nodded appreciatively. The centurion looked spit and polish enough to have been with the Emperor's own.

"Then I transfer to the Sixth Legion."

"Why?" Germanicus asked.

"To go home to Germania and see my father die. Three years there. Four in campaigns against the new barbarians."

"How did you find them?"

"The copper bastards be absolute masters of the ambush," the German said respectfully. "Then three years in Hibernia."

"My old command with the Third, then?"

"No, after you, sir."

"Ah, and what did I leave you men?" This was a weathervane question. Germanicus could sense the man's instant discomfort. Hibernia was a mess no matter who governed it. This German was too salty a dog to go stepping on toes, but too old a soldier to bother buttering anyone up. "Were things improved on the island?" Germanicus asked.

"I was glad to be gone, sir." Rolf stopped in a circle of light on the platform and took a moment to get his bearings. "This be where I was standing. And Paulus be directly across the Artery from me." The legionary's last position was now obscured by the procuratorial rail-galley.

Germanicus looked around as if there might be some material fact dangling in the air like a spider. "How did Paulus seem at supper?"

"No change from usual."

"Was he irritable?"

"No more than always."

Germanicus leading the way, they passed through the rail-galley to the opposite platform where the legionary had been pacing. There was nothing but a light reddish spot on the ice where the man had fallen. "Did you see Paulus just before the rail-galley came between you?"

"I did."

"And what was he doing?"

Crow's-feet sprouted at the outer corners of the centurion's eyes. "He be looking at the rail-galley, what be coming quick. But all of a sudden he look behind him—like somebody creeping up to surprise him. Then the Bos–Parthian come between us. Next, the rail-galley be gone, and Paulus be dead and down."

"What did you do?"

"I sound the alarm."

Colonel Marcellus crossed through the rail-galley with heat in his face. "Procurator!"

"Do you have news?"

"Aye," the colonel said gravely. In the naked overhead light he was a ramrod-straight figure with a hawkish nose and moist, brooding eyes the color of cork bark. His gloved fingers were like plumes of white feathers—royalty ran through his Parthian ancestry.

"Wait in my quarters," Germanicus instructed Marcellus, then looked hard at Rolf. "What do you think of this *massing* business?"

"It just *be,* sir. Two days before tonight, this *zaim* went 'bout like a cock, boasting he be ready to kill a Roman without laying a finger on him."

"What is the talk in the barracks?"

"The men say the *zaim* did it for sure. No doubt in their mind, Procurator." The centurion squeezed his brow into furrows. "This be my advice—don't let the *zaims* get back their old power."

"I have no intention of allowing that. As for you, get your kit and advise your tribune you'll be attached to my staff until I say otherwise."

"Sir, my tribune be a very young officer what don't know his way about yet."

"You have your orders, centurion."

The man jolted to attention.

"Board my rail-galley within the half hour. Dismissed."

The German trotted down the platform to keep the deadline, his drooping mustaches adding to the impression that he was miserable. Staff duty was no assignment for a man who loved the field. Especially *procuratorial* duty.

Marcellus rose from the couch when Germanicus entered the car, despite the fact that the procurator muttered, "As you were, as you were."

"Epizelus has come up with certain findings of interest, sir."

"Such as?"

"The legionary's venereal disease was in remission. It was not a factor in his death."

"That will please his parents. What else?"

"What the man did die from is called an aneurysm."

"Which is?" Germanicus asked, reclining on his own couch and taking a sip of vinegar from his canteen.

"As best as I can describe it, sir, a section of blood vessel in Paulus' head ballooned out and exploded."

"Charicles, bring the colonel some wine," Germanicus called to his aged manservant. "Odd way for a young fellow to die, what, Marcellus? Did you mention *massing* again for me?"

"I did. The doctor knows of no such thing in medical science. He asks that you refer such 'ethereal questions' to Colonel Crispa."

There was silence between the men at the mention of the woman.

Charicles padded down the aisle from the smoky mess, the tip of his tongue protruding from the corner of his mouth as he balanced a wine serving set on a tray. "Good evening to you, gentlemen." He smiled as if he had made a jest. But it was not his own remark that amused him. It was Marcellus' reference to Crispa.

The old man had been listening to Marcellus and Germanicus for some minutes. He was certain that he alone knew that both these officers loved the pale, blonde Scandian beauty. And no wonder: for all her high rank, she was a sensual girl with alluring, nearly haunted eyes—aquamarine in color. "Will there be anything else, Procurator?"

"Nothing for me. We'll be taking a centurion on with us. See that he has a place to bunk."

"Would this be the German?" Charicles asked with distaste.

Germanicus patted the stooped back of the servant. "Suffer change cheerfully, old friend. It's the only way I know to have peace of mind."

"But a *German*, sir."

Marcellus emptied his cup in a single draught. "Well, I must be off to check on the refueling. Any further orders, sir?"

"Yes, find out where the hades Crispa is."

"At once, Procurator."

Alone, Germanicus unhitched his breastplate and laid it aside. He had felt foolish with Marcellus. It angered him that his feelings for Crispa showed, although they had been transparent ever since she had appeared at his headquarters in Hibernia, a thin tribune with eyes too large for her face, much too knowing for her years. She had seemed to him the beautiful daughter of another world, arrived in the Empire only to be unblinkingly fascinated by all around her.

But the procurator had never set the wheels of his affection into motion. He had a keen sense of how, once started, the momentum of these passions could not be slowed.

And he had a wife in Ostia. Her health was delicate. He would not buy his pleasure at the price of her pain.

Two more months and he would be back home, retired. This would be for the better. He would let the days trickle away as he sat at the point of the headland, under the olive tree whose leaves in winter were scorched by the salt spray. It was here his son's ashes were hidden. He had lied to his wife, Virgilia, saying that the young tribune's ashes had been sprinkled over the Tiber at its outlet. This was so she would have no spot on which to focus her grief.

But as his time of service became shorter, his resolve to leave Crispa untouched became as taut as a bowstring pulled to its limit. Not that he lacked willpower. When it was brought to his attention that he was spending too many of his free evenings in his cups, he quit wine and never again touched anything stronger than vinegar. Furthermore, when Epizelus told him that continued smoking of lungweed might do away with the need for a pension, Germanicus took the clay pipe from his mouth and smashed it.

It was almost as if he enjoyed parting from things he desired.

His fidelity had become a comic legend; the legionaries under his command had composed a ballad in which Germanicus, upon finding both Helen and Cleopatra nude in his chamber—"a brace of lovelies," as it went—severely warned both that there'd be no wrestling in his bed.

All would have been simpler had Crispa not told him how she felt about him.

It had happened during the Hibernian civil war. Germanicus was ordering an inspection of a garrison on the west coast of the island when a troubled look crossed Crispa's face. This tribune was ordinarily so dutiful and eager to please, Germanicus stopped talking, then asked, "What is it?"

"Do—do not go, sir."

"What?"

"Not today," she said, her eyes now moist with embarrassment.

Germanicus smiled so the others would not become infected with whatever was upsetting her. People who must endure invisible dangers day after day become as superstitious as shepherds. "Come, tribune," he said cheerfully, "you ride in my sand-galley." As he had led the way down the marble steps of his headquarters, a momentary illusion had startled him: the sun had a drop of blood in it.

Charicles knocked on the bulkhead with his brittle knuckles. "Procurator!"

Germanicus was jarred from his memories. "Yes?" His heart was already racing because of the edge on the old man's voice.

"Marcellus sees fire to the north!"

"Where is he?"

"On your *ballistae* defense deck."

Germanicus rushed down the aisle, then drummed up the metal stairs to the platform on the rear of his car. Marcellus was staring off over the snow-blanketed roof of the station.

"Intermittent high explosive flashes right over the station antenna, sir."

"When was the last one?"

"Forty seconds ago."

Germanicus leaned his forearms on the railing. "Who in the name of Mars can be engaged up there?"

Marcellus made no reply.

"You don't think . . . do you?" the procurator asked.

"The wireless operator has been tapping out her signature for the last ten minutes—as ordered. No answer."

Suddenly there were orange bonfires that had dazzling lives of a few seconds, and then deep-throated crackling from the darkness.

This was always how a revolt began: One isolated Roman unit taking it on the nose and giving the barbarians a cheap victory. Nausea cut a riptide across the lining of Germanicus' stomach. He had not wanted to give her a field command. "Get down to the communications car, Marcellus, and personally direct the scan. Those bastards couldn't find thunder with an ear trumpet."

"Aye, sir."

Charicles brought him a marten cloak and a large cup of

warmed vinegar. "She can take care of herself, good sir," the old man whispered.

"Jupiter, I hope so." Germanicus savored the bitter liquid. There were more orange flashes in the north.

They were the same color as those he had seen outside the sand-galley window that day in Hibernia when he had ignored Crispa's warning and gone on the inspection tour anyway. Within seconds the sand-galley had been reduced to a scorched hulk on the road. Crispa and he had barely escaped the flames through the rear hatch, their hair singed.

They were caught in an ambush so fierce they simply huddled against a stone wall and waited to die. The blasting of the *pili* and the hiss-aah-hiss-aah of the Greek firers, which squirted oily bolts of flame across the sky, combined in a noise like cascading water.

Crispa's eyes were hard on his.

Suddenly a tribune and a centurion gave up their cover and stumbled across a rocky potato field, hoping to outflank the mass of attackers. But an arc of fire hissed out of a copse and embraced them with flaming arms. They collapsed as if they were made of sparrow bones and rice paper. In minutes there was nothing left of them.

"Damn!" Germanicus growled.

"It's all right. . . ." Crispa kept repeating to him. ". . . All right . . . all . . ."

A handful of legionaries decided their chances were better anywhere other than where they crouched, and as a single frightened body, leaped up and ran away from the blood splattered road.

"No!" Germanicus shouted. "Stay here, lads!"

But it was too late to save them from the *pili* hailstorm. Germanicus closed his eyes. Then he filled his sight with Crispa and smiled hopelessly. "If ever again, tribune, if ever again . . ."

Several yards distant, a wave of Greek fire surged over the wall. Germanicus felt this man-made *simoom* blow in front of his face. He thought of Carthage in the summer, freshly cut melons dripping in the hot sunlight, the eager eyes of the Numidian whores . . .

Crispa rested her fawnskin cheek against the back of his hand. She kissed his fingers. "I love you, Germanicus Julius Agricola."

"Pipes, *pipes!*" the legionaries along the wall began crying, making the unlikely couple jerk back from each other.

How flushed she looked moments later when they were rescued by a century of Pict irregulars returning from a fortnight's leave in a state brothel. The hundred soldiers tripped over the hems of their woolen skirts as they stumbled along, but they were still savagely disposed enough to put the Hibernians to flight.

Germanicus ignored Crispa as he took charge of the separation of slaves from those who, because of their ingrained surliness, were fit only to be crucified on the spot.

For days after the ambush he had been careful not to look her way.

Now over the snowy roof of the Firat Station the northern sky lit up like dawn. Germanicus winced. A sand-galley had been demolished. *Let it not be hers*, he silently prayed to Juno.

In Hibernia he had learned things about Crispa more shocking than her love for him.

Two months after the attack on the road, she and two of her fellow officers had been kidnapped from an inn by Iberian mercenaries who, fed up with service on the gloomy island, revolted to the man. The first tribune, a dark-eyed girl with Etruscan lineage, was bled to death in sight of the others. The second, the renowned Scilla, suffered torture without betraying the location of a reserve armory. His courage impressed the rebels; it alone saved his life.

Crispa was sexually abused.

During the endless undulations of the Iberians' lust, she cried out that their leader would break out in sores, bleed from every orifice of his body, and vomit the sacs of his lungs before the night was done. Strangely enough, the man took sick shortly before dawn. His fickle comrades took no chances. They beheaded him in renewed obedience to the Emperor Fabius and a nineteen-year-old Scandian tribune with aquamarine eyes.

It was the first Germanicus had ever heard of *massing*.

Marcellus came pounding up the stairs. "It's her," he said, out of breath.

"What does she have with her?"

"Some armor and a handful of praetorian instructors. But it's a training century. Green as grass."

"How are they doing?"

"Their wireless operator is too excited for me to tell. It's either a triumph or a rout."

Germanicus sighed. "Very well. What do they have here at Firat?"

"Three armored centuries, four infantry, I believe."

"Good, we'll need the sand-galleys. Contact the commander. Requisition two of the armored groups and start north. By the way, where *is* the commander?"

"In his quarters all evening. Not feeling well."

"We'll see if fresh air improves him. Put him in the lead sand-galley—my orders." Germanicus knew that the first armored craft in a formation was most likely to be firebombed. "Bypass Firat village. I will deal with this *zaim* later."

"Aye." Marcellus' gaze darted between the distant battle and Germanicus' face. The colonel licked his lips. "And where will you be, sir?"

"The flashes are moving northeast. I'll take this rail-galley east twenty miles, detrain my sand-galley, and head north from there."

"Your safety concerns me. Perhaps the Empire would be better served if I went on this reconnaissance."

"Now what harm could possibly befall me with that magnificent beast at my side?" Germanicus gestured toward the German centurion, who came grumbling across the icy stones of the platform toward the procuratorial car, his kit hoisted over his shoulder. "Are you ready to fight, man?" Germanicus called down to him.

"Hail Kaiser!"

CHAPTER II

"THERE HE BE!" Rolf shouted. In his excitement he stamped the iron plates of the armored vehicle with his foot.

"Turn right," Germanicus ordered the operator, who began twisting the guidance lever as if trying to wrestle a tree trunk out of the ground.

"Again he be!" Rolf cried. "Hard right!"

Germanicus and the centurion crouched at the crystal window on the prow deck of the sand-galley. Their breaths kept fogging the surface of the laminated quartz sheets, making the snowy plain outside appear watery.

Germanicus had last seen *ballistae* fire in the distant north ten minutes before. But now he had stopped looking for it. He and his two comrades were in their own hot water.

"Left now!" Germanicus barked.

"Left, sir?" the operator asked.

"Hard left, hard left!"

"Aye, sir!" The operator had no lateral vision from his seat in the bowels of the craft. The sand-galley was not designed to chase firebombers across the Anatolian plain at night.

"This one tires." Rolf swiped at the window with his sleeve.

"Fire coming from right!" Germanicus barely had time to warn the operator to clang shut the air intake before broken glass tinkled against the hull. The world outside throbbed in orange flame. Within seconds, the right bulkheads were too hot to touch.

"Are we losing our air?" the operator kept asking. "Are we losing air?"

"There be the bastard what pitched it, sir!" Rolf growled.

"Let's not be played with, centurion. One at a time."

"Are we losing air?" The operator's voice was now a dry rasp.

"No, man. It held," Germanicus replied. "Half left."

"Half left, sir." Then the operator added as if he'd known all along, "Intake was closed when we took it. And it was smack against the vent!"

"Look at the poor fool run. He should just lie down in the drifts and let us pass." Germanicus shook his head. "Hard left, hard, hard!"

The runner churned the snow behind him. His half-frozen rags fluttered in the blizzard. He glanced back at the sand-galley, which was gaining on him. His face was pinched by the cold. He looked back again—and again.

"Faster!" Rolf shouted.

"All I've got, all I've got," the operator apologized.

"He pulls away from us again." Rolf appeared ready to leap off the deck and throttle the operator. "Faster!"

"Here's how to slow him down," Germanicus said. "Legionary, turn off your lights."

"Aye, sir."

The seconds ticked off in blackness.

"Now back on."

The runner stood flat-footed in front of their prow. First confused, then elated, by the sudden darkness, he had stopped bolting across the snow. Now he saw how he had been tricked. There was no hope left, and the panic dribbled from his eyes. He showed the palms of his hands to the roaring sand-galley. It was the greeting of a man who knew he was about to die.

There was a thump against the forward armor plates. Then Germanicus felt only the smooth glide of the tracks over the blanketed land.

Rolf stroked his mustaches with agitated fingers. "One."

"Take the second barbarian with the *ballista*," Germanicus said. "That will warn any others out there not to toy with us."

Rolf climbed into the cramped turret a half level above the prow deck.

"Begin concentric circling," Germanicus ordered the operator.

"Circles inward, aye."

"Let's give our bomber a 'Gift from Gaul,' centurion." Germanicus handed the German a flat-nosed missile from the magazine.

"Ah, *fléchettes*," Rolf grunted.

The foil-skin canister contained five hundred tungsten darts. Each was the shape of a tiny arrow, so sharp it could nearly slip through a man's hand by virtue of its own gravity. Originally they had been dipped in hemlock and called "Cupid's Kick," but the poison proved superfluous, and they were too vicious a weapon to keep so affectionate a nickname.

The operator slowed to change gears.

"Don't let up!" Germanicus blasted at him. "Do you want to be cremated?"

Rolf squinted against the glare of lights on the snow. His task required extreme skill. The sand-galley had been personally designed as a siege weapon by Emperor Fabius. It was equipped with a single piece of artillery, but the placement of supports in the frame of the craft limited the rotation and elevation of this *ballista* to a few degrees. It had been assumed that the target would always be stationary, dead ahead.

"There he is!" Germanicus cried. "Forty-five right!"

"Forty-five right, aye!"

Rolf's field of vision, less wide than the operator's, was no more than a bouncing spot of light against the darkness. He sweated at his station, and his face took on a red cast. All the heat from the engine and the flashfire attack had collected in the elevated turret.

"Left, left, and we've got him." Germanicus pressed his fingertips against the bulkheads until the blood went out of them.

"Left, left! Give me a bigger piece of him!" Rolf screamed, thrusting his face against the twin grommets of the optical aimer. "Ach, the bloody lens be steamed!"

"Check for defroster failure, legionary!" Germanicus hoarsely whispered. "And left now too!"

"Defrosters are back ordered, Procurator."

"Magnificent." Germanicus took an unsatisfying breath. "Is intake open?"

"I be dizzy!" Rolf cried like a man who has but a few seconds left in his life.

The operator was slouching deeper and deeper in his seat. "I kept them shut, sir. I—I thought because of the immediate . . . the immediate threat . . ."

"Open it!" Germanicus crouched on the deck and shouted in the legionary's colorless face. "Open air intake!"

"Aye . . . aye . . ." His limp fingers floated toward the control.

Then a gush of cold, sweet air began to revive them.

"Fire coming!" Rolf pounded the bulkheads with his fists to get their attention. "The bastard be lighting a bomb!"

Germanicus threw himself against the window. "Right at once, man!"

"Right, aye."

Frantically Rolf swung the *ballista* right and left again and again like a man trying to shoot a ghost. "I have no picture. No picture."

"Hard right!"

Then the *ballista* thundered against the night.

Germanicus thought it peculiar how a great noise momentarily blinds a man, thumps the light out of his head. He could see in the next instant, but he was familiar enough with *fléchettes* to know that the petite arrows would seem to disturb nothing in their path. No snow would be kicked up. A man pierced up and down the length of his body would stand fully erect as if spared. Then the horror would dawn on him that he was soaked with blood from five hundred tiny mouths. And he would drop dead as if from the shock alone.

"A miss," Rolf groaned.

"Close intake," Germanicus ordered. "We're going to take another hit." He felt oddly indifferent.

Rolf was shoving a new canister into the breech.

"Orders, sir?" the operator asked.

The *ballista* blasted again, rattling the tinny guts of the sand-galley, and again the German centurion threw up his hands at his luck. "I be cursed!"

"Here it comes," Germanicus said quietly as if he had muttered, "Here comes a butterfly." He closed his eyes. One of these bombs was certain to reach its red fingers into the volatile belly of the craft. Good Jupiter, there were a thousand gallons of fuel aboard. It struck him as funny—a pathetic glimpse of his secret nature—that all this was really just to see Crispa again.

A drop of hot liquid glanced off Germanicus' cheek. He looked up and saw the sweat collected on Rolf's bare elbows.

Like men afraid of scaring off their good fortune by antici-pating it, not one of them wanted to be first to suggest that the firebomb had plopped harmlessly into the snow. But when an eternal minute had passed without the sound of glass shattering against the hull, they all smiled at each other like the custodians of a delicious secret: Life is sweet.

"Direction, sir?"

"I've lost him," Germanicus said. "Wait—movement there. He's gone into a culvert. It's covered over where he popped in. I see now—it's a bridge. Straight ahead. We're on a road."

"Dead on, aye." The operator looked pained. "Sir, these little bridges on back roads won't support our weight."

Germanicus saw that the legionary still had acne. "Yes."

"We were instructed at the Campus Martius—"

"I'm sure you were. Open intake."

"—to call an enemy out of hiding to surrender and—"

"You have your orders!" Rolf bawled from the turret.

"Dead on, aye." The operator's face was now flushed.

Germanicus patted the youth's shoulder. "We learn to adapt everything out here. Even our honor, I suppose."

"Aye, Procurator."

The sand-galley climbed the approach to the bridge. The three men inside the vehicle held their breaths as if their chests were about to be crushed. The prow of the craft sunk a few feet. The operator found its lowest forward gear, then gunned the sand-galley out of the depression it had just formed.

"I can't let fire attacks be made with impunity," Germanicus said.

Rolf muttered, "Two."

"We did this...thing...for the benefit of his friends still out there in the drifts." Germanicus opened his canteen and offered it around. "But, gods of mine, I don't like it. I don't like killing brave men without bloodying my hands."

"Give me the old *pilum* to mix things up, Procurator," Rolf called down, meaning the spear originally of that name and not the powder piece that had replaced it.

Germanicus slapped the centurion's boot. There weren't enough like him. There had never been enough like him. "Keep an eye out. And, legionary, don't let your speed slip. That's how we purchased the last attack."

Then, feeling spent and somewhat ashamed, Germanicus crawled and ducked under machinery and conduit. Avoiding the poorly insulated exhaust tube that was always good for a burn, he made his way aft to his mouse lair of a cabin. He lay down on the five-foot bunk without removing his boots. It was useless to try to get comfortable.

Bad things were on the way. Inexorably, events were grinding toward war in the East. But if this genuinely concerned him, why did he feel a curious relief? Was it that much of a consolation to be back in the field and away from the woolly-headed thinking of Nova Antiochia? Indeed, the only thing the provincial capital had given him was a corn on his middle finger as large as a dove's egg—from writing edicts to keep a ceiling on the price of grain. He knew that the factors snarled at the mention of his name as they swirled spiced wine in gold cups and plotted and plotted. The inflation could be damned as far as they were concerned. Food riots were less of a concern—the legionaries would handle any civil disturbance. It was fitting that Mercury was the god of both tradesmen and thieves. Absently Germanicus took out and rubbed the pendant he wore on a chain around his neck. His wife had given him this gold head of Minerva long ago. The goddess's eyes were emeralds. They sparkled brilliantly.

"Pardons, sir." Rolf stooped at the entry. He looked humble for the first time.

"What is it? More flashes?"

"No, sir. My . . . my old corporal be retired on an Empire tract in these parts. Before, I did not know we would pass so near."

"And you fear for his safety." Germanicus sighed. If Crispa were in real trouble, he could do little with one sand-galley. Effective help would arrive with Marcellus in the late morning. It was his love that drove him north toward the *ballistae* lightning. Germanicus knew he must say yes to Rolf to prove to himself he was still a man of restraint.

"He be a Jew from Palestine," Rolf continued. "With a barbarian wife. But that never be enough in times like these."

"Legionary!" Germanicus bellowed.

"Sir!" the operator replied from the forward section.

"Steer as the centurion commands."

"You are truly of the House of Julius." Rolf's eyes became soft with moisture. "You be born in Germania?"

"At Mogontiacum, where my father was serving. Wake me when we arrive at this tract."

"Aye, Germanicus Julius Agricola."

Germanicus closed his eyes. All sound faded from his ears.

As he napped he dreamed of Crispa's mother. He had never known her. But in the dream he could see the silvery hair that frosted the horizons of her face. As she turned her head against the Scandian summer sun, he recognized her to be the fountainhead of Crispa's beauty.

Germanicus had known Crispa's father from school days. He remembered him as an agreeable but moody boy who liked wine too much even at a tender age.

But it was her handsome Scandian mother who appeared again and again to him in his fitful sleep. Sometimes she begged him to save her daughter. He did not know what this meant. "Dear woman," his hollow dream voice said to her, "I can only do what I can do."

Her husband had served as the Emperor's envoy to the throne of Mithridates XIV. She had been no match for the vicious intrigue of the Parthian court. She killed herself after a tryst with her barbarian lover was betrayed by a jealous slave.

Often Crispa traded places with her mother in these dreams. And her lover became Marcellus, Germanicus' Parthian adjutant.

Germanicus had never been told directly that Crispa and Marcellus were lovers. To ask even Charicles would have been beneath the procurator's station. So he lived on the tongue-tattered edges of a rumor. Confirmation of it, he was certain, might break his heart and kill him. He could not stand the thought of her being with another man—especially one as arrogant as Marcellus. In secret, Germanicus loved her that jealously.

Again her mother's face shimmered against the waves of his sleep. "We have survived . . . though my heart . . . is wracked," she said, her voice deeper than usual.

"What . . . what do you . . . ?" Germanicus mumbled.

". . . survived . . . my heart is wracked . . ."

"Wracked?"

"No, *tract*, sir. We be arrived at the *tract*."

Germanicus blinked into Rolf's stare. "How does the place look?"

"No light shows from the windows."

"That can be a good sign. Your corporal is being careful."

The forward hatch was stuck from the heat of the firebomb. It took both their shoulders to pry it open.

Outside, the winter air made Germanicus cringe in his cloak. Silently Rolf laid his *pilum* on the topside deck. Then he muscled up on his long arms and swung his legs over the top. He lowered a hand to help Germanicus, who refused it with a grin.

The operator had parked the sand-galley directly in front of the dun-colored house so the *ballista* could blast the door if needed. The turret now clattered over an oil-thirsty track as the legionary lined up the optical aimer.

Germanicus waited on his haunches beside Rolf.

"Nothing moves," Rolf said, his words hanging in the air as if frozen there.

"They might think we're barbarians."

"Aaron knows the sound of a galley."

Somehow they didn't feel the need to announce themselves. Their hope of finding the retired corporal alive was thin.

Rolf stood at the ready, *pilum* locked in his hands, while Germanicus thrust the heel of his boot against the brass latch. In a shower of splinters, the door gave.

Instantly both men ducked inside—all who served in Hibernia quickly learned this way to enter hostile houses.

Behind them the door groaned shut on the wind. Then there was unnatural silence.

The interior of the room was completely black. Germanicus flicked on a hand torch. Its round beam bounced around the walls.

"The table!" Rolf stumbled backward.

The torch sputtered and went out. Frantically Germanicus tapped it against his palm. But it was no good.

A coal popped in the hearth. Germanicus felt his throat close. He threw open the door. Fed by the air that gushed in, a bright lick of flame squirmed out of the embers. In seconds the fire came back to life. The room glowed in russet.

"Aaron!" Rolf cried. His eyes had become goose eggs.

Without knowing he had done so, Germanicus had drawn his short sword.

They had collapsed onto their family table—all except the boy with auburn hair who had leaned back into his chair as if to take a short rest. Their meal of grain and mutton had grown cold.

A moan rose in Rolf's throat. "Aaron, his wife, his sons—how?" He began kneading the front locks of his reddish hair with his fingers. "Where be their wounds?"

"There'll be none. Not a scratch on any of them." Germanicus' torch came back on. He pointed it into the stunned eyes of the Jewish veteran, who seemingly might open his mouth or blink at any moment. Germanicus dared not study the children—three boys by a count from the corner of his eye—for fear he could not bear the sight. In his dreams he somehow forgot that his son had passed the tender grace of ten years and had died in battle at twenty-one.

"Massing. It be a *massing."*

"Perhaps." Germanicus knew it could also be a poisoning, but did not say so. He shared Rolf's conviction.

"Why him? His family?"

"They were the lowest fruit of Rome on the tree. So they were first to be plucked."

"But he be no longer in service!" Rolf seized his friend's head and began sifting through his curly black hair as if searching for a hidden puncture or slash. Then, just as abruptly, he gave up with a groan and strode out the door.

"Jupiter," Germanicus said.

Inside the sand-galley minutes later, Germanicus said to the silent centurion, "I won't have their heads show up in some marketplace for the *zaims* to mock."

"Aye." Rolf nodded and moved aft to be alone.

Germanicus gave the word. The operator ignited the Greek firer. A spray of greasy flame shot toward the dwelling. It rolled through the door in hissing cartwheels and exploded the structure with a crackling roar.

The fire could still be seen when they were twenty miles away. It was grimly beautiful even at that distance.

Germanicus crouched at the prow deck window again, watching for more orange bursts of *ballistae* and flinching each time he saw them.

After a while the murdered family was no longer on his

mind. He was thinking of a time in Sicilia, long before he was married. In the course of complicated maneuvers he had become separated from his century, although he had always suspected his legionaries of sneaking away from their green tribune, barely holding their laughter behind their palms. Tribunes were invariably the pampered sons of rich families—the military rank itself had almost been devalued to an honorific; there were two hundred of them to the legion, as opposed to six in the days of the Republic. Germanicus chanced upon a shepherdess with warm eyes and a liquid smile. With bony hands she drew him into the brush. His fingers fumbled to release his sword belt. It was incredibly foolish of him; she might have been in collusion with bandits.

It was with the same sense of reckless abandon he now slipped into the north of Anatolia.

CHAPTER III

SHORTLY AFTER TWO in the morning Germanicus located Crispa's camp.

And nearly lost his life in the welcome.

As his sand-galley rumbled out of the darkness, Crispa's captain of the guard ordered a barrage of Greek fire. Germanicus' operator scarcely had time to muscle the gears into reverse before wave after wave of flame came out to meet them.

"Rolf!" Germanicus shouted.

"Aye, sir?"

"Try the wireless. Give those fools the watchword." It occurred to Germanicus that the legionaries in the camp might already know the identity of their target. He had always expected to be assassinated, as his father had been. But would Crispa ever allow this treachery? "Back off, legionary, before the idiot in charge decides to train his *ballistae* on us."

And at that instant, huge *ballistae* projectiles began thumping the icy ground around them.

"Son of a whore!" Germanicus covered his ears with his hands and opened his mouth. "Back, lad, back!"

The operator accelerated so quickly, Germanicus was thrown headlong against the window, bloodying his teeth.

"Permission to dice the beggars with *fléchettes*," Rolf requested.

"Denied—for the moment." Germanicus spat red.

The sand-galley scurried back into a stream hollow. The operator cut both lights and engine. The shelling stopped. Germanicus eased up the hatch on a patch of sky with stars clustered as thick as grapes. The wind rustled through the dry grasses along the stream.

"*Vesta ... Vesta*," Rolf kept repeating into the voice tube until the word grew sluggish on his tongue.

"Leave off," Germanicus finally said. "Get up in the turret."

"Aye," Rolf answered eagerly.

"Tell me, is there rumor of a plot against my command?"

Rolf scratched his ear. He never liked to pass on barracks scuttlebutt. And it was dangerous to slander anyone in the Roman world. Yet he sensed that this might be different. "Aye, but these troops in Firat District be loyal."

"Who then wants me out of the way?"

"It all be just talk, Procurator." Then Rolf escaped into the turret and did not glance back down.

The operator looked sick with fear. It had been a long night for a new man. "What—will happen next, sir?"

"They'll send out a patrol—sappers probably—to try to blow us up."

"But we're *Romans*."

"Thank Mars, at least someone around here knows that." Then Germanicus stood halfway out of the hatch and listened. Ten minutes later he heard footfalls crunching across the snow toward him.

"Legionaries!" Germanicus called out in a calm voice. "We are soldiers of the Empire."

But for the wind, the plain was silent again.

"We have come in a sand-galley to see Colonel Crispa."

There was a snort somewhere out in the snow. A young voice said, "Galley, my buttocks, wrapheadie. We saw you pull up in a Bull Elephant—a Bull Ellie lorry with a mount tied on."

"*Vesta*." Germanicus ground his teeth together. "The challenge is *Vesta*."

Silence.

"Don't you lads know the watchword?"

Sheepishly one of the voices out there said, "We had no time to tap Nova Antiochia for tonight's word. What with you attacking us and all."

"*Shines*. The word is *shines!*" Germanicus slapped his palms against the armor plates. "*Vesta shines!*"

The first voice whispered, "It's *Vesta shines*."

Another whisper argued, "We can't take our bloody watchwords from the wrapheads."

"He sure talks like someone from home."

"Why, the capital's crawling with foreigners what've nothing better to do than learn our habits. At the public expense too."

"Legionaries, legionaries—" Germanicus tried to interrupt in a fatherly tone. The whispers now sounded like arrows being whisked back and forth across the darkness.

"Wait, wait," a new and more assured voice chimed in. "I know how to handle this. I heard it done on public wireless 'fore I joined the sappers." He cleared his throat. "Hey, you there!"

"Germanicus Julius Agricola here."

More insistent whispering: "Do you think it's really him?"

"Well, if it's old Germanicus, the worst he's been known to do is kick a man in the ass."

"You joke!"

"Not one bit. He did it to a legionary in Hibernia."

The youth who had learned to handle this from the public wireless now quashed his comrades with a "Sssh!" that could be heard a mile. "You there, what claims to be the good Procurator Germanicus—" Then he whispered aside to his friends, "That's just in case it happens to be the old bag of shit."

"Yes," Germanicus said wearily.

"Tell me this: How many fights had One-eyed Tullus before he hisself was slain?"

"Fifty-two," Germanicus answered. Gladiatorial contests had been a passion of his youth. "And he was defeated by a fighter nicknamed the Carthaginian because no one in Rome could stand him. He took off Tullus' arm at the elbow with the first blow."

Silence.

Germanicus filled his cheeks with air, then sighed.

Renewed whispering: "Anyone know how many fights Tullus had before what's-his-name from Carthage town hacked off his elbow?"

"You mean you asked and you don't know?"

"Well, I didn't expect him to come up with an answer so quick. Anyone?"

"Tullus fought before I was born!"

"I never even heard of the Carthaginian."

"You, Lartius, go back and ask the cook. He should know. He's almost twenty-three."

Germanicus could take no more. "Listen to me. I will order my operator to turn on our lights. I will then come forward with no weapons. You remain where you are until you are sure who I am. I am coming out now."

Germanicus leaped down into the snow and stamped out from the sand-galley in a blaze of noon.

If he died here, he knew he'd have to hide his face in shame from the Styx ferryman—killed after thirty-two years of service by a gang of excited children.

"Halt, there!" someone said from the right with forced sternness.

"It's him, what? I saw him once in Rome with my mother. Right beside his cousin, old Fabius hisself."

"The procurator was with your mother?"

"No, fool, I was."

A corporal with boils on his forehead came prancing out like a young stag in rut. "Most sorry, Procurator. But we learned our caution at the Campus Martius," he said brightly.

"Allow me to teach you more."

"How's that, sir?"

Germanicus kicked the legionary so hard in the rump the boy came limping back into camp a half hour behind the others.

Near tears, the captain of the guard explained that the wireless man had never passed on the information that Germanicus was coming from the Firat garrison, and that the procurator's sand-galley looked exactly like a captured Bull Elephant, a tracked lorry, the tribesmen had been careening around the plain for the past week.

"Where is Colonel Crispa?" Germanicus asked coldly.

"We have no idea, sir."

"What is going on here?"

"Well, most of our century was out training at dusk when they were ambushed by barbarians. There was bad confusion at first because the boys thought it was just the praetorian instructors dressed up as wrapheads like they do sometimes. But then there were so many of them."

"How many?"

"Dozens."

"Oh, Jupiter." And Germanicus didn't get the meat of the story until a praetorian instructor marched in at the head of a handful of walking wounded. He was admitted into camp without a hitch because everyone knew the bite of his tongue.

"Show's about over. Not that we won, Procurator." The veteran soldier eagerly accepted Germanicus' offer of vinegar. "Two hundred—no more—jumped us at sundown three miles north of here."

"Which way were they headed?"

"South—Artery bound, I'd say. We turned them northeast, and the chase was on. Hard to keep the lads together at this point in their training. Ten killed. More wounded."

"Where is Crispa now?" Germanicus asked.

"Twenty miles northeast. We here rode our transport until it broke down just over the rise."

"Is the colonel well?"

"When I left, aye—and holding the show together too. But they had just come upon some firebombers, most likely covering the retreat of the others. That's when they got one of our galleys. I don't know which one."

"Why were you sent back?"

"The colonel wanted a salt to check on the camp."

Germanicus nodded. "Good. After you've seen to your wounded and rested an hour or two, relieve the captain of the guard. Help is on the way from Firat. I don't want them engaged by our own legionaries—again."

"Aye, sir—Hail Fabius!"

The last orange flash erupted at four. Then the sky went black as oil. Germanicus paced back and forth across the snow beside his sand-galley until he had packed a hard trail of ice.

At five it occurred to him that he might tell her that he loved her. The universe seemed monstrously large and cold under the wilderness sky. And suddenly, telling her seemed like a sensible thing to do.

Finally a pinch of winter dawn showed over the turret of the sand-galley.

Germanicus had just gone back into the craft to warm himself when his scabbard began rattling on a metal shelf. Then he felt the deep vibration in the plates of his skull.

Crispa's century was returning.

He lay down on his bunk and stared out the small porthole.

One by one, like a string of dark beetles, the sand-galleys rolled into the bivouac, took up defensive positions in a wide circle. Operators bled the fuel lines and cut the engines. Then Germanicus could hear the wind soughing through the leafless poplars.

Legionaries began alighting from the sand-galleys. They staggered slightly on cramped legs in the snow. Here and there bodies were hoisted out and wrapped in blankets. Then they were hurried from sight. Germanicus was reminded of ants secreting away their larvae.

How strange for the living to look upon the dead. But how much stranger, Crispa had once said to him, for the dead to look upon the living.

He watched for her without success until his eyes began to burn. That dreadful electricity began to snap along his nerves toward his heart. He had last felt it at the news of his son's death.

Germanicus was preparing to find out where the morgue had been set up when among the silent sand-galleys a hatch clanged open. A blond head showed through it.

Germanicus briefly closed his eyes.

She came zigzagging through the trees, hair dusted in gold by the rising sun. When her enormous lovely eyes finally saw him, she smiled. "Hail, Procurator! Are you well?"

"Yes, and you, Colonel?"

She climbed aboard his sand-galley and dropped through the forward hatch into his arms. "Fine but exhausted. What a bloody time to have a training century!"

He dared hold her for only a moment. She felt so incredibly good. He folded his hands behind him. They were trembling. "Some wine—or will you breakfast now?"

"Wine? Jupiter, I'd sleep for a week on a cup." Her aquamarine eyes held him for a moment. They seemed to pierce all his secrets with sharp affection. There was a crescent of dried blood on the back of her neck. Without asking, he knew it was not hers. "We have a problem, Germanicus."

He said nothing for a moment. He found it strange to feel as heady as he did. "Yes, there's *massing* being done."

"That as well?" She looked taken aback for an instant.

Forward, there was the shuffling of weary feet—Rolf's. Crispa glanced that way with irritation. And the noise stopped as if on command. "Who's that?" she asked Germanicus.

"A staff centurion."

The shuffling continued, then Rolf appeared at the entry. The rims of his eyes were redder than usual. "Pardons, sir, but request permission to use the camp mess."

"Granted, if the colonel so allows."

"My pleasure, centurion." She was so marvelously assured of herself; it delighted Germanicus, who—however reluctantly—had offered her his patronage when it was argued that a woman could never handle a field command. "Inform the captain of the guard you are my guest. Please draw a meat ration."

"My thanks, ma'am," Rolf said.

The centurion kept stealing glances at Crispa. At first Germanicus thought that the man's interest might be sexual—whatever the restraints of military discipline, she had a magnetic pull at this distance. But it soon came to Germanicus that Rolf was troubled by something he saw in her face.

"Is that all, centurion?" Germanicus asked.

"Aye, Procurator." Rolf exited the sand-galley without delay.

"Come sit on the bunk before you fall down," Germanicus said to her.

She stroked the sheet with the flat of her hand. "How good this looks to me."

"In the past twenty-four hours, there've been two possible cases of *massing.*"

"Where?"

"One at Firat Station. A legionary under this centurion. Another on an Empire tract south of here. A retired veteran. And his family. They killed his family."

"Oh, Germanicus." She rubbed her eyes with her fingers. "There's another *jhad* coming."

"Yes, yes."

"My dreams for a week now—strange, bloody. I'm tired of waking up depressed."

"We've got to respond to the *zaims.*"

"But which one?" she asked.

"What do you mean?"

"Only one *zaim* is at the heart of this *massing*."

He took her hands and rubbed the skin over the thin bones with his thumbs. "This is a bog of contradictions!"

"Words, words, Germanicus—they're not the coinage of my realm." She tried to moisten her lips with the tip of a dry tongue. "Somewhere out in this wasteland, a barbarian priest has latched onto a secret as hot as a phosphorous spark. Suddenly he's become a Great Fire from which all the lesser *zaims* are lighting their torches. . . ."

"And running bloody wild through the province."

"Trying to set fire to every piece of Roman tinder they can find."

"The legionary at Firat and the retired veteran?"

"Yes, and probably dozens more we haven't learned about yet."

"Then this is just the beginning."

"No, just the opposite. I think there will be fewer and fewer from now on."

Germanicus sighed in exasperation. "Good Mars, Crispa, you've lost me again!"

"Our Great Fire is no novice in these matters."

"What makes you think so?"

"Please—" She put his question on ice with one glance. "This *zaim* knows he has only so much heat at his disposal before the power goes to ashes again. Soon he must call back all his followers."

"Why?" he asked.

"To throw their torches back into the blaze. To unite their energies in one conflagration. Then to loose this against one target. A lone Roman in a high place. And this will be a *massing* of the *zaims*. All will share in this man's death."

Each hair on his neck was buzzing in its follicle. "Who is that Roman?"

"I don't know."

These words were spoken in such an offhand way, her eyes so curiously blank, he felt slightly betrayed. "Can you give me any idea who this chief *zaim* is?"

"No."

"Where can I find him?"

"I don't know." She fluttered her hand around her face as a sign of confusion. "I have some sense he's farther east. But

I don't trust the feeling yet." She eased back against the bulk-head, eyelids now swollen with sleeplessness. "He drifts in and out of my dreams. Just a glimpse now and again. That's all. Give me time."

"Describe him."

"Dream people are never seen face to face—always from the corner of a misted eye."

"I beg you, Crispa."

She was silent for a moment. "He has a beautiful white beard. Luxurious and creamy like a summer cloud. And the air around him is purple."

The mention of this color touched a feather to his memory. But he could not recall why. "What is your overall impression of the man?"

"Power. It butts up against my own power like a crashing wave. Pounding, withdrawing in a fray of foam, pounding, withdrawing—growing more insistent all the time."

"Can you see . . . what will happen?" His jaw was strangely twisted to the side.

"I know only that—and please don't ask why—if you travel to this *zaim* on foot, all will end well." Crispa stretched wearily. "I hear that you were in Rome last month for the dedication of the new temple of Mars."

"I was." He leaned back and exhaled.

"How is your wife?" The tips of her fingers vibrated for an instant—just as his had.

"Well enough. She's still recovering from her illness."

"You must give her my regards when you see her again."

"I will. She always asks about you."

Crispa shut her eyes. "Did you see the Emperor?"

"Briefly. He looks fit."

"He is the vainest man in the Empire."

This careless talk set Germanicus' teeth on edge. "Crispa, an old legionary once gave me excellent advice. He told me to say dangerous things only amongst my closest friends. Then he added, 'Those who say dangerous things have no close friends.'"

"I'm sorry," she said simply. "I'm tired. So tired."

"Yes, that must be the reason."

She sank down against the sheets only recently wrinkled by his body. "I love this bed."

He waited until her breathing had grown deep and regular, then drew the blanket up to her soft chin. He wanted to stroke her cheek with the back of two fingers, but finally resisted the urge.

CHAPTER IV

AT NOON, THE sky the color of pewter, Colonel Marcellus arrived at the perimeter of Crispa's camp. He jutted out of the open hatch of the sand-galley that led an armored maniple, the equivalent of two full centuries in strength. His heroic pose was in obvious imitation of the brass Poseidon of Artemision.

The galley on his flank had been scorched by Greek fire. A man with only one feature left on his face—a hideously gaping mouth—swung on a chain from the craft's *ballista*. Shrunk by heat, the dwarfish body was like a burl pulled out of the flames just as it had begun to break down into snowy ash.

By wireless Marcellus ordered the maniple to halt well beyong the pickets' *pili* range. Two craft did not respond and had to be signaled by hand to stop. He cursed in his father's language. To him, the sounds on a wireless were the cosmic music of morons. He preferred the direct authority of the hand—in all matters.

Leaving the sand-galleys to rumble at his back, he marched up to the captain of the guard, who—to his surprise—was a praetorian centurion instead of a tribune.

The soldier saluted neatly but remained distant in manner. Marcellus knew his features were being read with the blunt fingertips of Roman prejudice. Rage pooled in his heart and began burning through his arteries like acid. He had first suffered this sensation in his childhood, most of which he had spent as a royal hostage in Fabius' court to insure the loyalty of his great-uncle, the Parthian king, to that eccentric despot squatting on seven congested hills he fancied to be the center of the universe.

"Colonel Marcellus, adjutant to the procurator."

"Greetings, Colonel."

"The watchword, I believe: *Shines*."

"Ah, forgive me, sir. The challenge: *Vesta*."

"No matter. If we don't know who we are, who will then?" Marcellus graciously smiled. It was always more profitable to have friends than enemies, especially among the Emperor's fanatically loyal household guards, who were now farmed out across the Empire to make certain Fabius was well loved. "You're new in Anatolia, what?"

"Yes, two months away from the Novo Provinces, sir."

"And the real wars." Marcellus removed his lambskin gloves and slowly began fanning himself as if it were July. "How I envy you. Real soldiering. Here, we're little more than *vigiles*, crying 'fire' in the night to scruffy savages who live in mud houses."

The praetorian grinned at the grisly trophy hanging off the *ballista* of the sand-galley. "Looks like you got to mix it up a bit this morning, Colonel."

"Just a bit," Marcellus said wistfully. "Where may I find the procurator?"

"He left camp afoot shortly after dawn with a centurion and two legionaries. They have not returned."

"His destination?"

"He would not say, sir."

"And Colonel Crispa?"

"The procurator's galley—sleeping." The man smiled as if expecting Marcellus to join him, but suddenly got the gist of something far different than he had anticipated, so he quickly let his eyes blur with indifference. He had not forgotten what the guard had taught him about survival. "How—how is the situation elsewhere, Colonel?"

"What? The . . . ?" Marcellus' eyes were piercing the procurator's sand-galley, passing through the armor like the white firebolts now being tested on Crete. "Oh, the bloody wrapheads are pestering us all over the map. But nothing all that . . . all that solid yet on their part."

"That's good. We'll need time to put these *massing* stories to . . ."

But Marcellus had drifted past him as if in a trance. The snow had thawed slightly at midmorning, but now a fresh northern wind refroze it, so the colonel crunched through the top layer of ice, his gaze never straying from the dark galley bedecked with the purple procuratorial flags. The hem of his cloak snapped against his calves in the breeze.

He must control his rage, the rational part of him argued for the thousandth time. Without self-restraint he could never be the man he planned to be. He had to learn to chill his rage at these times.

But she had finally done it. The Scandian whore had achieved her precious goal.

He ignored the salute from the legionary posted outside the galley and heaved himself up onto the foredeck, then dropped through the hatch. His cloak flopped over his head and shoulders, making him look like a coal-eyed druid rushing to a sacrifice. He burst into where she slept, his Iberian short sword before him at the end of his rigid arm.

This is where it had been performed. The flawless skin of her upper breast was exposed to the pale light. He could barely keep from screaming.

He knelt beside her. The tip of his sword dented the white of her throat.

"I love you," he whispered, already beginning to weep. "Forgive me."

But this was too much. Surely even she would understand that. It was really enough that she lanced him again and again with her confidences about Germanicus.

But just when her eyelids began to twitch, close to opening, he flung aside the sword and dropped his chin against his chest.

A red tint to his vision trickled clear.

"What is it, my darling?" She showed no alarm.

This made him weep even more bitterly. Somehow, he knew, he would never bring this thing to a conclusion. She would. "Do not lie to me. Did you . . . ?" His voice broke.

She tilted her head back so her throat was fully exposed and laughed.

"Do you want to drive me mad?!"

"I have no need, Marcellus. Your blood is full of madness." Then she wrapped her arms around his neck and drew him down to her. "But how I dearly love my crazy Parthian."

He resisted her pull, sweat showing on his upper lip and the ridge of his forehead. "Did you do it?"

"No, I dropped off here after a sleepless night—that's all." She frowned and let him go. "You should have no fear of *that*."

He raised a hand as if to strike her. She continued without flinching.

"Germanicus wouldn't. But if I thought he might, I would ask."

"Why do you torture me?" Marcellus groaned.

"Because I won't lie to save your feelings—no one's feelings. I love Germanicus Agricola. Not as I want you. But I will love him to my death—and beyond."

"Then how can you plan *his* death?"

Her fingers shot forward and covered his mouth, pressing savagely against his lips while he sucked air in through his nostrils. "Take care, Parthian. Do you want us to share twin crosses before the sun goes down?" Her hands fanned out over his smooth, brown cheeks and held him steady as she floated up to his mouth. "What is your short sword doing on the deck?"

He stared back at her and said nothing.

"Don't play these games to sweeten our lovemaking," she said. "It won't be you to take my life. I already know whose honor that will be. I heard from the Sibyl at Ephesus. She has never been wrong."

CHAPTER V

GERMANICUS LED THE reconnaissance back into the encampment. The eyes of the men were glazed with fatigue, and their strides were six inches shorter than what they had been ten hours before. Shoulders hunched, Germanicus felt the setting sun on his back. He turned to face it—a pearl slowly picking up speed as it sank through a glass jar of olive oil—and then his gaze dropped to the snow and his patrol's outbound track of that morning.

One of the men who had helped stamp out that bluish trace with his feet would join no more patrols. His name would be recorded in a dispatch and forgotten in a month. There was an injustice to dying in a minor skirmish. Death was imperious only if it occurred in the course of an imperious event. Otherwise it smacked of the trivial, although the individual valor of a man might be equal whether he died in a nameless bushwhacking or the stand at Thermopylae.

Germanicus had no more started to remove his breastplate than Marcellus trotted toward him across the drifts. "They've blasted the Great Artery!" he shouted.

"Where?"

"Near Firat Station."

"Is it down?"

"Completely," Marcellus said. "Both rail and pipeline. And the fire is out of control."

Germanicus shook his head. The Great Artery was a brainchild of the Emperor Fabius. It consisted of a four-foot-diameter pipeline with an iron trace for a rail-galley perched atop it; a communications wire was stretched from trestle to trestle. Spanning half the world, this network unified the Empire. But when the barbarians did their periodic mischief one blast was enough to close down a branch of the system for several days while repairs were being made.

An explosion on the Bosporus–Parthia line was a slash at the Roman jugular. Within minutes the Empire's stream of black blood dwindled to a trickle snaking across the bottom of the pipeline. Within hours the Aegean refineries stopped humming. And within days the skies over Rome cleared to a pristine degree not seen since Etruscan days.

"Break this bivouac. We'll return to Nova Antiochia at once. I'm sure the factors are already frightened to death."

Marcellus wiped his lips with the back of his hand. "Colonel Crispa would have your ear on this matter first."

"Where is she?"

Marcellus pointed toward the clump of naked poplars at the center of the camp. "In briefing."

Quietly, betrayed only by the squeaking of his boots on the now hard frozen snow, Germanicus slipped through the branches but stopped twenty feet away from the colonel, who was lecturing two sheepish-looking tribunes.

"Look here what you did," she said, drawing with a stick in the snow. "Making your flanking movement too wide, you exposed two galleys in your own century to fire attack. If you expect to remain in my command, you'll . . . ." Suddenly she seemed to feel Germanicus' gaze on her. She looked up. ". . . you will pay greater . . . attention to the safety of your comrades."

"Yes, ma'am," they said weakly in unison.

"That is all."

"Yes, ma'am." They wasted no time marching away.

Germanicus was smiling. He recalled when, as his adjutant, she had begged for a field command as if the fate of the Empire depended on it. Perhaps it did. Trust her to know. "Marcellus said you wanted to talk to me before we return to Nova Antiochia."

"We must not go back to the provincial capital."

"Why?"

She drew closer, eyes darting nervously. He savored her natural scent. It was delicious. Was it Juvenal who had written that no perfume was the best perfume on a woman?

"I've had a dream."

She said this in such a way that it made him stand straighter. "Yes?"

She appeared unable to answer for a moment.

"Go on. I didn't make it to this ripe old age by being fainthearted."

"Forgive me, Germanicus, but this dream has nearly broken my heart." She bit her lower lip once—hard. "I dreamt you will be assassinated in your headquarters."

"Under what circumstances?"

"I saw you sleeping. Two dark figures stole out of the *peristylum* . . ."

His mind's eye watched the pair of assassins softly pad across the worn stones of his courtyard garden.

"The guard was bribed. He abandoned his post at the *vestibulum* for the warmth of the kitchen and waited there in the company of the bakers for the deed to be done."

Germanicus could smell the bread being baked.

"The figures sneaked into your chamber. In the first pink light of dawn, two knives flashed."

Germanicus saw that the sun had dipped into a clear strip between the overcast and the horizon. The snow was glistening. "Who?"

"I don't know."

"The assassins—are they barbarians?"

"I saw no faces."

"Well, well." The hair prickled on the back of his neck. "So someone wants a new procurator."

"There's only one way to avoid this: travel."

"Where am I to go?"

"I dreamt of a huge mountain rising from the plain . . ."

"And?"

Frustration knitted her brow. "I don't know. It rather reminded me of Mount Aetna."

"What business could I possibly have in Sicilia?"

"No, it's just that it looked like Aetna."

"Did you see the ocean?"

"No, but there was a river far below the mountain. My feeling's strong this is all to the east of us."

"Like Aetna . . . but east . . . a river." He was about to scratch the side of his head when his hand froze in mid-flight. "Agri Dagi," he said. "The mountain you saw in the dream is Agri Dagi."

"Do you think?"

"Has to be. And the river is the Aras. It all fits, Crispa. That district has always been a hotbed of religious fanaticism."

"If you feel so strongly about it, Agri Dagi must be the place."

For a fleeting instant their eyes met, and he had a suspicious feeling, which he quickly put aside. "What does this mean?"

"You must go there at once."

"If we're in for another *jhad*, I've got to be accessible to my commanders. That district is remote."

"A grave is even more remote," she uncharacteristically snapped, then looked away.

"Well, it's a lucky place for me."

"Yes," she said hopefully, turning back.

Indeed, Agri Dagi was lucky for Germanicus. He had served the first four years of his career in the shadow of the awesome volcano.

While hundreds of his comrades had frozen to death in their thin blankets, or were butchered by rabid tribesmen during the Great *Jhad*, or suffered the agony of viper bites—staring at their swollen limbs while death slithered through their veins, he had survived. Better still, he had survived with honor.

Germanicus had earned the admiration of the Senate and the sweeter adulation of his fiancée by defending a critical pumping station along the Bosporus–Parthia line. He did this with fewer than sixty men against more than five thousand barbarians. To the present day the Emperor compared Germanicus' holding of Agri Dagi Station with Thermopylae.

"Very well," Germanicus said finally, "give the order. We connect with a rail-galley east of the damage at Firat. We go to Agri Dagi." He drummed his dry canteen with his fingers. "I'm dying for a drink."

Crispa handed him hers.

"No, thanks, Colonel. Vinegar's my weakness."

"Then drink, Procurator." Rose came to her cheeks with the admission that she had picked up one of his habits. This moment of girlishness bewitched him, and he longed to touch her face. They began walking toward his sand-galley.

"You must tell me something," he said.

"Anything."

"Had you ever *massed* prior to that time in Hibernia?"

The ugly memory clouded her eyes. "No."

"Then how did you know you could do it?"

"I didn't. It was like accidentally learning to make fire. I just stumbled on it, but once I had made a spark ignite into flame, I knew I could do it again."

"I wish I understood this thing."

"Oh, I still don't really know what the fire is. But that doesn't stop me from using it." Smartly she returned the salutes of a brace of legionaries. "At least you realize it exists as a force. That's more than the Emperor seems capable of."

"I can attest to that. He thought me overwrought when I brought up the subject. Perhaps that's why he's pressing me to retire. 'Cousin, it's time you come home to rest,' he said. I felt like a fool."

"He and his cronies fear Germanicus Agricola."

"Why? I'm comfortably low in the Julian line of succession. I have no political ambitions."

"Cowards are always wary of the brave."

He handed back her empty canteen. "I care very much for you, Crispa. So it distresses me to hear you talk this way. Soon a new man will stand in my place. He may not be so lenient."

They parted and did not speak to each other again while the camp was being broken.

As usual, when the order to roll was given one of the sand-galleys refused to budge. The engine coughed languidly, then died away once and for all. Its exasperated crew stripped the interior of their gear and exited from the rear hatch, cursing. They divvied themselves up into other galleys. Hatches clanged shut. Engines revved. The column lumbered forward, two crafts abreast, forming a line a quarter of a mile long.

Five minutes later the abandoned sand-galley exploded into a fireball that festooned the sky with black streamers. White ptarmigan were spooked out of hiding to beat their wings against the wake of the shock wave. Germanicus thought they looked like the ghosts of birds.

Sharing a forward hatch with the procurator, Rolf shouted over the massed engines, "That be the only part of these machines what work!" He was referring to the automatic destruction device attached to the fuel reservoir of each sand-galley. "With permission, I go below to rest now."

"By all means, centurion." Germanicus was glad to be alone for a while, the cold wind singeing his cheeks. Rolf's remark made him smile.

The bloody sand-galley.

Rome was teeming with armchair generals who thought the craft a wonder weapon, guaranteed to succeed where men might fail. That reliance, Germanicus knew, was dangerous.

Since its invention by the Emperor himself, size and weight had replaced reliability and mobility as the production standards. The current model was eight feet longer and two tons heavier than the original design. Germanicus recalled watching Fabius tinker with that first machine in a quartz-marbled atrium of the palace, the god Vulcan at his feverish labors. "This, cousin," he said as he took a wrench from a platinum tray held by a slave, "will resuscitate the Empire for another hundred years." It bothered Germanicus that Fabius visualized the Roman world as a near corpse in continuous need of mechanical aids to keep it breathing.

Germanicus glanced over at the sand-galley beside his and found himself trading looks with Marcellus. For the blinking of an eye, the obsequious mask slipped from the Parthian's face and Germanicus saw a frank hatred that made his stomach lurch. But then the colonel saluted and smoothed over his lips a smile that bordered on reverence.

Germanicus nodded and snuggled down into the privacy of his thoughts again.

The reason for equipping the sand-galley with an automatic destruction device was a private joke to the military people of the Empire.

It had all started with a signifer of Greek extraction named Draco. He was doing service in the Novo Provinces when it suddenly occurred to him that he was entitled to retire. Straightaway he stamped off to the *quaestor,* explaining in a firm voice that after twenty years of loyal performance he wanted to go home to Attica. The *quaestor* thought this was well and good, but his records documented only nineteen years of service. Unlike his ancient namesake, Draco had no use for rules. A former boxer in the Panathenaic style—with scars on his face from the lead bosses on the knuckle straps to show for it—he had the unconscious habit of squeezing and releasing a fist as he talked, and the angrier he became the more noisily he sucked in air through the large nostrils of his often broken nose. In reinforcing one of his arguments he banged the table so hard that the *quaestor's* wax tablet and electrum stylus floated up in a local shortage of gravity.

Enough, the *quaestor* finally insisted: no record, no retirement.

That night, as the story went, a drunken Draco was beating his native camp follower when he had a thought that stopped his raging hand in mid-flight. This was not the result of an abrupt compassion for the woman. It was the realization that he had been both wounded and decorated for his part in the Crossing of the Borysthenes during the Sarmatian Expedition, and every schoolboy knew that this costly winter fording had occurred on the fifteenth of January exactly twenty years prior.

Again Draco marched off to rattle the *quaestor's* table. The functionary promised to look into the matter, which he did at his convenience, but was able to report back to the Greek only that there was no record of his participation in the action. Did he have the decoration or some other proof? Of course not. The silver medal bearing Fabius' grateful countenance had been pawned long ago, but Draco retained one souvenir of the battle. He hiked up his tunic and revealed a scar on his left buttock. The years had bleached the purple out of it, and he offered the sight as prima facie evidence that his word was good. The *quaestor* countered that Draco could have scars all over his ass, but that still was no kind of confirmation.

This was all the Greek was built to withstand. He showered a hailstorm of oaths on the man and, before he himself knew what had happened, planted the handy stylus in the *quaestor's* back.

So it came to pass that one of the most experienced sandgalley signiferi in the Novo Provinces sprinted over the brush and flinty rocks into the great wild land. In an hour there was a price on his head.

The deserter was almost forgotten two winters later when his old armored century was on patrol in the arid pinelands south of the Great Red Chasm. A snowstorm forced the sandgalley crews to make a hasty bivouac for three bitterly cold nights. When, on the subfreezing morning of the fourth day, they had dug out their craft—careful not to touch the frigid metal with bare fingers—the legionaries had a new problem. Five of the sand-galleys would not start. Catering to the phlegmatic engines proved fruitless. Fearing the arrival of another storm on the westerly wind, the commander had no choice but to leave the craft where they rested like the snow-dusted carcasses of bison. He planned to dispatch a maintenance *decuria* to recover them as soon as possible.

But these beasts came stampeding home before Roman mechanics could ever reach them.

A few weeks after abandonment the five sand-galleys came roaring into the garrison at Nova Petra, *ballistae* belching flame and topside decks aswarm with grinning natives. Inspired by strong drink, the barbarians were able to raze the barracks and fifty yards of aqueduct, then round up a dozen delighted camp followers of their race, before the legionaries overwhelmed them by virtue of superior discipline and sobriety.

Among the prisoners was a seething fellow with features uncharacteristic of the others. While his nose was flat like the norm, it appeared to be more the result of contact with a fist than the design of nature. He had a curly black beard, whereas his comrades had hairless cheeks like boys. This was no tribesman. "Hail, Draco," his former commander mocked him, "chieftain of the unwashed."

The Greek had found refuge among the new barbarians, gone about his business naked in the summer and in animal skins during the winter—just as his hosts did. He took a bride, tired of her, then secured a divorce simply by dumping her possessions outside his portal. He repeated this custom with a number of different women and found it quite stimulating. The native village, he explained like a boastful child, was stuck to a cliff wall like a dollop of mud. It was a city on Olympus.

Within a week of finding the galleys in the pinelands, he had organized native crews and trained them to a jerky but adequate level of competence. Then he rolled off toward Nova Petra to take his revenge.

The commander wanted to know how he had started the frozen crafts. Draco laughed in the officer's face. But during the final hours of his crucifixion, he revealed the answer.

Draco had ordered his charges to build fires under the sand-galleys. Ten minutes of this man-made spring, and each craft rumbled to life.

Germanicus had thought at the time that the lesson to be learned from this tale was not that automatic destruction devices were required but that resourceful noncommissioned officers should not be crossed without good cause. An imperial investigation confirmed that Draco had been eligible for retirement. Still, the Emperor's staff had not seen the issue in the same light as Germanicus and other officers had; they were doggedly sure there was a technical solution to every human problem.

Germanicus wearied of the cold and passed through the galley to his bunk. Flopping down on the mattress, he was asleep in minutes, oblivious to the clanging of the tracks and the growl of the engine.

He was dreaming that the fingers of a priest were fitting a coin between his teeth, fare for Charon, the Styx ferryman, when . . .

"Procurator."

Germanicus opened his eyes on Rolf's face. The sand-galley was no longer moving. "Yes?"

"We be at Firat village. Colonel Marcellus awaits your orders."

"Hand me my sword, man."

Snow roiled down the alleyways between the squat mud dwellings on wild spurts of wind.

Marcellus trotted up, puffing steam. "Sir, I've cordoned off the village with the century."

"Good."

The colonel impatiently stubbed the ice with the toe of his boot. "Then what is your pleasure?"

"Where is Colonel Crispa?"

"Behind us, Procurator."

He turned and beheld her. Forgiveness seeped through the corners of his smile. He found it impossible to be angry with her for long, even for her frank mouth.

Cheeks pinched red by the cold, she saluted as vigorously as a cadet. "At your service, sir."

"Thank you, Colonel." Germanicus led the two colonels inside the perimeter of legionaries. Their cloaks drawn tightly around them, the soldiers looked like bats who had wrapped themselves in their wings. "Marcellus, I want each male over the age of thirteen taken to the square. Tolerate no resistance."

"Aye, Procurator." The Parthian passed the order on to the centurions, who began bawling against the storm, directing men and sand-galleys into position.

"What will you do?" Crispa tried to put Germanicus between the wind and her.

Germanicus was silent.

"If you kill him, the power of the *zaims* will grow. It will be an admission from us that the legionary was *massed* against."

"I know."

"But it's just as dangerous to do nothing."

A blast of air made them jerk their faces to the side; it felt like being peppered with ground glass. Germanicus peered through a crack in his fingers as a sand-galley's *ballista* flashed over the rooftops. A roar followed the impact of the projectile on the other side of the village. "Why must they resist even when there's no hope?"

Crispa said nothing.

The couple paused at a yawning door. The glow of an oil lamp invited them in out of the blizzard.

Minutes before, a meal had been set on the table, and aromatic vapors seeped from chunks of lamb atop a mound of steaming rice. Germanicus barked at a legionary immediately outside to shut the door against the slogging lines of prisoners being prodded toward the square by Romans. Then he gestured for Crispa to sit opposite him. Each idled the left hand in the lap and ate with the right, as was the native custom.

They smirked at each other, feeling a bit mischievous for pilfering another man's supper. "Do you remember," he asked, shaking rice grains off his fingers, "when one of the factors in Nova Antiochia was selling his millet on the black market—and I was not certain which one?"

"I do," she answered.

"You told me—without hesitating—which of them was guilty."

A piece of roasted meat steamed in her fingers.

"How did you know?" he insisted.

"I just knew."

"I confronted the bastard, and the shock was enough to reduce him to tears. It convinced the other factors they couldn't hide their crimes from me. The black market dried up for months—in grain, at least." Thoughtfully he chewed on a lamb rib. "Do you think you could do it again?"

"You mean here?"

"Yes. Can you tell me which ones blew up the Great Artery?"

"I don't know, Germanicus."

"Are you willing to try?"

She slowly nodded, eyes glistening, then let her gaze drift over the food on the table. "This is what it is to be Roman, isn't it?"

"What do you mean?"

"Always sitting down to someone else's table."

"Yes," he said simply. He had long since stopped trying to deceive himself.

The snowfall was easing up. It quietly shimmered down like tiny flakes of mica. The barbarians had been forcibly organized into uneven ranks by the legionaries. They stood stiffly in their ragged coats and trousers. Their breaths came in frosty bursts.

"Procurator!" Marcellus said. "I have detained the *zaim* in a nearby house. We were lucky to catch him. The beggar was packed and ready for a trip east. Two of my best interrogators are at him. We'll get to the bottom of this *massing* thing."

"Don't harm him," Germanicus said, then leaned down and whispered to Crispa. "Are you sure this is not the *zaim?*"

"Without laying eyes on him, I know he is not the Great Fire of my dreams."

Marcellus hurried off—probably to prevent a slow murder already in progress.

Germanicus began reviewing the barbarians one by one. He held Crispa's elbow in the palm of his hand.

They stopped in front of a boy who could have been no taller than four feet or stouter than a hundred pounds. Germanicus brushed the snowflakes from the child's eyelashes. "It is not Roman to punish brave soldiers," he said in the most common Anatolian dialect. He felt certain that the many dark eyes opposing him understood each word. He shoved the boy out of the formation and motioned for him to be gone into the night. The child fled. "But saboteurs, those who attack the Great Artery and exasperate the mother who suckles them, will be punished as surely as the sun rises each morning over Agri Dagi."

Germanicus let a silence hover over the moment. A fresh

gust of snow filled the spaces between the assembled villagers. "Can you do it?" he begged Crispa in Latin.

"I—I need some light behind them. That day at Nova Antiochia—the factors had the sun to their backs."

"Colonel Marcellus!"

"Aye!" the man cried, returning from the house where the *zaim* was detained.

"Place two galleys behind these people. Ignite on all forward lights."

In moments an artificial noon lit up Firat's square. A dozen suns flared from the bows of the grumbling craft, casting the whitewashed minaret into a marvelous spectacle: a gleaming tower of ice.

Crispa confronted the first barbarian. He smiled in an insipid way, surprised that it was but a girl the mighty Empire was pitting against him. Her eyes blurred to a strange dreaminess, and she parted her lips slightly. She avoided the man's pupils and instead seemed to take in an impression of the whole figure before her. "No," she said without warning, and moved down the line.

Germanicus sighed a cloud of vapor.

She spent more time on the next barbarian. The man was effete-looking. He had moist feline eyes, so Germanicus was caught off guard when Crispa finally said, "Yes . . . I'm afraid . . . yes."

"Centurion!" Germanicus called to Rolf, who rushed forward without so much as a thought showing in his face. "Slay this one!"

Then Germanicus anxiously fixed his attention on the next barbarian in line so he would not see the sparkling fall of the short sword.

Shock plowed through the men of Firat like a hammer blow.

"No," Crispa said, continuing her review, and again, a no, and still another no, until they were well along the second rank. Then Germanicus could tell by the change in the set of her jaw that another conspirator had been uncovered.

"This one, centurion!" Germanicus said without waiting for Crispa to speak.

She dug at the thin lines in her forehead with her fingertips. "I don't—"

Suddenly two men broke from the back rank, and the dazzling night was filled with shouts of legionaries. Germanicus clenched his teeth against the belching of the sand-galley *ballistae*, which did little more than to punch dusty holes in a hovel wall and deafen the foot troops while the two barbarians ran toward the darkness. It was finally *pili* handheld by legionaries that downed the would-be fugitives. Marcellus trotted out to dispatch them with his sword. Germanicus found his eagerness crude.

"Thank Mars they ran," Crispa said. "I was beginning to have trouble."

Germanicus massaged her shoulder. "Thank you." Then he faced the cowed barbarians with a renewed sense of authority. "Such is the power of Mother Rome: to know who is guilty and who is not. Colonel Marcellus, the rest may go."

"But their *zaim*, sir—"

"He with them. If he were responsible for any act against the Empire, he would already be lying with the dead in the snow."

CHAPTER VI

THE BLACK NIGHT whistled past the open *ballista* platform. The two-day storm had spent itself, and Germanicus' rail-galley now rattled eastward under a sky rife with huge stars.

Crispa pressed against Marcellus, nestled in his cloak, on the swaying deck.

He hissed a string of words into her ear on a gust of delicious warmth. "Two stations from here a Parthian tribune will ask to see the procurator on the concourse. It is imperative we get the old man outside there at Mus."

"No, no, no," she whispered, clutching the cloak in her fists.

"As soon as he shows from his personal car, a squad of Parthian mercenaries will fall on—"

"No!"

"Listen! They will fall on Germanicus and those loyal to him. To save yourself, salute and bow your head as the slaughter begins. The mercenaries have been instructed to spare all who do this."

She tried to shield her face with the cloak from the numbing wind. "Fool! Don't attempt what can never be!"

He became rigid in her arms. "Do you mean to betray us?"

She closed her eyes. "No."

"Then why talk this way?"

"I know so much more than you, my darling."

"What then?"

She covered his mouth with her chilled lips.

Behind them the iron door groaned open, then slammed shut. Unwiped, a dab of his spittle froze on her cheek.

Backlighted by the lamps in the car, his breeze-tossed hair full of reddish gold, the German centurion Rolf stood glaring at her.

She felt terror as the angry eyes bored into her, fully expecting him to suddenly turn on Marcellus and her like some wild animal. The steam trickling out of his mouth was more like smoke; it seemed as if her racial kinsman had a fire raging in his belly.

But the centurion merely said, "The procurator ask to see Colonel Crispa."

She eased out of Marcellus' arms. "Tell him I come directly."

Then the German saluted and marched back into the car.

"I'm afraid," she said.

"Why? The old bastard adores you."

"Yes—tonight."

He squeezed her arms with his hands until she softly groaned. "Give him no cause for suspicion, woman."

The young tribune remained rigidly at attention, although Germanicus had gently commanded him to stand at ease.

"So the commander at Tigris Station suggests I remain where we are now." Briefly, pain kneaded Germanicus' heart in its cold fingers; this boy carried himself much as his dead son had.

"Yes, sir. One of his armored centuries is heavily engaged against barbarian saboteurs just a short way down the Great Artery. He fears for your safety."

"Thank him for his concern. But advise him that as long as the line remains open we are rolling through."

"Aye, Procurator. Hail Fabius."

"Hail Fabius." Germanicus prevented the young officer from withdrawing by raising a hand. "Which tribune are you?"

"Marcus Junius, sir."

"You remind me ..." Germanicus' eyes grew deeply sad. "Good night, Marcus."

A while later Charicles stole in and pouted in the least lighted corner, as was his habit when upset. Germanicus glanced up from a proposal to restore the monument to Alexander at the River Granicus, which had been recently vandalized. "What is it?"

"The stove don't work. And I don't know how the procurator expects me to make a decent meal with no fire."

"Improvise."

"Improvise, the procurator says. What would he have me do? Build a fire of camel chips on the bloody deck?" he muttered.

"Out!"

The old man turned back at the door. "Oh, Colonel Crispa is here as you commanded."

"I'll see her."

Her cheeks were chafed crimson by the wind. "Hail, Procurator."

"You look frozen to death."

"I was out on the platform for a breath of fresh air."

"You'll be out there again before the hour is done," he said. "Sand-galleys are battling some tribesmen ahead."

"Do you want the *ballistae* manned now?"

"Wait. No sense having our people too numb with cold to shoot well." He suddenly dug his fingertips into his temples. An eyelid wildly fluttered for a moment.

"Are you ill?" She took a step forward.

He took a gulp of vinegar from the cup and ignored her question. "You, of course, are familiar with the village a few miles north of your training bivouac."

"Is that where you went this morning while I slept?"

"Yes." He began to breathe easier. "Forgive me for borrowing two of your legionaries without asking. And then losing one of them."

She waved off his apology.

"But I would have learned little," he continued, slurring the edges of his words, "had I gone parading in there at the head of a full infantry cohort."

"What did you learn?"

"I'll need your help to understand."

She smiled at his need of her gift. "Of course."

"We hid ourselves in a stand of poplars on a bluff overlooking the village just as the tribesmen knelt down on their rugs for the noon prayer."

As Germanicus proceeded to describe a scene common to all of Anatolia at midday, Crispa grew visibly restless. "But what is unusual about . . . ?"

"Something was terribly different." An eyelid twitched again.

"Please tell me, Germanicus—are you ill?"

"It will pass. I felt much worse an hour ago."

"Let me summon Epizelus."

"No, I think I know what brings on this condition. I'm trying to tell you about it."

"I'm sorry."

"You see, the villagers weren't kneeling south toward their holy city. They'd turned to the west."

Her breathing became so light it would not have stirred a feather. "What in that direction warrants their devotion?"

"Not devotion—their rage. It's Nova Antiochia."

"Now *I* don't understand."

Charicles shuffled in on feet livelier than usual. "Sir, pardons, but the tribune who just arrived here insists on reporting flashes in the eastern sky." The old servant screwed up his face. "Is the procurator suddenly interested in lightning for some reason?"

Germanicus snorted and for a twinkling felt like his former self. "That will be the skirmish with the barbarians ahead. Have the tribune tell Colonel Marcellus I want all *ballista* platforms manned within ten minutes. How many armed cars have we?"

Charicles' lips silently counted before saying, "Fifteen."

"Good. That's enough to show them a fight."

Crispa prevented Germanicus from rushing out by holding his forearm. He found this bold. His gaze scolded her.

"Please," she said, "what makes you think the villagers were bowing toward Nova Antiochia?"

"It's the seat of imperial power in this part of the world." He strapped on his short sword, sorely wishing his station would permit him to carry a *pilum* and actively "mix it up," as Rolf put it.

"What difference would that make to these poor ignoramuses?"

"Crispa—we are talking about a *massing*." He slipped past

her into the shockingly cold night.

Rolf was wrestling into the harness of a portable Greek firer. He showed his big square teeth to the procurator. "We push through, sir?"

"Better to let them blow up the Artery at our tails than in our faces."

"Aye."

Crispa was at his elbow again. "Don't tell me you think they're *massing* against you!"

"Then whom, Colonel?"

She made no reply. Her eyes darted back and forth.

He pulled her behind the *ballista*. "I trust you as I have trusted few human beings. You say go to Agri Dagi, and I go directly—against my judgment. Now I must have some answers. You alone can give them to me."

"I would never let you come to harm."

"Why are the villagers involved in this? I thought *massing* was something left to the Great Fire you spoke of."

"Remember how I told you that all the torches would be thrown back into the bonfire? This is the beginning of that. And the effects of this will soon be evident."

"What effects, Colonel?" Again his eyelids began twitching. Then the irises floated upward like balloons, and for an instant, only the whites of his eyes showed.

Crispa kept from screaming by gnashing the cloth of her sleeve with her teeth.

"What effects?" He spun around and barked, "Tribune! Where is Marcellus?!"

"I don't know, Procurator."

"Find him!"

The young officer sprinted off. The preparations of the two-man *ballista* crew became more frantic.

"Germanicus," she whispered in his ear, "it's dangerous for you to imagine you are their target. You can make yourself ill." The rushing air had whipped tears to the outer corners of her eyes.

"*Imagine?* When a hundred men whine deep in their throats and point their hates toward Nova Antiochia—"

"What makes you so certain they are concentrating on the provincial capital?"

Rubbing his temples, Germanicus sighed. "Crispa, you become tiresome."

Her face smarted at his remark. "Where, sir, would you station me for battle?"

Seeing that he had stung her, Germanicus reached out, gathered and squeezed her gloved hands. "Here, Colonel, here. Fight by my side."

"I ask for nothing more."

A shadow cut off their light from the car's interior. "Colonel Marcellus, sir, as you—"

"Where have you been?"

"I'm sorry, sir. There are citizens aboard, tragedians en route to Poppaeus' garrison."

"Why weren't they put off at the last station?"

"There was no word of danger ahead or I would have. Their comfort is provided for in the forwardmost car."

"Inspect all platforms. See they are in readiness." The procurator gave his back to the colonel.

"Immediately." Scowling, the Parthian passed around Crispa as if she were five times her actual size.

"Flare on the right!" a legionary shouted.

Everyone mobbed that side of the platform to watch a white fire float down and wink out like a seed of light plowed under the night by the gods. Where it had dropped behind the horizon the moon now gracefully rose, igniting billions of ice crystals into brilliant spangles. The desert became an inexhaustible trove of gems that glistened all the way to Parthia.

Germanicus prayed that the commander at the next station had observed the regulation to shut down the petroleum flow while the Great Artery was threatened. The commander two garrisons behind had not taken this precaution, and the resultant conflagration had required four hours to contain before repairs could begin.

A rail-galley had not been exploded in six years, but the confusion and destruction visited on the Romans by such a blow was certainly an inducement to saboteurs. Uneasily Germanicus thought of the thousands of gallons of raw fuel passing directly under the cedar trestles on which the galley rolled.

They rounded a hillside, and Germanicus saw a vista that filled him with disappointment.

It looked as if a Titan had emptied his brazier. The landscape was littered with embers. Each coal was a smoldering sand-galley, its armor plates glowing cherry-red from internal fires. "No wonder the commander here wanted me to halt down the

line!" Germanicus fumed. "He's being whipped—and no wonder, the way he's spread his galleys over half of Anatolia!"
Then he stilled an eyelid with his finger.

The rail-galley skidded to a stop, the locked wheels throwing
showers of orange sparks. Two men boarded the procuratorial
car from a freight siding. The first Germanicus recognized as
the tribune-ranking adjutant of Dulius, commander of the Tigris
garrison. Behind him waddled a native-born Anatolian who
had held the post of *quaestor* in this region until it became all
too obvious that his only aptitude lay in personal grooming
habits.

"Hail, Procurator," the tribune said. "Marcus Dulius sends
his warmest regards."

"Where is he?" Dulius was a harried little man in Germanicus' estimation—one of the least respected of his garrison
commanders.

"Unreachable, sir—but in the area."

"You have described a dead man to me."

"I meant to give no such impression. It's just that, Procurator, there has been such . . . such—"

"Confusion."

"Exactly, sir." The man was too advanced in years for his
junior rank. His face was puffy from rich foods—no legionary
to survive a day's march on a handful of grain, this one—and
his nose was heavily brachiated with tiny purple veins.

"Bad times, *pasa*. Awfully bad times," the Anatolian muttered, tufting his oily beard to a point.

"Is the pipeline shut down in precaution?" Germanicus asked
the tribune.

"Oh, quite, sir."

"Your losses?"

The tribune searched the wasteland behind his eyes for good
news.

"Out with it, man," Germanicus snapped.

"Thirty-five legionaries and four officers killed. Twice that
number wounded. Nine sand-galleys destroyed, two badly
damaged. A century all in all."

"Awfully bad times for the old policies, *pasa*."

Germanicus faced the silken Anatolian. "What in the name
of hades is your function?"

"Why, a liaison between the Empire and the barbarian com-
munity, *pasa*. You see, I am both a loyal citizen of Rome and

an adherent to the Prophet. So, I am very, very sensitive to—"

"Magnificent work you've been doing."

"Sand-galley under attack!" Rolf cried.

Germanicus seized the optics out of the German's hands. He focused on a craft three hundred yards out in the snow. It was surrounded by more than a dozen barbarians. Bombs flickered in their hands. The rag fuses squiggled in the dark like glowworms.

The Roman crewmen were ducking in and out of their hatches, firing *pili* instead of relying on the *ballista*'s narrow field of fire to keep their attackers at bay. But this desperate tactic prevented the legionaries on the rail-galley from helping them; it was impossible to mow down the barbarians without raking the exposed decks of the craft.

"What's wrong here?" Germanicus asked, noticing that the *ballista* on the platform had not been turned so it could be fired at the earliest opportunity.

The legionary complained that the weapon could not be budged along its track.

"Kick it."

"Kick . . . it, Procurator?"—as if he'd been asked to fly.

"In the breech!"

The soldier did so. Grudgingly the mount grated across the rusted teeth of the cogwheel track.

"Shoot a flare at that galley to get the crew back inside," Germanicus ordered.

A white dart wafted over the plain at the craft. The Romans barely had time to pull down their hatches before a shower of phosphorus was upon them.

"Now kill those barbarians!" Germanicus cried.

The length of the rail-galley erupted with the fiery discharge of *ballistae* and *pili*. The moonlit shapes of the tribesmen fell away. It was as if their souls had been revoked suddenly by an angry god. The wicks of their firebombs sputtered out in the snow.

"Excellent marksmanship," Germanicus said. "Signal that sand-galley to approach us."

"Aye, sir." Rolf broke a torch out of his cloak.

Germanicus became aware of Crispa at his side. For a fleeting instant this seemed the best of all possible worlds: a night as translucent as obsidian, this lovely Scandian girl rubbing the back of his hand with hers, and the indefinable thrill of battle. Then he saw lines drawn across her face in the topography of worry. "What is it, Crispa?"

"I have a sensation . . ."

"Yes."

"Something is about to happen."

"What?"

She cringed. "Throats slit . . . shadows creeping up to the Great Artery . . ."

"Centurion, post sentries around us," Germanicus said. "Let's keep on our toes, lads."

The thin space between his body and Crispa's disappeared. In the privacy of the *ballista*'s moonshadow, she gently rested the side of her face against his breastplate.

Incongruously he found himself thinking of his wife, Virgilia.

She was not well. Her vigor had been seeping out of invisible wounds for more than a decade. Her once soft brown hair had become spun glass, and her fingernails were the color of resin. What was it that wasted her away year after year? Her surgeons were baffled and their only suggestion now was to remove four inches of her tailbone before it wore through the taut skin.

That musty couch in her bedchamber must crucify her, she who had run along the uppermost tier of the amphitheater at Nimes, wearing a wreath of sunflowers, her pretty mouth overflowing with laughter. This was a June meadow of a girl blighted before her time.

And now, when he was seconds away from closing his arms around his precious Crispa, he was ashamed that his thoughts leaped ahead to the day Virgilia would finally die.

His mind's eye watched the flames wiggle up out of her pyre. But something deep inside would not let this fire liberate him. Like the flimsy ashes that floated up on the heat, he made it only as high as the tops of the cypress trees before crashing down to a garden turned gray by her absence. That day in Nimes—and many others of joy—held him down with a sweet gravity he might never transcend. He was inevitably victimized by old memories.

Germanicus softly moved Crispa aside.

The sand-galley rumbled up to them. The forward hatch opened, and a centurion crossed from the craft to the *ballista* platform of Germanicus' car.

"Hail, Procurator!" The man wore a huge grin of relief.

"How did you become separated from your century?"

"Orders, sir."

"Explain."

The centurion glanced at Dulius' adjutant. "We was on night patrol, Procurator, when all of a sudden we come on a band of wrapheads carrying boxes and whatnot toward the Great Artery. We scattered them right off. Then, as I live and breathe, we was ordered to split up and pursue the bastards. Even a pack of wolves won't do that, sir. Well, our sand-galley no sooner goes its way than a million bloody wraps leap up out of the snow. That's when the slaughter of good crews begun."

"Who gave the order for the crafts to separate from each other?"

"Colonel Dulius, through this tribune standing here, sir." Contempt tugged at the corner of the centurion's mouth.

"Now, Procurator," the adjutant piped up, "it was not humanly possible to anticipate the barbarian ruse."

The Anatolian shook his head. "Yes, *pasa,* these are insidious times."

"Tribune, what is the primary objective of all imperial soldiers in this region?"

"Defense of the Great Artery."

"Tell me then: How can you be taken in by any ruse as long as you remember what you must defend?" Germanicus spun angrily on his heels.

"Centurion—"

"Sir?"

"Does your wireless work?"

"Hit and miss."

"Well, however you do it—regroup what's left of your century down here along the Artery where they're needed."

"Gladly, sir, but with only being a cent—"

"The beauty of our profession is that remedies may be prescribed for all exigencies."

"I don't rightly catch your meaning, Procurator."

Germanicus turned to Dulius' adjutant. "Surrender your insignia and short sword to this centurion."

"The man's father was a freedman!"

"All the more reason to win back your place of honor before the night is—"

Germanicus stopped short. A cry of horrified surprise was

escaping the throats of the legionaries on the *ballistae* platforms. Twenty years prior he had heard exactly the same exclamation from the imperial family. The Emperor's son had slipped away from his attendants and was stamped to death by Fabius' favorite racing horse, made skittish by the child's approach. But now it was a different kind of calamity: A group of barbarians clad in white raced down the sloping approaches to the Artery, scampered up the trestles as agilely as apes, and flew into the end car of the rail-galley. They had silenced the Roman sentries without so much as a gurgle being sounded.

This swift penetration of their defenses stunned the Romans, and Germanicus now rushed to rally them. Grasping the disgraced tribune, he shouted as if to a deaf man: "Form a squad and get down there. Stop them before they get to the next car!"

Rolf was already leaping over the roofs of the rail-galley, the blue ignition flame of his Greek firer flickering in the breeze, when Germanicus called to him: "Let's not cremate this galley ourselves, centurion!"

The German shrugged as if annoyed that his procurator's mind could be occupied with such petty concerns.

Pili fire reverberated in the last cars of the rail-galley. There came the rainlike noise of *fléchettes* passing through metal. Germanicus stooped beside Crispa. "Damn their plan—it's a good one. They'll use the rear car for cover while they attach an explosive device to the Artery. Colonel, form an element of those forward *ballistae* crews who have no field of fire, then deploy along the right flank."

"Aye, sir."

He clutched her thin, bony wrist. "Do not stretch your courage—and my nerves—too tautly."

She flashed a smile at him, then was gone.

The former centurion he had just commissioned as a tribune was bellowing at him from the forward hatch of the sand-galley.

"What is it, tribune?"

"Sorry, Procurator, my engine won't restart."

"Then assemble your century here as best you can by wireless." Germanicus withdrew to the other side of the platform and massaged the sides of his head. After a few minutes it occurred to him that young Marcus Junius was staring at him. Germanicus had the eerie impression that his dead son's eyes were trained on him. The last line of Sophocles' *Oedipus Rex* was being whispered by his mind's voice: ". . . let none presume on his good fortune until he finds life, at his death, a memory without pain."

"How old are you, Marcus?" he asked this pup of a tribune.

"Twenty-one, sir."

They turned at the sound of glass being shattered.

Crispa and her squad had been slogging through waist-deep drifts, trying to get beyond the captured car, when the barbarians smashed out the windows and splattered the snow around them with shot. The legionaries flopped down out of sight. Germanicus thought he would go mad with anxiety until he saw the colonel briefly lift her head to get her bearings.

The detail would advance no farther.

Damn, but he had to admire these bold saboteurs. They had nestled into the safest place from which to attack the giant—right between his toes. All the *ballistae* on a rail-galley, except the unit mounted on the rear car, could discharge only to the sides. The barbarians had robbed Germanicus of his most effective weapon.

He saw the newly commissioned tribune abandon his sand-galley, and armed only with a *pilum*, trudge off to find his command among the flaming wreckage of battle. "So his wireless is out too," Germanicus muttered with respect. "But that does not stop the son of a freedman."

"Procurator!" a legionary shouted. "Colonel Crispa signals to us!"

Germanicus climbed onto the roof of the car. Crispa indicated to him that something was happening down the line, and he peered in that direction. "Oh, Jupiter!"

A second team of saboteurs was huddled around the pipeline two hundred yards distant, working furiously in the moonlight. Their comrades on the rail-galley covered them as they readied the explosive. What Germanicus would have given for an operational sand-galley—and how he doubly swore against the absent Dulius for letting the barbarians make their way in force to the Great Artery.

Then one by one, like spirits sniffing dawn, the barbarians dropped their tools and trickled away into the night.

The seconds pounded against Germanicus' eardrums like iron hammers. The blast knocked him off his feet.

It seemed to him that he had been floating in the air for hours, gently bouncing off the stars, feeling the worries of a lifetime evaporated away into space, when he realized with bitter disappointment that he was lying in a dent in the soft metal of the rail-galley roof. His buttocks were very sore.

The breach in the Great Artery flooded the sky with smoke. The fire would rage until all the standing oil in this section of the pipeline flowed out.

"Procurator?" The eyes of the young tribune peeked over the edge of the roof. "Are you . . . ?"

"Yes, I am."

Then Marcellus' eyes appeared; they reminded Germanicus of the gaze of a predatory cat. "Sir, they have taken hostages."

Germanicus sat up. The skin on his face and the palms of his hands was still tingling. "Who?"

"Dulius' adjutant and one of our corporals, Clarissa Varro."

Unaided, Germanicus leaped down onto the platform, then led the way toward the barbarians.

The Anatolian returned from negotiating with the saboteurs. He crouched beside Germanicus behind a marble bas-relief, the only partition in the second-to-last car that had not been riddled by *fléchettes*.

The Roman hostages were bound together with cord at the foot of a barricade the barbarians had erected with overturned couches. Two arms projected from the jumble of furniture and held knives against the throats of Dulius' adjutant and the female corporal.

The adjutant was smiling with colorless lips. Germanicus admired him for it. Faced with the equal futility of courage and cowardice in this situation, the man had chosen courage if only because it was aesthetically superior. Germanicus saw this in that smile, and he wondered how, within a single hour, two souls—one fearless and one timid—could inhabit the same skin. He grinned at the adjutant, who seemed to take further heart from it.

The Anatolian at his side reeked of musk. "Well, *pasa*, how fortunate that I, an adherent to the Prophet, am with you, yes? Our dealings with these people require a touch as soft as the petals of a rose—if we are to save the Emperor's brave soldiers."

Germanicus felt like spitting. "What did these renegades say?"

"They demand that you sever their car from this rail-galley and proceed from the area at once. Adamant—these people are adamant, *pasa*." He leaned forward and whispered, "I was raised in the same village as their leader. Believe me, he is most dangerous. He is capable of carrying out the threats he makes against the two poor *lictors* who so nobly carry the *fasces* in Anatolia for our godlike Emperor."

"What will become of my people?"

"He assures you they will be released within a short walk of a Roman garrison if . . ." The man paused with a deprecating smile.

"What?"

"If word comes to him that Mustafa has been released from the praetorian fortress at Nova Antiochia."

Mustafa was a notorious rebel who had seen most of his sunrises from the windows of Roman prisons.

"I see," Germanicus said.

"While accommodation in this instance is contrary to my feelings as a loyal citizen of Rome, I must admit, *pasa*, that there are certain advantages to this proposal."

"Such as?"

"Well, it will pacify the hotheaded factions. And the more responsible of my people will be assured that their ethnicity is respected by the procuratorial government."

"The night on which Mustafa was last released he went straightaway to the Temple of Hadrian at Ephesus and blew off the head of Dulius Aelius' statue."

"That was seven years ago, *pasa*. We have a saying—"

"I'm sure you do." Germanicus tapped his lips with a finger. "Very well, I'll disconnect the car."

The Anatolian grinned wide with delighted surprise. "Excellent judgment under the circumstances. Your Julian blood becomes more evident with the passing of each year."

Germanicus gestured for Rolf to join him on the platform. He whispered in the centurion's ear, then Rolf reluctantly shed the Greek firer. At first his eyes were sad. Then, before he took a *pilum* from a legionary, they became cold. He began creeping over the roofs toward the rear of the rail-galley.

"Marcellus!"

"Procurator!" His voice came from the next *ballista* platform forward.

"Signal the operator to detach the last car."

"Aye, Procurator."

"You cannot imagine the benevolence that will spring from

the hearts of my people because of this order, *pasa.*"

"Do not underestimate me, *quaestor.*"

The man beamed at the mention of his former title. "How can one underestimate a son of Aeneas?"

The coupling clicked open.

"Roll backward, Marcellus!"

"Back . . . ward, *pasa?*"

"Sir?" Marcellus asked, torch in hand.

"To the rear!"

The Anatolian was propping up the corners of his smile with needles. "Which of their precise instructions is met by our going backward?"

There was a quick jolt. Everyone on the platform lurched and tottered for his balance. The long rail-galley began to inch toward the fiery break in the Great Artery. The heat intensified as the pillar of flame loomed higher and higher and the galley gained speed. Then Germanicus ordered, "Full stop!"

The myriad iron wheels of the galley squealed to a halt with the sound of a pig being dragged to slaughter.

But the uncoupled car continued on its way alone.

"Centurion!" Germanicus cried, his eyes clouding with moisture from the terrible anticipation of what was coming. This one word was all he had to shout. From the last Roman-held car, Rolf discharged his *pilum.*

The Roman hostages slumped to the deck, pierced to death by *fléchettes,* saved from feeling any further horror. The knives held against their throats fell out of the hands of the astonished saboteurs behind the barricade. Rolf kept them inside the car by riddling the couches with every round he carried, and Crispa's squad prevented the use of other avenues of escape by raking the smashed-out windows with volleys of shot.

"Pasa, oh, *pasa!"*

Germanicus held out his hand as if he wanted to blot out the coming sight.

The car grew smaller against the mountain of fire and smoke. Then it was swallowed up. A breath later, the already troubled night sky was shattered by a flash of orange lightning and an unnatural peal of thunder.

The silence on the rail-galley was ghastly. No one seemed capable of breaking it. Germanicus barely noticed that Crispa had come aboard and was standing near his side, hushed like all the others.

"Sir," Marcellus said at last, "a formation of sand-galleys approaches."

"Signal their leader . . . secure the area . . . transport the wounded . . ."

"Pasa, I fear terrible repercussions of th—"

Germanicus seized the Anatolian and heaved him off the platform into the drifts below. The man came up choking on a mouthful of snow.

"You'll make a rebel of this man!" Marcellus protested.

"Do you think I am a blind man in my own province, Colonel?"

"No, of course not, Procurator, I merely—"

"Make a report of a posthumous promotion. Dulius' adjutant died well."

"To what rank, sir?"

"Tribune."

"But he *held* the rank of tribune."

"I know. I said he died well. He lived like a niggard. He never spent a *solidus* of his courage—until now."

CHAPTER VII

THE RAIL-GALLEY BEGAN to slow for Mus Station. Germanicus' breathing grew shallower and shallower in the overheated car. His mind was drifting toward wakefulness. The lights of the station flashed across his eyelids. He awoke feeling depressed but couldn't recall what he had been dreaming of. "Mars," he prayed, "give me command over my sleep."

The door clicked open, then shut.

He wondered if he was fully awake, for he fancied that a human figure was creeping toward him on cat's feet so softly he could hear only his own heart pounding.

"Who goes there?" Germanicus asked in a whisper. He did not rise to get his short sword from the couch because he suddenly felt sure this was all a fantasy. And he did not want old Charicles to turn the lights on a procurator spinning around wildly, striking at the darkness with his blade, shouting at phantoms like a drunken gladiator. Still, Germanicus' skin was rough with gooseflesh.

The figure sat on his bed. The mattress sank slightly. Then he knew that this was no dream.

"I felt . . . you might need me. . . ."

Germanicus pulled Crispa down against his bare chest. She covered his mouth with hers. An overwhelming sense of privacy, as if they had stolen away to some hidden kingdom, began winding down the helix of his soul like a drop of hot wax spiraling around a burning candle. At that instant he could have disappeared inside her and left no regrets behind.

She began kissing his ears and eyes. "I love you, Germanicus."

He came as close to admitting his love for her as he ever had, but then groaned against the smoothness of her cheek. "We have our loyalties . . ."

"I am a willing traitor to everything but you."

Then a knock at the door made them both sit up.

"Yes?" Germanicus asked.

"Colonel Marcellus, Procurator."

Crispa's body went taut in Germanicus' arms. "What is it?" Germanicus said.

"We've arrived at Mus Station, sir. We received word earlier that an officer in the garrison here begs your attention—briefly."

"Very well, give me a minute or two."

Crispa got up and moved across the chamber. She stood in the shadows, avoiding his eyes.

As Germanicus stepped out onto the icy paving stones of the station platform, he recalled what he had been so recently dreaming about. It had been his father's death. The man had been assassinated.

Far down the vacant concourse a lone legionary was pacing away the night. He passed under a light. He did an about-face and started back toward Germanicus, who now turned his ear toward a new sound coming from the opposite end of the platform.

His hand gravitated toward the hilt of his sword.

Whoever was approaching from that direction was sniffing the air excitedly. Germanicus thought he could pick out the clinking of iron nails on the stones. Then there was no mistaking a hearty sneeze in the darkness.

Germanicus was steeling himself for the worst when he suddenly chuckled under his breath at this cutthroat sneaking up on him.

A lean dog came scratching along the ice on his nocturnal

prowl. With considerable loneliness, this brought home to Germanicus that he was in a foreign place and not Italia. With over one hundred and ninety million people crowding the narrow peninsula of the mother country, there had finally been no room for the needs of both dogs and people. Two legions had fanned out across city and plain to slay every canine in their path. Only a few breeds necessary for shepherding chores had been permitted to survive.

He petted the animal on its ragged nape and smiled. "Well, it would be fitting to dispatch a dog to kill a cur, what?"

Now the heavy boots of a man scuffed along the stones in hurried approach.

Again Germanicus squeezed the hilt of his sword.

Marcellus sprinted out of a breezeway straight for Germanicus. Despite the early morning cold, he was sweating. "Procurator!" he called in a strangely tense voice.

"Where is this officer who braves the dark to see me?" Germanicus saw that Rolf had quietly come out of the rail-galley to stand beside him.

Marcellus stopped ten paces short of them—instead of three, which would have been more natural. His eyes were glistening. "My pardons, sir. The centurion on duty reports the tribune who desired to see you waited until two, then decided we might be delayed until morning."

"So?"

"They all marched back to the garrison."

"They? I thought just one officer wanted my ear."

"Yes, but he turned out his century for you to review."

"What?" Germanicus vented steam out of his nostrils. "Turned out for inspection half the night? Suppose those men are engaged against the barbarians tomorrow night? That would mean two full days without sleep, wouldn't it?"

"Aye, Procurator. I'll convey your displeasure to—"

"Isn't it enough the tribesmen are exhausting my legionaries without imperial officers further wearing down the lads?" An angry Germanicus went back aboard. He passed Crispa in the passageway. "Any dispatches from Nova Antiochia?" He did not stop to meet her eyes.

"Yes, the Emperor wants to know our situation here."

Germanicus waved off Charicles before he had time to voice some complaint. "Tell the Emperor all remains under our control, Colonel Crispa."

"Is that all?"

"All he would want to know. Any other news?"

"There was a riot last night in Ephesus—contained now."

"Very well."

"And an assassination in Syria—a corn factor."

"That will soften the prices for a while." Germanicus rushed past the entrance to his quarters just as the rail-galley lurched onward again.

"Sir, your quarters—this door."

"I know, Colonel," he said uneasily. "I can't sleep. Are the tragedians still forward?"

"First car, yes."

"Do they have musical instruments with them?"

"A harp and a flute, I believe."

"I long for a little diversion, Colonel." Germanicus finally turned his head to look back at her. But she was no longer behind him.

"The height of barbarian sloth!" Marcellus fumed on the *ballista* platform, eyes swollen with fatigue. The winter skeleton of a birch forest shot past in the light of the setting moon. "The Parthian bastard was just cold and bored. That's why he shuffled back to the garrison!"

"I told you nothing would come of it."

He studied Crispa in silence for a moment. "Why do you stand so far from me?"

"I am exhausted."

"All the more reason to want my comfort."

She listlessly walked into his waiting arms.

"When I was born, Crispa, the auspices revealed that I would either become a powerful king or die young. I am no longer young, my darling." He chuckled ominously. "Now let the Great *Zaim* pluck this Roman functionary out of my path."

She was weeping.

"What is it?"

The rail-galley curved along a bend. They watched the lights spatter on in the forwardmost car. They held each other.

"I did not mean to wake you all," Germanicus apologized. "Forgive my intrusion—I thought you might be too restless to sleep."

"Ah, but we are, Procurator—especially after such a heroic

struggle taking place under our noses," a middle-aged man said, fingering his salt-and-pepper beard as a sign of obsequiousness. "So great is our fortune that our senses are still intact, sleep would be ingratitude to the gods."

"Who are you?" Germanicus asked.

"Demetrius of Delphi."

Germanicus smiled. By the look of this man's nose, he was more likely "Darryle of Londinium" than "Demetrius of Delphi." But Greek pretensions were winked at, and it was considered in bad taste to challenge even the most brazen claims to Mycenaean blood. On the other hand, groundless claims to patrician heritage usually resulted in blows and, occasionally, homicide. It amused Germanicus how some Romans gave greater concern to their origins than their final destination.

"How many compose your company?" Germanicus asked.

"Twenty, sir, of the most sensitive talent in the Empire. This allows us the luxury of an Aeschylean chorus of twelve."

Germanicus found himself enjoying the moment. "I thought all the best companies have a chorus of fifteen, as Sophocles prescribed."

Demetrius looked crestfallen as he confessed, "Two of our most veteran actors deserted us at Massilia. Another died in Corinth of . . . a fever."

"Love's burning fever, it was, guvnor!" a mawkish voice said from the company. "Or the blistered butt of it!"

"Enough of that," Demetrius barked. "But, as you now know, sir, we had fifteen for a while."

"Still, quite a company."

And indeed they were: The young men draped themselves across couches pilfered during the night from other cars. Ranging in race from Armenians to Zadracartans, all nevertheless shared a common cast to their appearance: a certain fastidiousness that went beyond careful grooming. A hoary-haired Celt had plucked his eyebrows into the shapes of two converging comets. Planting kisses on his neck was a Parthian who sported a perfectly trimmed beard and wore a mummified asp around his head as a fillet. A Macedonian half dozed as he patiently rubbed oil onto his depilated chest. The youth had painted his face crimson with a dye made from crushed *kermes*, a scale insect.

Germanicus was mildly surprised to see Marcus Junius from

his staff sitting beside a Sicilian boy who, with his liquid, dolorous eyes, could have passed for a pretty girl of sixteen. The tribune appeared so uncomfortable at being discovered in his dalliance, Germanicus felt moved to wink at the officer to assure him he would not be censured. Except when such behavior interfered with duty, he would voice no objection. He refused to forbid to others what the royal family openly dabbled in from time to time.

"Well," Germanicus said, "good night to you all."

"Procurator, may we honor you with some small entertainment?" Demetrius gestured for Germanicus to take the couch he had been occupying.

"I don't mean to keep you up."

"We shall be waiting impatiently for the cheer of dawn whether you go or stay."

Germanicus sat. "If you insist, then."

The aging tragedian rubbed his hands together. "Now what is the procurator's pleasure? Something from the classics? Perhaps a Gaulish nothingness play?"

"Do you have an oration in your repertoire?"

"A speech?" Disappointment dulled the man's eyes. "Do you desire a particular oration?"

"No, but I should like music set to whatever you offer."

Demetrius' eyes became lanterns again. "Ah, music! I have got the most extraordinary thing for the procurator. It is fresh from the mental forge of our genius Emperor, who plucks forms out of the eternal fire as deftly as a *colonius* picks apples."

The Celt padded forward with an incredible piece of hardware.

"What in the name of Pluto is that?" Germanicus asked.

"Why, it's a *harphlutium,*" Demetrius explained, very much the proud owner. "A harp and a flute united as one in brass. The Emperor has such a flair for intertwining purposes in his inventions, yes?"

"Do you play often for the imperial family?"

"We have not yet had the honor."

Germanicus breathed a little easier. Tragedians and musicians were notorious spies. He pointed to the elongated tube on one side of the triangular frame on which a dozen strings had been tautly stretched. "This, by virtue of the fingerholes, I take to be the flute portion?"

"Yes, it can be identified by the flared bell that stops it at the end."

"That I took for a copper chamber pot," Germanicus muttered. There was forced laughter. "And what sound does this piece here produce?"

"I'm afraid that is a handle, sir," Demetrius answered. Again laughter—but more genuine than before. "But, good Procurator, wait 'til you have seen this splendid ancillary feature. Cups, gentlemen."

Eight lead vessels shot under the instrument. The Celt smartly twisted the projecting mouthpiece a quarter turn, then blew until his cheeks turned purple. Demetrius fiddled with a small valve on the lower side of the harp frame. Suddenly the valve became a spigot from which eight ruby squirts of wine sizzled into the bottoms of the cups.

Applause.

Germanicus cocked an eyebrow. "Marvelous. And can this cow be milked for music as well?"

"Of course, Procurator."

The company made room for the musician to heft the ungainly *harphlutium* onto his hip.

As soon as the youth began to play, Germanicus saw what purpose the wine served: It was nothing less than an anesthetic to be ingested in numbing quantities before the torture by sound. "Enough, please," Germanicus said through a pathetic grin. "A musical fascination, no doubt, but my preferences run to the traditional at this hour of the night."

"But, sir, with a little patience you will come to appreciate the *harphlutium*," Demetrius said.

"Permit me to save the pleasure and my patience."

An *un*hybridized harp was strummed in the back of the car. It sounded like an old friend clearing her throat.

"There we are," Germanicus said warmly. "And how about that oration?"

"Directly, our good governor." The would-be Greek quietly announced to his company with a clap of the hands, "All right, lads, *The Captain of the Gate*—the abbreviated version." A little fog of the northern isle was seeping through his Phocis accent. But it had dissipated by the time he raised his arms in supplication to the heavens and dedicated a brief prayer to Mars.

His appointed chorus began:

"Then out spake brave Horatius,
The Captain of the Gate:"

Demetrius' hands swooped out of the air like eagles. Then
no longer was he a swollen-faced old fool with rouge on his
cheeks. He was a soldier of Rome, already deprived of one
eye, facing with but two comrades the massed Etruscan forces
of Lars Porsenna at the foot of a small wooden bridge over the
Tiber:

> *" 'To every man upon this earth*
> *Death cometh soon or late.*
> *And how can man die better*
> *Than facing fearful odds,*
> *For the ashes of his fathers*
> *And the temples of his gods? . . .*
> *" 'Hew down the bridge, Sir Consul*
> *With all the speed ye may;*
> *I, with two more to help me*
> *Will hold the foe in play.*
> *In yon strait path a thousand*
> *May well be stopped by three . . .' "*

"Aye," Germanicus whispered.
Demetrius cocked his arms and rammed his fists against his
hips:

> *" 'Now who will stand on either hand*
> *And keep the bridge with me?' "*

Germanicus' nerve endings were thrilled by the common
cry of "I—I—I!" that rocked the car until the men courted
hoarseness. He felt only a bit ashamed of being swiftly ma-
nipulated by such a backwater company. "Well done," he said,
admitting to himself that this was the perfect night for diversion.
"I am glad we please the procurator."
"Whose words do you speak?" he asked.
"Ah—those of Publius Vergilius Maro, I'm sure." The actor
frowned. "Do you know some other source?"
"Yes, a barracks ballad I loved in my youth." More forced
laughter attended this remark. It grieved him to think that once
he had been something of a wag, able to make his fellows

laugh with natural ease—a pleasure now denied him by his rank. "I jest, good Demetrius," Germanicus said. "I'm sure we borrowed our bold song from old Publius." He craned his neck. "Tribune!"

Marcus Junius came to attention. "Sir!"

"Wine from my stores for all present if you know the author of this declaration."

"I will try, sir." His face flashed pink as hands began pummeling him with encouragement.

"'Both to do and to endure valiantly is the Roman way.'"

The young man hesitated long enough only to wet his lips. "Livy, sir."

"Correct he is."

And the tribune was off at a dead run to find Charicles and the keys to the wine storage, the cheers of the actors on his heels.

Germanicus leaned back, smiling. "Of course, the entire tale is suspect."

"How is that, Procurator?" Demetrius asked.

"Another version has Horatius surviving his stand."

"Forgive me if I prefer my version—this hero does not have the poor manners to be honored in the flesh for his valor." The old actor pointed with glee at Germanicus' tribune, who came staggering in, his back bent under a hogshead. "You cannot imagine my delight, Procurator, to be in the presence of such an accomplished scholar of the Empire."

"I'm no historian." Germanicus held out his cup for Charicles to fill it with vinegar. The old servant scowled at the company as he shuffled out of the car. "Let's just say I've taken a peek at the past through the crack of a closed door."

"I beg to differ with the procurator," Marcus Junius piped up, "but he is regarded as an eminent historian. At the Campus Martius, we pored over his treatise, *The Critical Trace: A View of Roman Survival*. Our mentors nicknamed it *The Lex Germanicus*."

"What is the gist of it, tribune?" Demetrius asked.

"The fate of empires depends on the flip of a coin."

Demetrius blinked. "I must be missing the point."

"Hear me out—the trick is to pick out those moments when the toss was really critical. An event that was important was not necessarily critical. For example, in the seven hundred and fourth year after the Founding—"

"Caesar defeated Pompey at Pharsalus," Demetrius finished for him. "And had it not happened as it did?"

"Caesar would not have come to power, of course. The next critical event was Octavian's naval victory at Actium."

"Wait, wait, my young Polybius," Demetrius said. "Why have we whisked past the murder of our god Julius Caesar?"

"His death was important, not critical," Germanicus interrupted. "He bequeathed us Octavian, or Augustus, as the Senate named him, who would have come to power no matter what the circumstances. By defeating Marcus Antonius at Actium, Augustus prevented the splitting of the Empire—that is when the fate of the world tottered on the tip of a pin." Germanicus took a sip of vinegar. His words caused a stir among the tragedians. In the nuances of Roman politics any comment not absolutely laudatory of Gaius Julius was somehow taken to be a republican sentiment carefully salted away in the imperial heat of the age. It was especially surprising that this was said so casually by a member of the Julian family. "Not that Caesar's untimely death was anything but a loss."

"Of course," Demetrius said.

"Of course," the tragedians echoed.

"The final critical moment examined in the treatise is the battle of Teutoburg Forest," Marcus said with a cocky smile, mooning over the lip of his cup at the Sicilian boy. "There, Augustus' forces under the command of Quintilius Varus thrashed the German tribes under Arminius—"

"Hermann," Rolf grunted, making a point of racial pride by using Arminius' German name. Again, he had slipped unnoticed into Germanicus' presence to be the procurator's shadow.

"By this victory," Germanicus explained, "Augustus extended the Empire to the Mare Suebicum in the north and the River Vistula in the east. In one fortunate stroke, we put the barbarian threat at an arm's length—I shudder to think how we would have fared against these tribes in the intervening centuries had Teutoburg been lost. And just as importantly, we swelled our legions with Germans—once disciplined, perhaps the best soldiers in the world—at a time when our own hardy stock was in danger of being depleted."

On the sea legs of a veteran rail-galley traveler, Demetrius skittered across the pitching deck to the wine keg. "Fascinating—where next can we find this thread through the bloody rag of history, Procurator?"

"I had gotten no farther than the reign of Tiberius when the Hibernian civil war broke out, and I had to devote all of my energies to the present."

The cup stopped halfway to the aged actor's lips. "You may find something interesting I heard firsthand from the Sibyl at Alexandria last summer."

"Not that idiotic tale," the Celt whined.

"Hush, child. The Sibyl insists that during the year 786 a most extraordinary thing happened. The fate of the Empire lodged in the wits of the procurator of Palestine—'just like a sesame seed stuck between his two front teeth.'"

"I can think of nothing noteworthy in that part of the world at that time—except that mysterious death of Julius Caesar Germanicus in Antioch."

"No, good governor. This involves no one as grand. He was not even a Roman."

"The procurator?"

"Oh, no, sorry to confuse you. I'm speaking of the man the procurator was called upon to judge. A Hebrew named Joshua Bar Joseph."

Germanicus shook his head. "Means nothing to me. What is his story?"

"He was brought to trial by the local religious authorities."

"His offense?" Germanicus asked.

"Certain heresies."

"Against our gods?"

"No, theirs—or I should say their single grumpy little deity."

Germanicus chuckled. "I'm sorry, but the Sibyl fishes in waters too deep for me."

"It tries even the keenest imagination, doesn't it?"

"What became of Joshua Bar Joseph?"

"He was freed."

"Then how could he have threatened Rome?"

"By dying at our hands."

"Dying?" Marcus was incredulous.

"Yes," Demetrius said. "The Sibyl claims that had he been martyred a new cult would have arisen to threaten the Empire."

"How?" Germanicus asked.

"The religious liberality of the Empire would have been supplanted by dogmaticism and, inevitably, political division."

"What makes her think this Hebrew could have converted us? We are not a hysterical people."

"The Sibyl does not think, Procurator. She perceives."

"Why was he released?"

"The wife of the governor persuaded him that this Joshua was a righteous man. She must have had Minoan blood, that one."

Germanicus slowly got up. He craned his sore back to find a wisp of dawn on the horizon. "Ah, first light. Well, I don't know."

"Your skepticism is usual, sir. For this very reason, the Sibyl instructed me to originate a drama fully explaining the incident."

"Perhaps if we find the time at Agri Dagi."

"That would be to our extreme delight. In the course of my research, I discovered the story had nearly rotted away in a dank atmosphere of legends."

"Unfortunate."

"But, with the aid of the Sibyl, my version now stands as the most plausible."

Germanicus limped toward his private car on a sleeping foot. "Take your rest, gentlemen. We are on the verge of another *jhad*. There will be no rest until it's over."

CHAPTER VIII

THE SUN BURNED through the overcast. A beam of platinum-
colored light slanted down from the sky and flooded the garrison
at Agri Dagi. The silver pieces on the dress uniforms of the
assembled praetorians glinted to life. Mist began rising from
the flat black stones on which the men stood.

The military band, which had been playing that German
music so popular in remote outposts of the Empire, now stopped
three full beats, then struck up the more stately *Emblem of the
Legion*. Standing before the main formation with the officers
of Germanicus' staff, Crispa shuddered. Was it the tune or the
icy breeze? She had just marched up from the comparative
warmth of the station.

The Great Artery ran squarely beneath the parade ground
in a reinforced tunnel with portals that were secured by double
iron doors in time of alarm. Access from the subterranean
station to the windswept terraces above was achieved by a flight
of travertine stairs. It was embellished with frescoes depicting
Xenophon's expedition to ancient Persia——Roman artists sought
to justify the present by glorifying the past.

Her gaze drifted to the gleaming weapons of the praetorians. She was reminded of the venal purposes to which these tools of violence had been put through the centuries: the emperors confirmed and then struck down by them, the conspiracies given authority by them, the innocent men and women forced to open a vein in a warm bath rather than face the public indignity of execution by this praetorian steel. And she knew she did not want to die. Not just yet. And for one reason:

Germanicus. He was reviewing the troops in his slow, methodical way. She thought he looked sad and tired. Who could imagine he would one day know the horror and the glory of . . .

Her heart missed a squeeze. Poppaeus, the rotund garrison commander, bounced into view. He embraced Germanicus and jarred the procurator with his shrill gales of laughter. "Bastard," she whispered.

Desperately, Crispa tried to think of something other than Poppaeus.

She trained her mind's eye on the village in which she had been born, an un-Romanized settlement in the south of the Scandian peninsula. The image she saw, she felt certain, was how it appeared on this winter morning. The high peaks of the snow-laden roofs loomed up out of the forest. The smoke from the chimneys was the same color as the ashen trunks of the birches. But all at once the sun became warmer and warmer on her face. The tips of the tree branches sprouted green, and the white drifts shrunk back into the shadows. Pungent spikes of swamp onion wiggled up through the duff.

"Ah!" She sighed. A wind balmy with spring was now rushing around her. Full-blown leaves trembled on their stems. Then she heard The Boy call from beyond the meadow. "Sigi!" she answered.

Kicking off her boots, she raced through the grass, blades sticking between her toes as she ran. With milky skin and hair the color of ripe wheat, The Boy was beautiful. His lust was frank; he had not yet learned to adulterate it with guile. Taking his hand, she joined him in dodging the wooden altars of the old graveyard. And they vanished into the silent forest.

Yet, how odd—in the sweet afterglow of their innocent pleasure—to tell those trusting eyes the incredible: He would be dead in another season, slain by the legionaries for joining the notorious Scandian Renegades. "How do you know such a thing?" his voice still asked.

Crispa returned to the Agri Dagi garrison with a disconcerting jolt. *Ballistae* thundered in salute to the procurator. She blinked and looked around her. The wind had shoveled aside the cloud cover, and the sun spewed glitter on the glaciers of Agri Dagi. The sight of the mountain took away her breath. The physical world was magnificent. She did not want to die. Not yet.

But that long-awaited night was coming soon. The Sibyl had said it would be during the full phase of the moon:

> *"Your ashes will abandoned be;*
> *Your spirit to the north will flee."*

Strange questions buzzed in her head. What would the first hour following her death be like? Would her spirit body, armed with a host of sublime senses, bolt aloft, fly north over the moon-flecked waters of the Pontus Euxinus, stream through the forests of Dacia like a gossamer shroud, and finally glide down to the little graveyard in Scandia to rest beside her mother's own specter? Still, there was a herculean labor to be accomplished before she could lie beneath one of those altars tilting over with antiquity.

Startled, she realized that Poppaeus had waddled up to her and was speaking.

". . . this *massing* notion, Crispa. I can't put any stock in it. Are we to become as superstitious as the barbarians?"

She calmly tried to return the gaze of his piggish eyes but found it impossible. She, who had found the strength not to tell her own first cousin that he was about to be arrested on a charge of treason, now wanted to scream the truth to Germanicus, who in his ignorance looked pathetically vulnerable to the dangers that faced him. The pressure of all this was becoming more than she could stand. "Good Poppaeus is right to be concerned about superstition," she heard her voice evenly say. It was as if an older sister had taken over for her. "But *massing* is not a superstition. It is a terrible weapon, and we must be wary of its power."

"What are we to do?" Poppaeus asked. "Sink into the kind of ridiculous behavior that marred our past—such as posting sentries around a corpse so witches cannot carve off its face?"

Germanicus' eyelid began fluttering. Pretending to shade

his eyes, he brought up a hand to mask the tic.

"Well, this is certainly an issue to occupy us while we dine on the most succulent Syrian lamb I've ever had the pleasure to serve," Poppaeus said.

With disgust Crispa stared at the man's person: the puffy wrists, the multiple chins sagging off his jawbone, and a rump as wide as a sword was long. His repulsiveness seemed all the more vile because she had a part in his conspiracy.

"What activity have you had here at the pass?" Germanicus asked.

Poppaeus smiled. "Not a peep from the savages."

"Where is Colonel Scilla?"

"On a reconnaissance."

"As he should be. Good."

A captain with soft-looking hands whispered in Poppaeus' ear, who then scowled and snapped, "Why wasn't I told?"

"I saw no urgency in it."

For Germanicus' sake, Poppaeus varnished a smile over his lips. "Forgive me, but Scilla returned an hour ago. One of his Scandian irregulars was wounded, and the colonel has been attending to him. He has been advised of your arrival. He will join us as soon as possible."

Just then Crispa saw Colonel Scilla striding down the stairs from the concourse toward them. He donned his ceremonial helmet, which had been tucked under his arm, then ran his fingers down the red crest to make sure it was evenly fluffed. Involuntary tears came to her eyes. The birthmark that splashed across his forehead and upper left cheek still made him self-conscious, which he attempted to offset with an aggressive walk and the habit of flexing his jaw muscles. The limp the Iberian mutineers had given him he could not hide. "Hail, Procurator," he said warmly, without affectation.

"Scilla!" Germanicus grasped the man by his sinewy shoulders. "How are things here?"

"We can expect a barbarian revolt at any minute."

Poppaeus cackled. "Sometimes I can actually see the black cloud hanging over your head, Scilla."

The officer brought his heels together in deference to his commander. "I mean only to give the procurator a clear idea of our predicament here at the most salient garrison along the Artery."

"Predicament? I would rather you refer to it as our situation. After all, we have not experienced the trouble they are having in less tightly run districts."

Scilla was close to saying something more when he thought better of it. He quickly turned his attention to Crispa. "Hello, Colonel."

"Colonel," she said softly.

They pressed their right palms together, then interlocked fingers. Once again she could smell the stench of renounced Roman uniforms smoldering in a corner of the barracks. She could see Scilla as he lay on the mess table, smiling at her as he waited for the Iberians to break his shinbones with an iron bar, gently warning her with his eyes not to fixate on their fellow tribune, who was floating lifelessly in the bathtub. "Courage!" his expression said. And she recalled how, after his legs had been crushed without making him betray Rome, he had writhed on the floor and watched what the rebels were doing to her. He had looked as if his soul was being smothered. Then his hand had reached out for hers. Palms touched. Shaking wildly, fingers intertwined. It was at that instant she had found the strength to *mass*.

"How is Lucius?" Crispa asked, her hand falling away. She referred to Scilla's blind freedman and mate.

After meeting the legal requirements by sharing ten years of unblemished fidelity and promising to will their estates to the Emperor, the two men had been granted a liaison, a homosexual marriage sanctioned by the state.

"He is well. And misses your good company. He says it was the only thing that made Hibernia bearable."

"I think of him often."

"He maintains you are the only person whose warmth he confuses with the sun's."

Poppaeus' voice prattled louder than all others. "Now, this light repast I've had prepared for your arrival is nothing fancy. Just something to keep your strength up against those pesky *zaims* until my banquet this evening. Then I will really fortify you with enough sustenance for a decade." Jovially he patted Marcellus' breastplate. "I will not fail to order a course of Parthian delights."

Marcellus smiled without feeling. "I will eat what my commander does." This was a shopworn expression of loyalty born of a spate of poisonings that had thinned the ranks of the Julian family in the last century.

"Nothing for me now." Germanicus began inching Scilla aside by the elbow. "With your permission, Poppaeus, I want a more detailed briefing from the colonel."

"Sir, it offends me you ask my permission at all. With the procurator, my acquiescence is automatic. And you will find my adjutant to be the most thorough of men. Infinitely thorough." As soon as Germanicus and Scilla were out of earshot, he grunted at Crispa and Marcellus, "And if Colonel Scilla weren't such an atrocious reactionary like our beloved procurator we wouldn't have a 'predicament' here. Well, no use letting our pleasure be spoiled. Time to eat, friends. The truth is, Germanicus' presence always keeps me from having any fun."

"He has the ability to inhibit us all. It's extraordinary."

"Dear girl, I find nothing extraordinary about a man who stamps out pleasure and fetters imagination wherever he shows his vinegar face."

"He is the essential Roman," Crispa argued, color rising in her cheeks. "That is both good and bad."

"Well, the essential Roman, as you say, has positively stagnated our culture."

Three abreast, they plodded up the icy steps to Poppaeus' quarters. Marcellus bumped against Crispa. She thought nothing of this until he did it again—and again. She fired an angry glance at him, and he backed off. As if with new eyes, she noticed the thick black hair in his nostrils, his obstinate barbarian jaw, and most detracting of all, the weak, brooding mouth.

She could not believe the times she had abandoned herself in joy to him. Even more unfathomable was the memory that she had given herself to him the first night they had met, shocking her closest friends with her brazenness.

But she would give herself to him again. This contempt now buzzing around her face like a cloud of gnats would clear. Then, once more, she would see him in hot golden light.

Below, Germanicus and Scilla were strolling across an observation platform. Crispa smiled. Each had clasped his hands behind his back as they talked.

She had first confided her feelings about Germanicus to

Scilla and Lucius in Hibernia: "He is not handsome. He is not always good company. But he attracts me. I don't know why."

"He exudes a great moral authority," Scilla had said, trying to fan life into the peat fire inside the cottage he shared with Lucius. "The Emperor mocks the sacrifices we make out here. You know—his damned excesses. But Germanicus redeems what we do—makes it all seem honorable and worthy. When he's in command, our administration of the world becomes a noble necessity." He frowned at the balky coals. "I too love him, Crispa. But my passion lies elsewhere. To confuse love and passion can be costly." Then he took Lucius' hand in a way that seemed quaint and modest.

Wheezing, Poppaeus called a halt on the first landing. He glowered at Marcellus. "What happened at Mus Station?"

"The tribune you trusted so highly grew tired of the wait and marched his men back to the barracks. I was ready to kill Germanicus myself, but his German bodyguard ruined that chance."

"So be it." Poppaeus chortled as if this all had been a trivial matter. "It was worth a stab in the dark."

"We should try again here in Agri Dagi."

"Don't be absurd, my boy."

"Poppaeus, you have the necessary forces!"

"Those forces might look to Scilla for their orders in the confusion of the moment. The mottle-faced little bastard enjoys a sickening loyalty from them."

"Poison him," Marcellus suggested.

Poppaeus screwed a fingertip into a dimple in his fat cheek. "I already am. I've been doing it for months—a drop at a time in his wine."

Crispa stumbled and missed a step. Marcellus had to catch her. She thought she was going to faint. She had not foreseen the death of her gentle friend, and she staggered under the weight of this new horror added to her burden. Crispa bit her lower lip so hard, blood oozed up the space between her two front teeth.

"Patient methods are best, Marcellus." Poppaeus' breath became even more labored. "This mountain will be the death of me."

"To think Germanicus would already be in his tomb had we succeeded at Mus."

"Well, I risked it only because had we failed, the commander there—not I—would have been put to the sword." The huge belly trembled with laughter. "And to think the poor fool knew nothing about it!"

Suddenly Marcellus jabbed the air with a fist. "We must be bold before it is too late!"

"To rush forward boldly is to wind up bloody. We should sit back and take our cues from the coming events in Rome."

They approached a cliff that crested over them like a black wave. At an opening large enough to admit a sand-galley stood two praetorian guards with jaded eyes. Crispa had the feeling that nothing would have relieved their boredom better than to butcher the next human being who strolled up to their post.

Entering Poppaeus' headquarters was a virtual walk into the underworld—the entire complex had been blasted and chipped out of the volcanic mountain. The effort had taken ten years and cost many Cambrian slaves, who were skillful tunnel miners, their lives.

As they padded down a long *vestibulum* Poppaeus drew Crispa and Marcellus against his body with his hammy arms. "This chamber was as gloomy as a catacomb, so I had it paved with fifty tons of obsidian." There was something sinister about the lustrous black tiles.

Crispa turned her ear to the music of falling water.

"Over this way, my dear," Poppaeus said, having noticed her reaction. Chuckling merrily, he led them aside down a passageway toward what sounded like a freshet tumbling out of the mountain. But when they reached a small concavity Crispa leaned against a metal railing, sickened by the sight.

"Here I come to meditate." Poppaeus dreamily viewed the cascade. "A dozen slaves were drowned when they blasted free this subterranean stream." Crimson spotlights cast the water into frothing blood. "I call it my Phlegethon room."

"Let's go," Crispa said weakly. It appeared as if all the blood to be spilled in the coming hours now gushed from a single wound in the world.

"With this water supply and ample food, you could withstand a siege here for a hundred years," Marcellus said.

Poppaeus tapped the side of his bald head to indicate that, he too, thought himself clever.

Beyond the obsidian-tiled *vestibulum* was a huge atrium, crammed with statuary gaudily painted in the Greek style and a ring of at least fifty couches. This, she knew, was where

Poppaeus did his formal entertaining. But when they passed through the great hall Crispa's heart sank, for she knew they would be feted in the commander's notorious personal quarters. Word had it that the only thing forbidden in these lightless dens was decency.

Two more praetorians had been stationed in the *tablinium*, or passage room. This pair had such unmitigated cruelty etched in their faces, they made their comrades posted at the portal of the complex seem as pleasant as vestal virgins in comparison. With lightning efficiency they relieved Marcellus and Crispa of their swords. "Why is this done?" Marcellus complained.

"Oh, children, let me eat with peace of mind," Poppaeus whined.

"Do you fear us?" Crispa asked.

The fat man smiled and said nothing.

She could scarcely hide her shock when a servant took Poppaeus' cloak and toga. Completely naked, the man acted as if nothing were amiss. He rubbed his hands together. "Now, who is ready for an appetite enhancer?"

"I am." Marcellus gamely ignored his host's lack of costume. He took a pipe stuffed with hemp from a slave girl whose gown revealed one of her breasts.

Crispa refused the offer. Even more than wine, hemp robbed her of that hypersensitivity she would so desperately need from now on.

"Recline on your couches," Poppaeus said. "And Crispa, it would delight me to see your body."

"I think not."

"Don't be embarrassed."

"I think not," she repeated woodenly. It made her feel ill at ease to have to keep her gaze above the man's swollen gut.

"The choice is yours, but I've heard about your excellent beauty—and hearing is not quite the same."

"She has named her choice," Marcellus snapped.

"So she has. The only demand I make of my guests is that they enjoy themselves."

Taking a cup of wine that she absently recognized to be of a celebrated vintage, Crispa lay on a silk-upholstered couch. The opulent atmosphere was nauseating her. But there was nothing to be done. The agony of it all: She would never have choices again!

The musky perfume hanging in the air threatened to choke

her. Whenever it had begun to clear out, silent servants appeared and sprayed more of the suffocating stuff from brass atomizers. These people shuffled around as if they had been recruited from the ranks of the dead, their youth scorched out of them by what Poppaeus had forced them to do.

She gasped.

Two evil eyes wiggled up from behind Poppaeus. The copper-scaled stem supporting them danced from side to side. "Don't be alarmed," Poppaeus said. "They're harmless in every respect."

At the mention of others of the same species, Crispa crawled higher on her couch and glanced from place to place on the floor. Then she recognized the coils in the shadows for what they were. The first snake she had seen now slithered up the crack between Poppaeus' mountainous buttocks and onto the pink desert of his back. He wrapped the obliging thing around his neck as if it were a scarf. "They are an accessory to good dreams."

"I thought that's what wine does." Marcellus popped a mushroom into his mouth.

"Oh, no. Wine promotes dreamlessness—as does poison." The Parthian stopped chewing.

Poppaeus giggled wildly. "You must forgive me, dear fellow, but I learned this manner of humor through my close association with the Empress Pamphile. Don't worry. Ours shall be a long and profitable friendship."

"What word do you have from the Empress?"

Poppaeus conspicuously kept silent until a slave had finished heaping steaming piles of blanched asparagus on his plate. Then, while munching on a juicy spear, he whispered, "She asks her friends to be careful as the day approaches. One heedless word can cost us all our heads."

Marcellus smirked. "Imagine Fabius' face when he realizes his own Empress has masterminded his overthrow."

Poppaeus raised his cup. "May he go to his death never knowing who or why."

"Has Pamphile heard you out about my proposal?"

"Oh, yes, and has granted it—in effect."

"What do you mean?"

"As procurator of Anatolia, I will be permitted to do what I please with the province."

"And?" Marcellus' eyes simmered with distrust.

"Haven't I already given you my word?"

"I learned the value of a Roman's word when I was a child-prisoner in Fabius' palace!"

"Rest assured—Armenia will be your *satrapy* to govern as you see fit."

"*Greater* Armenia—which means the parts of Cappadocia and Parthia we agreed upon. Have you forgotten so soon?"

"What? Oh, no, no. I spoke thusly for brevity's sake."

"Do not be brief when you describe the size of my realm, Poppaeus!" Marcellus gestured with a fist, knocking over his cup. "Did you make these new boundaries clear to the Empress?"

"There was not time to delve into details."

"This matter is no detail!"

"The woman is reshaping the world, man!" Then Poppaeus quickly lowered his voice. The serpents had become agitated. They slid under the couches. "How can she be expected to settle each question herself at this time? She has entrusted me to make guarantees for her as the need—"

"I want my assurances directly from her!"

"It's too late. She's hours away from seizing power. Do you want to jeopardize hundreds of lives with your impatience? As soon as all is resolved in our favor, we shall go to Rome and petition her for the creation of your little kingdom."

Stuffing his mouth with more mushrooms, Marcellus mulled this suggestion over in brooding silence.

Poppaeus smiled at Crispa. "Now, the Empress and I did find time to discuss your request. She found it touching you asked only for a Scandian temple to be dedicated in your mother's honor. She said this will silence forever the gossip that sours the sweetness of your mother's memory. Did you know they were girlhood friends?"

"I know only that she was jealous of my mother's beauty."

"Pamphile is envious of no one," Poppaeus said.

"Even the gods can be envious."

"What we can agree on, dear girl, is that Pamphile will rule in an enlightened manner."

Crispa glared at him. "And what will that be?"

"Opening up the gates so change and growth may pass through."

"What change?"

"Crispa, the long journey has left you argumentative. Need

I remind you that we have not had an innovation in our form of government since Julius crossed the Rubicon? Or that our doting senators still gabble in a Latin Cicero would be comfortable with?"

She was ready to say that all the tyrants of the Julian genes had, in the rosy flush of newly won power, promised an enlightened reign, even a return to the Republic in due time, but the argument suddenly seemed useless.

"Let's keep the proper perspective in this." Poppaeus scooped up a snake and stroked its head with a finger. "Pamphile vows to give procuratorial governments greater control of their own affairs. Meaning she will not skim all the cream off our enterprises as Fabius does."

No more than ten years of age, two naked Parthian slave boys bowed before Poppaeus. Their greased bodies glistened in the lamplight.

"Ah, my little wrestlers. Get on with it—quickly."

They lunged into each other with vigor. Arms and legs intertwined, and the boys toppled to the floor with the firm thud of young muscles.

"Do not dillydally!" Poppaeus warned them. "Tell me, Crispa, what are the auspices for our venture? You hobnob with the Sibyls."

"The Sibyl at Ephesus is the only one I know."

"Well, what does she say?"

Crispa looked carefully toward Marcellus, "She says that some fires look cool until we step on them."

"Sounds like something a bloody Sibyl would mumble." Poppaeus called for a servant.

"Sir?" an old man whose ears were missing said too loudly.

"These boys are irritating me. Look at this!"

They were rocking back and forth in each other's embrace. "Arm them with steel," Poppaeus said.

"But these are not gladiators, sir. They are not trained in swordplay."

"What better teacher than experience? Arm them!"

"Aye, sir."

Wine dribbled down Marcellus' chin as he eagerly waited for the contest to begin.

"May you never be a king," she whispered so he could not hear.

"What is that, my darling?"

"Nothing," she snapped.

Their small penises shrunken with fright, the children confronted each other with short swords in their hands.

"Begin!" Poppaeus shouted.

Crispa buried her face in the couch rugs.

"You've done a good job defending the Great Artery here, Scilla," Germanicus said proudly.

"We've learned the hard way how to do it. A static defense isn't worth a damn."

"Not until your back is against the wall." Germanicus tried to recall what the scene had looked like when he and less than sixty legionaries had defended the pumping station against an army of tribesmen during the Great *Jhad*. The snowy hump of Agri Dagi was the same, of course, as was the birch-covered cone of Little Agri Dagi seven miles to the southeast of its grander sister. The jagged volcanic mountains ringing the pass still evoked that loneliness he had felt so keenly as a young tribune at war. The old pumping station was now a ruin, and the new facility had been built higher on the slope in the saddle of the pass, where it could be more readily protected behind a wall bristling with *ballistae*. Below, the pasture that in the same day had been velvety with spring growth, and then churned into a field of red mud by the battle, was now a sea of cream, as if all that violence had never been. The breeze whistled for the silent ghosts to show themselves.

His eyes followed where the Great Artery declined away toward the Parthian city of Tauris. From there two spurs departed for Sarmatia and Scythia. This region was indeed the crossroads of the eastern empire—Rome's lifelines were strewn across its desolation.

"Are you thinking of twenty years ago?" Scilla asked quietly.

Germanicus nodded.

"I've never heard you say a word about that day."

Germanicus' eyes drifted toward the pasture again. "I saw a slave gather the points of a dozen spears in his chest in order to save the *decurion* he served. A slave!" He snugged his cloak around his neck. "How could I ever do justice to such an avalanche of courage?"

"When the snow melts, you can find all kinds of things

down there—broken teeth, bits of bone, rusted sword tips . . ."

Germanicus shook off his reverie. "You said you expect a rebellion at any minute."

"Without a doubt."

"Give me reasons."

"My native sources tell me the black-market price of a *pilum* has gone right through the ceiling. Ambushes on our forces have doubled in frequency. Last week a prisoner seized for a minor offense killed himself by beating his head against a wall—rather than face interrogation."

"Just like before the Great *Jhad*."

"And that's not all, Germanicus. *Zaims*—hundreds of the holy beggars—are beating a path up here from the plateau. Which leads me to a matter only you might understand."

"Yes?"

"The bastards are up to *massing*. They did the trick on one of my centurions, I'm sure. Poppaeus would hear nothing of it, saying I was filled with superstitious trash and that the man had died of a heart attack. Poppaeus should have been there to see Crispa . . ."

Germanicus felt the unnerving spasms begin in his eyelid.

"Are you all right, sir?"

"Yes, go on."

"Yesterday, I went out to check on the small village along the Aras River. The wrapheads there were doing the damnedest thing. You know how precise they are about facing their holy city when they pray. Well, that city is south, not west, of here. These rug-kneelers were fixing on due west."

Germanicus felt his heart sink. "Were they making a whining noise deep in their throats?"

Scilla struck his palms together. "I knew this couldn't be an isolated incident!"

"I'm afraid not. A legionary dropped dead at Firat Station— all the signs point to a *massing*. The same fate befell a retired legionary and his family."

"You fought a major skirmish to get here, didn't you?" Scilla asked.

"Yes."

"May I be frank with the procurator?"

"When haven't you been?"

"Anatolia is ready to blow up any second. What the hades

are you doing out here now?"

Germanicus studied the stone walls of the old pumping station. He had the expression of a gravely ill man being shown his sarcophagus for the first time. "Two reasons, my friend—and I trust it to go no further. First, Crispa had a vision that I'd be assassinated in Nova Antiochia."

Scilla gasped. "Who plots against us?"

"She doesn't know but believes I am safer near Agri Dagi."

"Trust what she says, Germanicus."

"I do or I wouldn't be here. Second, I believe I'm being *massed* against. That is why you saw the barbarians turned toward the west—the capital, my seat of power."

"No doubt they'd love to make the procurator their next victim. But why necessarily you?"

"Suddenly I have ailments I can't explain."

Scilla smiled with encouragement. "I've felt poorly myself the last few months. Does that mean I'm being *massed* against? You will enjoy thirty years of Ostian retirement after I am ashes." But the eyes of his former adjutant could not lie to Germanicus.

"There is something more. Crispa dreamed of a powerful *zaim* with a beautiful white beard."

"Good Mars!" escaped Scilla's lips in a hush. He spun around to face the mountain.

"Is he up there, Scilla?"

The colonel nodded fiercely. "There's a chasm on the northeast face. In its shadows, at the foot of a glacier, is a barbarian redoubt. We call it the . . ."

"Purple Village," Germanicus said.

"You know of it, then?"

"Yes. And that's what Crispa meant when she said the air around this Great *Zaim* is *purple*."

"Well, we hear it's a bloody fortress. I doubt we would live far enough up the trail to see its minaret."

"I was there once," Germanicus said without explaining. "It would be suicide to go in force."

"A reconnaissance, then?"

"That is what we must do, good Scilla."

The colonel stared at Germanicus. "I'm afraid the altitude has made the procurator heady."

Germanicus chuckled—it was refreshing to hear such bluntness from a subordinate. "How else then?"

"Send a native emissary. Wait for this great one to come to us."

"At the head of five thousand warriors? No, I don't have time."

"Why must you see him?"

"I have to end this *jhad* before it begins. Otherwise, years of work are thrown away, and Anatolia becomes another Hibernia. I must talk to the man face-to-face. If I fail to convince him, I may have to kill him. Whatever the case, Crispa assures me that all will end well if I go on foot to see this Great *Zaim*."

"End well for whom?" Scilla slumped on a low stone wall and smiled. "Do you know what you are asking me to do? Please tell me, Germanicus, that you know."

"I do, my friend."

Scilla slowly came to his feet again. "Then enough rest. Our only chance to get near this impossible citadel is with my best special squad. We were getting nowhere until we put aggressive patrols out in the snow. And at night. It was hard to break that safe-and-sound-by-dusk mentality that came from centuries of building nice stout fortifications in wild lands where it got very dark at night."

It heartened Germanicus to hear Scilla speak confidently. "I understand you've put your lads on skis—just like the Scandian Renegades."

"Sir, my lads *are* Scandian Renegades."

"The gods protect us," Germanicus muttered. "Reformed of looting and other bad habits, I hope."

"Not entirely."

"Oh, Jupiter, Juno, Janus . . ."

"But they fight like no men of war you've ever seen," Scilla said. "Mention the Purple Village and you won't get a legionary out from under his bed."

"I have no quarrel with unorthodox soldiering."

"You might when you rub elbows with my Scandians. They're not ordinary soldiers—even for this forsaken place. I let them go their own way as long as they get results for me."

"I trust your leadership."

Scilla shook his head. "Very well. When do we go—tonight?"

"No, now."

"I'll get my people together," the colonel said without blinking an eye.

"I want to take a centurion from my staff along. A good man. He's a German."

"My Renegades will have him for breakfast."

"Not this one."

CHAPTER IX ·

FOR CENTURIES, Rome allowed the successive ruling clans of
Scandia to come and go like storms across the tundra. The
Empire did not dip its boots in northern slush because the
barbarian warmaking was internecine, and the one time an
imperial cohort was called upon to help one ragtag nobleman
against another, the legionaries mutinied. Emperor after emperor had turned his back on what was assumed to be a frozen
wilderness sparsely populated by half-starved barbarians with
hair the color of fire.

This was before the discovery of iron ore.

Three months after the find, two full Roman armies arrived
on the muddy heels of the Scandian spring to crush the barbarians "by the turning of the birch leaves," according to their
commander, Lucius Maxentius. But Maxentius failed to wrap
up the campaign in a year, let alone a summer, so he was
replaced by Severus Carcalla, who vowed to whip himself daily
until victory was his; and he was replaced by Commodus the
Elder; and he by his son, the Younger; and he by Marcus
Valerian—until nine years and three hundred thousand le-

95

gionaries had been gobbled up by a country that had not yet surrendered a pinch of iron.

It was said that Scandia was mining Rome for blood.

Valerian's fortunes were already at their lowest ebb when a key garrison mutinied, and at last he felt forced to make a decision that haunted him until he opened a vein one evening and trickled away from his burden.

As early as the four hundred and first year of the Empire, the historian Gallienus concluded that no weapon will ever be outlawed immediately after it is invented. No matter how terrible its potential, the device will be used at least once because of "some desperate necessity of war."

So it was with *portaplague*.

Roman commanders refrained from using this biologic agent for twenty years after its development—until Scandia—when Gallienus' assertion was proved correct.

Imperial officers, legionaries, functionaries, and their barbarian wives and camp followers were inoculated. Then non-exploding canisters were lofted by *ballistae* into the areas held by the rebels, where the children scooped them up as soon as the metal was cool and, like all booty, carried them into their camps.

Sixty percent of the Scandian people were eradicated. All resistance collapsed without the loss of an additional legionary.

Had it ended there, Valerian might have been able to live with himself. He was a simple man who was readily consoled by his wife, children, and garden.

But he had loosed an evil that was ten times easier to incubate than contain.

The Scandian peninsula had been under the twin hammers of war and famine so long there remained no livestock or game on which to observe the effects of *portaplague*. Even the great reindeer herds had gone into the grousing bellies of men.

So it baffled the *coloni* of northernmost Germania when their cattle and sheep bloated up and perished overnight. They blamed anthrax, forest spirits, the gods, and finally—with the anemic anger of men who have lived their lives under a tyranny—the Empire, although never the Emperor himself.

But by this time the blight had spread all the way to Transalpine Gaul, where human cases began to appear. In less than a week *portaplague* leapfrogged down the calf of Italia to Rome. Their leaders apparently unable to do anything, the people dusted off the old superstitions, and the sky over the Forum Romanum became yellow with sulphur smoke.

The Emperor's physician, the principal medical authority, later excused himself at his public trial by claiming ignorance of Valerian's activities in Scandia. This might have been true. But, nevertheless, he had failed to implement a vaccination program, although it was proved the virus had been identified as *portaplague* in Cisalpine Gaul.

Six hundred thousand died and were laid out in the streets for collection—among them the wife and two small children of Marcus Valerian. Another two million perished in the provinces before the disease had run its course.

All this had taken place the year Germanicus was born.

The pathetic thing, Germanicus thought as he exchanged his dress uniform and light armor for the snow-white suit and kepi of an imperial mountain irregular, was that Valerian had been a good man and a capable general. He had just lacked imagination.

Germanicus stopped his hurried preparations for the patrol and tried to remember what had launched this mental excursion. "Ah, the Scandian Renegades," he whispered aloud.

Valerian had rounded up the nine kings of Scandia to make them surrender for all time.

The day had been steel gray from horizon to horizon. The wind whistled around the shields of the legionaries. Suddenly, just when Old Balder was scribbling away the freedom of his people, the young *jarls*, or earls, overpowered the praetorians guarding them and gained weapons in the blinking of an eye. More than a hundred Romans died as the Scandian noblemen hacked their way to the forest on the cheers of their kings.

There was no explanation for such delirious behavior—at least not to Romans, who had not known subjugation since Hellenic times.

Who could blame these *jarls* if they took to the wilds and lived off plunder from Roman outposts? Sliding on their skis beneath stars as big as apples, they gave a personality to Scandian outrage, and the common folk nurtured them despite the imperial penalty of crucifixion.

The bastard sons of these men became known as the Scandian Renegades. They were less sure than their fathers of the reason for the rebellion but were just as venomous toward foreign rule.

However, Polybius predicted the outcome of this revolt two thousand years before it occurred: "... when the sons of these men received the same position of authority [as their fathers] ... some of them gave themselves up with passion to avarice and unscrupulous love of money, others to drinking and the boundless debaucheries which accompany it, and others to the violation of women or the forcible appropriation of boys; and so they turned an aristocracy into an oligarchy...."

The attitude of this second-generation leadership was the conceit of oligarchies that their members are superior to those who serve them. It became clear to the people that the scions of their *jarls* were superior only in their excesses, the greatest of which were butchery and looting, often exercised against their fellow countrymen. The Scandians began looking to the Roman procurator for order and safety in their daily lives.

Within fifty years the Renegade movement degenerated from a devoted partisan army to a horde of drunken brigands. Having forced the Romanization of Scandia with their licentiousness, the Renegades saw no disloyalty in fighting for the Empire as long as the pay was good.

Scilla handed Germanicus two wood frames. Each enclosed a latticework of stretched animal gut. "Beaver tails," he explained in the musty air of the supply chamber.

"What are they for?"

"Walking on the snow."

"We used to push through it."

"We are not the iron men of yesteryear, Procurator."

Rolf deftly fitted the contraptions onto his boots, then began assisting Germanicus.

"Do you ski, centurion?" Scilla asked.

"No, Colonel." Rolf seemed to take the question as a racial slight. His eyes declared that a legionary *marched* where his Emperor sent him—on his knees, if necessary—but never frolicked on waxed hardwood slats. Apparently a pair of beaver tails was as far as he would compromise with the elements.

"Very well, then. You, the procurator, and I will make do on tails. We can—"

"But do *you* ski?" Germanicus interrupted Scilla.

"Expertly. But I'll stay at the center with you. My Scandian Renegades will cover our flanks."

Outside, the midday glare made Germanicus think he had stepped from the supply room onto the flaring surface of the sun. Squinting, he pulled the twin smoked lenses down off the brim of his kepi and over his eyes.

"This way, sir," Scilla said, "if you'd like to slip away with no fanfare. My Renegades will join us on the snow."

One by one they lowered themselves down the face of the wall in a hoisted cage. The endless belt that conveyed it automatically activated a bell to alert the sentry. This Scilla silenced by wrapping a woolen sock around the clapper.

Then the imperial patrol struck out into the wilderness.

An hour later Germanicus gazed back at the garrison. Crusted with huge black scabs of lichen, the *ballistae* fortifications looked intimidating enough, but he knew only too well that these defenses were far from impregnable. He meant to commend Scilla for ordering vigorous patrol around the clock, but then he thought of Crispa down there and the note he had left for her, commanding her "to protect all procuratorial interests in my absence." Now he regretted the officious tone of this missive; somehow it insinuated perfidy on her part.

From the slope above came a sound like water being poured over hot coals. Rolf unslung his *pilum*.

"Wait," Scilla cautioned him.

The uncanny noise drew nearer.

"What be this?" Rolf had hardly finished speaking when a shadow skirted over the drifts into their midst and stopped with a splash of ice.

Rocking back and forth on his skis, the Renegade was tall and mountain lean. His oily blond hair was drawn into a ponytail that swung down to his waist. He had blackened his prominent cheekbones with charcoal. This made his blue eyes appear more deeply set than they were. His body was athletic in a careless-looking way; no Olympian narcissist, he slouched rather than preened. Weapons and skis were the only aspects of his person that were well cared for.

"Procurator, may I introduce Corporal Hagg from the first squad of irregulars," Scilla said.

Reeking of the honey liquor Scandians consumed by the hogshead, the man was well on the way to being drunk. He returned Germanicus' regal stare and barked, "Hah!"

Scilla had to restrain Rolf until Germanicus motioned for the centurion to hold back.

"Hah!" the Scandian repeated.

Scilla had to pull Rolf back all over again.

As smoothly as the beaver tails allowed, Germanicus approached the Scandian. A closer inspection revealed the barbarian's eyes to be red with ruptured blood vessels.

"Hah!" The man refused to budge an inch as the procurator's face came toward his.

"So you're from Scandia, Corporal Hagg."

The blue eyes glowered from their bone caverns.

"I was there once, Hagg. In the summer. Very beautiful. Especially the lakes. But I didn't care much for the insects. Big fellows, aren't they? And hostile." Germanicus smiled engagingly, and for the first time the Scandian seemed a bit off guard. "Well, I found out there was only one way to deal with the nasty beggars. Slap them right when they least expect it. Just when they're trying to draw blood."

Then, with no warning, Germanicus raised the wooden beaver tail and kicked the Renegade in the scrotum. The man doubled over, his knees and forehead striking the snow at the same time, skis clattering as they crossed.

Scilla smirked behind a finger. "Hagg, I should like you to meet Germanicus Julius Agricola, Procurator of Anatolia and General of the Legions."

"Just one question, Colonel." Germanicus turned his back on the moaning Renegade. "Did he know who I was?"

"Oh, no, Procurator. In that case, he'd have been ten times as rude."

In the space of a few breaths, the Scandian went from moaning to laughter. This indignity was just another symptom of a universe he found hopeless. "Yer-mahn-eee-kuz!" Hagg said between guffaws.

"You see," Scilla explained, "it's a contest among them to see who can be the most offensive to the Romans."

"How does this chap rank?"

"I'm afraid he's a small fry. Perhaps seventh of twelve."

"Grand," Germanicus muttered.

"There's one—Jann's his name—who's rather exquisite at the game."

"Is he their leader?"

"They don't subscribe to our idea of leadership. Everyone's supposed to be of the same heart and mind. Leadership would be superfluous. The concept is *Roman*."

"How do you get along so well with them?" Germanicus asked.

"I told Jann I'm a Hibernian."

At three, just when the sun floated behind the peak, the imperial patrol came to the edge of a region that looked impossible to traverse.

Germanicus' lips grew thin as he recognized the vista before him.

Through the ages, fingers of frost had pried into cracks on the face of a cliff, unloosing great hunks of basalt. Year after year these monoliths had tumbled below to shatter. Eventually a jagged heap a mile wide was formed, honeycombed with dens and caves that were dark with shadow even at high noon. A hidden stream chuckled deep within its bowels and issued sulphurous mist up through the rocks.

"Here's the first reason we've never been to the Purple Village," Scilla whispered. "Jupiter, what a horrid piece of territory."

Germanicus could hear the skis of other Renegades slicing across the snow in an upslope flanking movement. "We called this Pluto's Villa in our day."

"We still do." Suddenly Scilla stared at Germanicus. "Pardon my boldness, but how could you have made it this far?"

"I will not pardon your boldness," Germanicus grunted. He could not admit that he and two other boy-officers had gone up to the Purple Village—not without disgracing the dead. The young tribunes had caught the fever of the Persepolis Trove—the legendary treasure Alexander had seized from the ancient capital of Persia and lost in transit to bandits between Ecbatana and Lydia. A rumor circulating in the garrison placed the trove inside the Purple Village. They made it to the forbidden aerie, but only Germanicus survived to recount the story to his fuming colonel. He was not court-martialed, because the commander was grasping at straws to save the reputations of the slain lads, who like Germanicus were of excellent families. So it came to pass that the young officers had been sent on a reconnaissance with secret orders.

Whatever the official lie, the experience had cured Germanicus of greed. Whenever his palm itched for gold, he forced himself to recall his two friends, whose bodies had never been recovered from the village.

Suddenly there was a scream from above. It was the cry of bottomless pain.

"Well, we've found the wrapheadies!" Scilla joined Germanicus behind the cover of a rock.

"That man be cut by a blade," Rolf said.

The screams dissolved into delirious wailing.

Scilla winced. "Good Mars, I know that voice."

"Whose?" Germanicus asked.

"I'm sure it's Hagg's."

Two Renegades sidestepped down the mountainside on their skis. They dragged a third Scandian—Hagg—between them. The man was now simpering as if nothing mattered—not even the loss of his forearm. His comrades had stemmed the bleeding by tying a length of rope around his bicep.

Germanicus recalled the gladiator Tullus, who had died of the same wound long ago.

"Yer-mahn-eee-kuz," Hagg said with a drunken sneer.

One of his companions, a crafty-looking man in his early thirties, plugged Hagg's mouth with the neck of a canteen. The smell of honey liquor was overpowering—like rotten fruit. "Forgive our brother, Procurator," this Scandian said in heavily accented Latin. The irises of his eyes were so pale, the blue almost appeared to be bleached out of them. "He's dying. But he's too much a beast to do it with decorum."

"You must be Jann."

"At your service. I am the bastard grandson of Balder, last chieftain-king of Scandia."

"I've heard of him."

"What Roman has not? He and eight kinsmen were marched down the Via Flaminia in chains."

"What happened to your man up there on the mountain?"

"A wrappie got him from a vug." Jann spoke of an air pocket in the lava large enough to conceal a man. "Hagg was pointing the way to go. A blade flashed out and took his arm—*pffft!*"

"Did you get their man?" Scilla asked.

"Not yet, Colonel. There was no way to bag him without letting Hagg bleed to death."

The wounded man's complexion was little different from the ice pillowing his head. He gnashed the knot in his ponytail with his teeth.

"Get that barbarian," Scilla ordered.

Germanicus held up a hand. "Wait—take him alive."

"Of course, Procurator," Jann said in his airy, sarcastic way. "There is no cause for vengeance here, what? Only a Scandian has lost his wholeness."

"There is no room for revenge on this mission," Germanicus said. "We must make it to the Purple Village."

"I spit—" Then Jann stopped.

The muzzle of Rolf's *pilum* was pressed against the Scandian's throat. "Spit and die, reindeer man."

"Please—do it. I would love you for it, German." There was an obscene willingness to die in the Scandian's eyes.

"Ach!" Rolf lowered his weapon, disgusted.

Jann gestured at Hagg as if to make a point and saw that the man was dead. Instantly his eyes brimmed with tears. A sob left his throat. He whispered in Scandian, at first passionately affectionate as he covered the dead man's gaping lips with his, and then bitterly as he made sidelong glances at Germanicus.

"Get that barbarian up there," Scilla said in a dangerous tone of voice.

Germanicus expected the colonel and the Renegade to exchange *pili* fire, but Jann quietly dried his cheeks with Hagg's ponytail and got up. "Aye . . . aye . . . aye."

"Bring him to us—alive."

Germanicus watched Jann chop back up the slope on the edges of his skis. "I hope they're worth it, Scilla."

"This is the worst they've been in a while. I'm afraid it has to do with you being along."

"How do you discipline men who don't care whether they live or die?"

"You don't. If they happen to be flowing in your direction, you use them."

"Otherwise?"

"You execute them."

There was the crackle of *pilum* fire.

Germanicus' mouth fell open. "You don't think the bastard went ahead with it to spite us, do you?"

Scilla was barely breathing. "If he comes back alone, I'm going to have to kill him."

Rolf grunted his approval.

"And the rest of them?" Germanicus drew his short sword.

"We'll just have to take our chances." Scilla shook his head. "We should never have come. It's just too big a temptation for them to lash out at a procurator—and a kinsman of the Emperor to boot."

Germanicus smiled with what he hoped was reassurance.

"Then we'll just take our chances, what?"

They could hear a pair of skis hacking footings down the face of the slope toward them.

Then a spray of ice stung their faces. When they looked back the Renegade stood above them, grinning, his colorless eyes shining.

A barbarian youth was slung over Jann's shoulder.

"Is he dead?" Scilla asked. His voice was calm, but he bared his teeth as he spoke.

The Renegade laughed.

"Is he dead!" Scilla shouted.

Jann dumped the youth in the snow, where he began to squirm with the first signs of returning consciousness. "He is— whole, Colonel."

Scilla blinked like a man who is trying to wake up from a bad dream. "Why did I hear a *pilum?*"

"A little joke."

Scilla whipped out his sword, and Germanicus thought, well, this was coming.

Scilla swung back. Jann refused to flinch. Just when he was an inch from cutting the renegade in two, Scilla turned the blade and slapped Jann's arm with the flat.

The crack sounded over Pluto's Villa.

Triumphantly Jann waved his arm to prove it was not broken. "Again, good Colonel. But this time hold the steel true."

The second Renegade, who before this had been obediently scouting the slope, now rocked back and forth on his skis beside Jann.

However tempted he might have been, Scilla had no opportunity to carry out Jann's desire.

At that moment dozens of tribesmen charged over the boulders at the imperial party, screaming as they came. The sky was a thicket of raised barbarian swords as the tribesmen reeled and darted among the rocks. Some rushed down in such a frenzy their *jamadani* unraveled from their heads and hung in the air like war banners.

Germanicus seized Hagg's *pilum*—protocol be damned.

Scilla broke his sword in skewering a barbarian who flew out of the gloom at him.

Rolf dropped several of their number in a defile. He did this with one good shot, which allowed the remaining Renegades to sweep down the same path and join the Romans in a mutual defense. "That be *fléchettes* for you!" Rolf shouted with satisfaction.

Scilla tugged at Germanicus' sleeve. "Look at this!"

"What?" Firing his *pilum* as quickly as he could, Germanicus was shocked that a veteran officer would take the time to remark on something in the midst of a fight that might well cost them their lives. But then he saw what had so captivated Scilla and said, "The crazy damned fool."

"The glorious fool," Scilla whispered, then shook himself out of this reverie in time to cut down a barbarian who had also seen the incredible sight on the summit of a nearby boulder.

There Jann the Scandian, bastard grandson of Old Balder, kicked off his skis. He began dancing as if he were impervious to *pili*. This strange man with no color to his eyes twirled and twirled in supple motion. His oily locks of hair floated out from his scalp. Drops of saliva slipped from the corner of his mouth and sparkled like pearls. His laughter became a sound somewhere between the screams of a mad woman and the howl of a wolf—all Germanicus knew was that it unsettled his stomach.

This specter entranced the barbarians, and most stood with their weapons dangling from their hands. Meanwhile the Scandian Renegades threw themselves into the opportunity for wanton slaughter. Jann's performance apparently had no effect on them.

One cobalt-bearded tribesman was actually dispatched with a Renegade muzzle tapped against his temple. He fell away, his face crowded with amazement, a spurt of blood keeping time with the fading beat of his heart.

Jann took a flask out of his dirty white suit. He filled his mouth to overflowing. The shimmering of the silver flask must have jarred one barbarian to his senses, for the warrior raised his *pilum* to his shoulder and let loose with a thunderclap.

A bloody rip appeared in the shoulder of the Renegade's suit. He flowed to a graceful stop and rested on his toes. He did not touch the wound.

"Save yourself!" Germanicus cried, surprised by the urgency in his own voice.

Jann addressed him with the same moist, hopeless look Germanicus had seen in Hagg's eyes as that man lay dying.

No one moved—not even the other Renegades. Their forearms were now painted with blood, which seemed to give them some wicked pleasure. To the man, they were grinning with very wet lips.

Germanicus could hear the hidden stream soughing far below his feet in the volcanic rubble.

The instant quivered between action and inaction in perfect silence. No barbarian budged because each assumed another was already in motion to kill the mad Scandian. No Roman or Renegade stirred because each was sure it was already too late to save the man. Jann looked no more alarmed than a child who has awakened from his nap to the music of birds.

Germanicus felt the suspense so heavily he could not lift his arms to violence.

Then the same barbarian who had stitched Jann's shoulder found his fighting wits once again and fired.

The flask exploded into shards just as the Scandian brought it to his lips.

"Down, Jann!" Scilla rasped, as if his urge of scant minutes ago to cleave the man in two had never been.

Jann opened his hand against the sky in simple acknowledgment that it was now empty of the flask. He appeared to find delight and magic in this turn of events. "Good, good," he said.

Finally his words broke the spell.

The massed *pili* of the barbarians crackled to life, and the Scandians began their awful hacking again. Jann ignored this and continued to stand on the boulder as if he were willing himself into a bronze statue.

The insanity of this scene made Germanicus ache to clasp his head with his hands and shout. Why did the barbarian marksmen keep missing the man who loomed above them? Something inexplicable was taking hold of these savages. They wanted nothing more than to kill this foreigner who, with his ski-borne hellions, had been tormenting them for months. But the power did not seem to be theirs.

While reason told Germanicus that Jann would soon spill over, dead, he felt that the Scandian was protected by the gods simply because he did not put much importance on his own destruction. The gods respected that. They had had a bellyful of human desperation.

Jann closed his eyes and smiled. The wind tossed his hair.

By this time the other Renegades had pruned the native

party to a third its former size. Roman soldiers, even veteran legionaries, might still have been chopping and gouging for their lives. But these Scandians were masters at doing no more to a foe than what was necessary to incapacitate him. In Hibernia Germanicus had seen a legionary thrash a corpse to a pulp while other rebels flitted around the Roman, merrily sticking him with their dirks.

A Scandian now felled two barbarians with one stroke, then ducked under a burst of shot that should have taken off his head.

The tribesmen began to notice the carnage being inflicted on them. By twos and threes they crept back into the dark spaces among the boulders.

The prisoner Jann had taken prior to the attack began to shudder, life returning to him with the tremors of a massive headache. "Guard this one, centurion," Germanicus ordered Rolf. He glanced up at Jann, who obstinately remained atop the monolith, surveying all below with the incurious aspect of a hawk who has already eaten.

As Germanicus' gaze dropped down again, he saw something that begrudged his respect.

The tribesman responsible for Jann's shoulder wound was inching toward the boulder on which the Scandian was so calmly perched. Obviously dying, the man left a bloody furrow behind him in the snow. An upturned knife protruded from his fist. Even at the distance of fifty feet, Germanicus could recognize the horrible concentration in the man's face. "Here's a born warrior. First to fire. Last to leave," he said under his breath. Then he aimed his *pilum* at the dogged barbarian and fired.

Nothing.

He scowled and laid it aside. "There's one coming for you, Scandian!"

No change came over Jann's expression.

Hearing Germanicus' words, the tribesman staggered to his feet. He glared back at the procurator with hatred, then began to lumber up a shute of loose rock toward Jann.

He vomited blood once, but that was not enough to make him give up heart.

Scilla came trotting up to Germanicus, his chest heaving. "What is it?"

Germanicus gave no answer other than to unsheath his short sword. Scilla spun around and trotted off, calling for any Scandian to bring his *pilum* at once.

The barbarian was now twenty feet and closing on Jann. Each step was obvious torture, and he began to stagger. Prayer after prayer tumbled off his lips.

Meanwhile Jann held fast. His smile was more obstinate than ever.

"Take charge of yourself!" Germanicus bawled. He took several heavy steps forward only to break through the icy surface of the snow and sink up to his waist. Exasperated, he hacked at the stuff.

"Procurator!" Rolf's voice boomed over Pluto's Villa.

Germanicus could not see the centurion. A stone buttress divided them. "Aye?"

"Do you wish me be there?"

"No, stay with your prisoner. This lunatic isn't worth our mission." Then Germanicus pulled himself out of the freezing hole and rushed onward again.

Only a few yards now separated Jann from his attacker. Germanicus scrambled up the shute, his lungs burning for air, and confronted the barbarian, who slowly rotated toward this new threat and snarled with yellow teeth. Then the barbarian made a wild lunge at the Roman that nearly cost him his balance. Germanicus swiftly struck back at the tottering man, and the barbarian found himself staring at a gash in his arm that rendered a glimpse of bone.

Jann feigned a yawn.

"Aaah!" the barbarian screamed in rage and pain, uncertain which gaping hole to plug with his fist, the new wound or the tear in his abdomen from which a loop of gray intestine protruded.

The tip of his knife flicked at Germanicus' face.

Germanicus made another strike, but it sliced only air. He knew he faced the desperation of a dying man—few things were as dangerous. He had the impression that Scilla was standing somewhere behind him but realized that this face-to-face fight made a *pilum* shot from outside the ring of death impossible.

When the two combatants had made a half circle, each crouched, and locking gazes with the other, Germanicus was tempted to run the Scandian through with his sword, but could

not do so without taking a cut himself from the tribesman.
"Help me, you fool!" he hissed at Jann.

The Scandian shrugged.

The other Renegades fanned out, leaping from rock to rock,
trying to find some vantage that afforded a clear shot. But from
every place they checked, either the procurator or Jann stood
between the barbarian and their sights.

"Give up, friend. You have fought well," Germanicus said—
or hoped he said in the mountain dialect he had shelved long
ago.

"*Inshallah,*" the man answered. Germanicus then knew there
would be no surrender. Paradise waited for the warrior who
died in holy combat.

Germanicus sucked in his belly as the knife flashed past
him and counterattacked before the tribesman could backhand
the blade into his groin on the return swing. The edge of
Germanicus' sword dug into the man's neck, severing the ca-
rotid artery. Germanicus was rewarded with a splash of blood
on the front of his white suit. The material began freezing at
once.

"*Inshallah,*" the dark lips quietly muttered. The barbarian
fell face down in the snow.

Germanicus' breath rattled in his throat. He sank to rest on
his haunches, and Scilla rushed to keep him from toppling
over. "Procurator!"

"Help me to my feet, good Scilla." The frigid air was like
acid to his lungs. Disgust nearly overcame him when he saw
how thoroughly soaked he was with the dead man's blood.
Teeth clenched, he squeezed the icy liquid out of his sleeve.
"I had forgotten . . ."

"Would you like a sip of vinegar?"

"Please," Germanicus said very seriously as if he had been
offered the crown to a kingdom. He nearly drained the canteen
Scilla had handed him. "Are you partial to this swill too?"

"No, procurator, the canteen is yours."

"Ah, so it is." He dipped his sword in the snow and frowned
as he pulled it out. It was still stained. Recalling the bravado
of his words to Rolf two days earlier—that he didn't like to
kill a man without bloodying his hands—he saw himself in
such a fatuous light his heart felt like a chunk of clay. No
recent death had affected him like this. "Mars, I feel low. So
damned . . . low."

"You handled your weapon as if it were a *gladius*," Scilla said, referring to the short sword from which gladiators had derived their name, meaning that Germanicus was this caliber of fighting man.

"I handled it as if I'd been trained in a butcher's stall." Germanicus had the queer sensation that his eyes were about to tear. He quickly checked the impulse before it bubbled up his throat and became a sob. "I loved him, Scilla—for just an instant I loved this one."

Scilla gripped his arm harder. "We should call a halt here. Nightfall is only minutes away."

"As you think." Germanicus saw that Jann had wandered off and stood against the darkening sky. "Why?"

"To humiliate the Emperor's kinsman."

"How?"

"To make you serve him, even briefly," Scilla said. "And you did that by saving his life."

"Is the price worth it to the fool?"

"That doesn't matter to him—to any of them. Life is nothing. Life under Roman rule is less than nothing. The message, sir, is simple: He and his kind are afraid of nothing. Not even the *pilum* and the blade. Jann is willing to die to plant this seed in your mind."

Germanicus slowly shook his head. "What good would that do?"

"Who knows, you may one day wind up governor of Scandia."

"No, thank you."

"See—he accomplished that much. And think of the import of his act if you become Emperor."

"Not this lowly cousin." Suddenly Germanicus realized that his ears were ringing. "Do they hate us that deeply?"

Scilla grinned bitterly. "When the Iberians captured . . ." All at once there was a tic in the colonel's voice, a disconcerting hesitation that made Germanicus look away. ". . . captured . . ."

"Crispa and you?"

"Yes. And when they were doing . . . things to me . . . one of them whispered in my ear. He had cruel, intelligent eyes and a pointed beard. The others called him 'Cicero' because he was so eloquent. And refined—the bastard had made the mimicry of patrician manners an art. The pain . . . the pain was so . . . significant . . . I didn't catch what he said then. Months later, when I was safely back in Rome at my mother's house, I awoke . . . screaming. It had returned to me what 'Cicero' had said. I finally heard the words. 'Hating you is my reason for being.'"

Germanicus began massaging his temples, trying to stop the ringing. "Was he their leader?"

"Oh, no, that honor belonged to a pig named 'the Valencian' after his hometown. And when poor Crispa finally *massed* against him . . . it was 'Cicero' who was first to repledge himself to the Emperor and suggest that 'the Valencian' be beheaded. It was his sword that did the deed." Then, as quickly as it had come, the hesitation left Scilla's speech. "It's the patience of a conspiracy that frightens me. It's insidious. And it's the kind of thing that wins out eventually." He pointed to the dead barbarian at their feet. "This fellow I can understand. He was direct, honorable in his rebellion."

"And he was cut down like a sacrificial ox."

"Aye." Scilla's eyes shone through the thickening dusk. His birthmark appeared darker than usual. "He failed in his straightforwardness. His comrades will fail in theirs. Then, finally, they will learn. They will become conniving like the Iberians, the Hibernians, the Scandians, and all the rest. Each will build a secret temple of hate in his heart and sneak off to it whenever his Roman master is not watching."

"Mother Rome, you have made me weary." Germanicus sighed.

Jann struck up an incongruously gay Scandian song with rocketing strains he took to the top of his register.

"What will be done with him?" Germanicus asked.

"No question—I must execute him."

"When?"

"Not out here," Scilla whispered. "The others would turn their claws on us in an instant." He fingered the jagged point of his useless sword. "We've made it this far only because of them."

"I know."

"We cannot go on."

"We must."

"There are nearly a *decuria* of Scandians left, Germanicus, and we are only three. A dozen barbarian ambushes like this one await us farther up the mountain."

"I have no doubt."

"Jupiter, I think of what we're doing and I get dizzy!"

"Again, my friend, I must go to the Purple Village."

"But how can we be certain you are being *massed* against?"

"We can't."

"And, if it is a *massing*, how do you propose to pluck the fuse out of it if we never make it alive to the bloody place?"

Germanicus grasped his former adjutant by the arm. "In Hibernia I ignored Crispa's advice and nearly lost my column to an ambush. Now she tells me to come east, so here I am—but not to sup with Poppaeus. I must go to the Great *Zaim* with the white beard she dreamed of. My mind does not question the wisdom of this patrol, Scilla—I am sure this is the only way to save the province from war and famine, perhaps the only way to save my life."

"These Scandians are about to mutiny!"

"I thought they had already." Germanicus tried to smile through his exhaustion. He patted Scilla's shoulder. "These northern rakehells have only a fresh acquaintance with cunning. We were first to taste it. We suckled it from the meat of a she-wolf."

"What are we to do?"

"Nothing for a few hours. Let Jann stew in his juices."

"Then what?"

Germanicus winked. But he did not feel like winking, and this front of good cheer was digging into his last reserves of strength. "Now to rest awhile." The ringing in his ears had become thunderous.

"Order Rolf to bring the prisoner and join us. Then announce to all the renegades—except Jann—that they've done well today and their procurator is pleased. They are at liberty to strip the dead of all booty and to keep the same for themselves. The mortally injured left behind by their comrades are to be slain with decorum. There is to be no torture. Each barbarian shall be given the opportunity to petition his god before the blade falls."

"I have no assurance the Scandians will obey these orders."

"I know, Scilla. But if we concede this last vestige of discipline, there is no hope left."

Frowning, Scilla nodded his agreement.

"Now promise them a month in a state brothel at my expense if they continue to prove themselves so fearless," Germanicus continued.

"But this smacks of a concession, sir!"

"Of course it does. We too can be cunning."

CHAPTER X

GERMANICUS WAS STARTLED out of a shivering half-sleep without knowing why. Blinking his frosted eyelids, he bolted up and first looked to the left, where Scilla was tucked between two sheltering rocks, and then to his right, where a watchful Rolf lay on top of his sleeping roll, an arm crooked under him as he listened to the night.

"What is it?" Germanicus asked.

"All be quiet, sir," the centurion answered.

That was it, Germanicus realized: the ringing in his ears had stopped.

As irritating as it had been, its sudden absence was even more alarming.

The moon beat down on a checkerboard of black stone and snow. The cold was eating out a lonely space inside him, and he began to feel much older than his years. He longed for the soft couch at his headquarters, the brazier Charicles set beside it when the nights grew chilly. He knew it was demeaning for a soldier to knead his resolve with such epicurean longings. But he also understood that middle age was a web of habits spun to nab a little comfort. He fondled the green-eyed pendant of Minerva his wife had given him, then let it dangle outside his suit.

"Centurion, tell me something?"

"Aye?"

"Your legionary who died at Firat Station, Gaius Paulus—did he complain of *sounds* before . . . ?"

Rolf's eyes widened. "Aye, a terrible ringing."

Germanicus said nothing for several minutes. "Where are the Scandians?"

"Now and again I hear one upslope and the others be down-slope somewhere in the stones. One be off on patrol two hour ago."

"What of our friend Jann?"

Rolf scowled in the strong moonlight. "You and the colonel just fall asleep when a mist float over the madman. When it lifts, he be gone."

Germanicus squeezed the *pilum* that had belonged to the Renegade Hagg. "How is the prisoner?"

"He work at his binds for a time but give up." Rolf gently kicked the sleeping form who earlier had resisted Scilla's interrogation. "This one be no more than a boy, Procurator."

"Wars are manned by boys. I'll keep watch now. Sleep."

"Aye." Without another word, Rolf flopped back and was breathing heavily within a few seconds.

Germanicus had been pressing his ear against the silence for the better part of an hour when something made his heart skip a beat. There was a strange noise far above Pluto's Villa. At first he misjudged it as coming from the cliff looming over them. But a few minutes of concentration convinced him that this was only an echo.

The real thing was from the sky directly overhead.

The barbarian youth awoke and rubbed the sleep out of his eyes with his fingers. He looked up. Then his smooth brown face went slack with wonder.

"What is it?" Scilla shook off his exhaustion. "Kill them if they . . ." His confused voice trailed off.

The Scandian who had been out on patrol sizzled in on his skis and spun to a stop. "Hah!" He shook his *pilum* at the heavens.

"There!" Scilla cried.

Germanicus tried to follow the colonel's finger out into space. But he spotted nothing. "What do you see?"

"I don't know what it is!"

The sound grew louder. It was like the rustling of a death shroud, or the wind prattling in the dry fronds of a palm, or— for spurts of a few seconds—a man slapping his chest with the heels of his hands.

"Where the hell is it?" Germanicus gazed from the Gemini twins across the Milky Way to Pegasus and finally to Polaris— all without seeing a thing out of place in the northern night.

The Scandian screamed, *"Spökke!"* then doubled over and tried to bury his face in the snow.

"What did he say?" Germanicus asked.

Scilla answered in a hoarse whisper, "A ghost. The man thinks it's a ghost."

"Is it still up there?"

"Aye. And coming down."

Germanicus began stamping around in circles, neck craned back, heart surging up his windpipe. "What does it look like?"

"White—with red eyes."

"It be invisible, I think!" Rolf shouted, unable to keep the fear out of his voice.

Jann slowly rose out of the shattered monoliths and stood as straight as a ramrod. He opened his arms to the sight above.

Scilla discharged his *pilum*. "Look out! Here it comes!" Involuntarily he dropped to his knees.

The approaching sound flooded Germanicus' head. His hands let go of the weapon and shot up to protect his face. Then it was on him. He felt as if he were being thrashed with hanks of rotten hair. The hot breath in his face was the very smell of death. It reminded him of the fetid air in his father's tomb, which had been the nesting place of pigeons until the burial.

The fingers of his right hand fumbled for his sword. He swung from the wrist, careful not to lop off his own nose.

"Halt! Halt!" he heard himself cry, now swinging wildly.

A screech from the thing made Germanicus reel backward and totter on his heels. Two ruby eyes, round and huge with cruel wisdom, bored through him. For the first time in a thousand combats he was terrified that he might petrify with terror.

The eyes stalked him again.

He flung the blade in a circle only to split the air with a swishing noise. The crimson eyes whisked back to let his blow pass by harmlessly, and then they swooped in with a vengeance, screeching at just the right pitch to erupt Germanicus' skin into gooseflesh.

He felt sharp, broken teeth rake across his forehead. Drops of blood collected in his eyelashes and trickled down the bridge of his nose. "What are you?!" he asked with a moan.

The answer came in the same rattling noise and a gust of unnatural breath blown in his face. Germanicus tried to retreat several steps in order to view his attacker, but the thing held fast to him with what seemed to be two skeletal hands. He got a glimpse of a fleshless nose before it bored into his shoulder.

Again he tried to separate himself from it with his sword. This time, however, the hilt slipped out of his numb fingers, and the blade twirled away in spangled cartwheels. Instead of slowing as it rose and finally falling back to earth, it continued upward until it spun into the mouth of the man in the moon— that lunar chimera first pointed out to him by his mother. *How odd*, he thought. Through his agony it also occurred to Germanicus that the sword had belonged to his father and, before him, his father.

The scrambling of his own feet tripped him. After a long, silent fall he lay with his back in the snow. The gigantic red eyes became everything: a universe of bottomless crimson. He felt the blood rush out of his head. Then came the blackness.

How odd to be in Rome. Germanicus does not feel it but somehow knows the air is warm. The month must be late May or early June. He slowly looks down at the toes of his boots. They are pointed at the familiar vault of the Pantheon. Drifting back and forth across the square, he tries to count the sixteen columns of Egyptian granite from one spot, but there is no single vantage from which they can all be seen at once.

Afar there is a rumbling din. It comes from the direction of the Via Flaminia. Germanicus finds himself floating off that way. A man scurries past. He wears coat and trousers like a barbarian. His face is hidden by his hat, which is some kind of cut-down *petasus*. So emaciated that his clothes hang off his frame, he does not notice Germanicus and disappears around a corner. Another new and strange foreigner in the capital.

It dawns on him in degrees, the way a man absently realizes his wife has changed her hairstyle, that Rome is different. Little things—street lighting fixtures, glazing in windows, letters and words on signs—have been altered since his last visit. Has the Ninth Ward of the city been turned over to some new barbaric race existing on the public dole?

He emerges onto the Via Flaminia, then reels back into a recessed doorway. Shock takes his breath away.

Marching north through the heart of the mightiest empire in the world is a foreign army!

He takes another quick look down the avenue. It is clogged with exhausted soldiers, horse-drawn carts laden with wounded, and peculiar mechanized craft of various types he has never seen before. What race are these men? Through the grime and dried blood on their faces, they appear to be of German stock.

Then he is heartened to think that this straggling horde has been defeated south of the city by a Roman army. Not exactly walking but not flying, either, Germanicus is propelled southward to greet the victorious legionaries, to cheer their brilliant commander. He stays flush against the walls and favors the shadows as he goes, but grows bolder when no one gives him as much as a glance.

He halts. Coming squarely at him is a barbarian soldier. He wears filthy olive-colored garments and a helmet shaped like a tortoise shell. His manner is that of a centurion. The weapon slung over his shoulder is made of wood and iron. It is sleeker than a *pilum*. Germanicus cannot believe his eyes. "Rolf!" he cries. At first he thinks that here is his centurion—the resemblance is uncanny. But then he takes into account small differences and suspects the man might be Rolf's father.

The German takes no notice of the procurator. He continues on his plodding way, shoulders hunched with fatigue.

Germanicus lets him go and passes into the Forum Romanum ward.

The retreat of cohorts dwindles to a trickle of soldiers with desertion in their eyes. Obeying the craven urge, some of them scamper down alleys. After this, nothing can be seen until elements of the army's rear guard come zigzagging up the way as if all the legions of Rome were on their heels. They leave off snipers who say farewell to their comrades like gladiators saluting the Emperor before they die.

Then there is a prickly silence.

Germanicus wafts through the Arch of Septimus Severus. It has suffered from neglect during this war, but even in good times the upkeep of the old palaces, temples, and monuments depletes a budget larger than Anatolia's. He is almost out in the sunlight again when he glimpses human shapes huddling in the transverse passage of the arch.

He approaches them—an old man accompanied by a woman, perhaps his daughter, and a small child. They too are dressed like barbarians. But there is a Roman cast to their features. Like dogs who spend a lifetime with one owner, have these strangers come to resemble their masters?

Germanicus has the inkling that, while he is invisible to them, they somehow sense he is nearby. The woman tries to stroke the gooseflesh off her bare arms. *"É freddo improvvisamente, papá,"* she says.

Her words surprise Germanicus. They are like a provincial Latin spoken underwater.

"Andiamo. C'é qualcosa di sospetto qui."

"Ma i Nazisti," the old man says.

"Per favore, questo non é un buon posto."

They pick up their belongings and leave.

The Forum—what in the name of Jupiter has happened to the Forum Romanum! Begging the gods to let him have revenge on the fleeing army, he is so dazed by the devastated scene that it is some time before he realizes the destruction is not recent. Pausing beside the Column of Phocas, he sees that the square is meticulously clear of debris. Grass and small flowers choke the cracks between the worn paving stones. The Temple of Saturn, the imperial treasury for nearly two millennia, is now but a *pronoas* bankrupt of its building.

The center of the universe has shattered and blown away.

He is terrified that at any instant the officers and legionaries he led to their graves, the rebels he executed for their fervor, every barbarian he slew with his own hands or ordered slain, will materialize among the stumps of broken columns and, pointing to the hollow shell of the Forum, ask what purpose their deaths served.

He has no answer.

He moves south again. Germanicus needs the reassurance he will gain by witnessing the victorious entry of the Roman legions.

His spirits have already sunk too low to be affected by the miserable condition of the Flavius Amphitheater. What mad emperor or drunken Gothic chieftain has stripped the world's most famous structure of its marble, travertine, and statues?

His first concern is how upset Manlius will be. His bookish older brother is charged with the preservation of imperial antiquities. He serves directly under Fabius in the capacity of royal adviser. This indignity to the great theater will surely crack his heart, the walls of which have already been calcified by worry over the deteriorating state of this or that monument.

Far above, a boot heel scrapes on stone . . . Germanicus is lofted up the crumbling stairway toward the sound and is delivered onto the third level. There, behind a masonry buttress, crouches a sniper. He aims his *pilum* through an arcade at the Alban hills.

As Germanicus eases up to his back, a look of fright crosses the barbarian's face. The man takes care not to glance behind him. Germanicus is moved to pity by the sense of loneliness that surrounds the solitary figure. He pats the barbarian's shoulder. The man jumps up, spinning wildly around, as if ice has been touched to his sweaty skin. The sniper is so rattled Germanicus vows not to lay a hand on anyone else he encounters in the city.

He departs from the amphitheater by floating over the head of the Colossus of Nero.

All that remains of the Circus Maximus is an elongated island of grass, marking the location of the *spina* around which mechanical chariots had thundered in clouds of dust and oily smoke. He hurries onward. He must get to the southern end of the city before his heart bursts.

Finally he arrives at the Porta Pia. He gazes south along the Via Appia, eagerly expecting the vanguard of cohorts that are certainly closing on the capital.

He does not have long to wait.

At first he thinks the craft is a sand-galley, but as it rumbles nearer and nearer the gate, he sees that it is more streamlined, less bulky, and outfitted with a weapon even more lethal-looking than a *ballista*. A white five-pointed star is emblazoned on its turret. Whose symbol is this?

Through a pall of smoke comes a string of infantrymen. Warily, with war-honed senses, each clicks his eyes toward Germanicus. But their gazes go right through him, and they continue scanning for phantoms behind walls, in windows, atop roofs. Those who walk within inches of him shiver for a few seconds.

Germanicus moans. This is no imperial army. Not even an

irregular century of ethnics drafted from the provinces.

Each of these men is like an *amphora* filled with a blend of wines: Britannican, Scandian, Hibernian, Sicilian, Iberian, Saracen, Gaul, Goth, even a splash of new barbarian blood.

Obviously two foreign powers have clashed somewhere in Campania. And for the first time in history, Rome is about to be invaded from the south.

But where are the Romans?

The flow of soldiers begins to thicken as it passes Germanicus. *Decurias* become centuries, which grow into maniples, which swell into cohorts, until finally a flood of green uniforms is stamping past to the same insistent beat. Half-starved dogs bark and nip at trouser legs. A league of nothing but troops of Britannico-Scandian stock march by. Following them come Balluchistanis, sporting spiked black beards and *jamadani* coiled around their heads. Next approaches a century of Jews, for several wear the Magen David, although the average looks as if he has a Sarmatian great-grandparent or two.

But where are the Romans?

Old men, women of all ages, and children creep out of hiding to line the way. They cheer and toss flowers. A grinning matron pours wine into any helmet that is held up to her urn. Her tiny husband kisses the fingers of the barbarian soldiers.

Germanicus scrutinizes the eyebrows, the ears, the hands, the coloring, even the gestures of the people.

At last he understands.

These *are* the Romans.

Defeat has dug gullies into their faces. It has dulled their eyes and thinned their lips. One rout could not have done this to them. Only centuries of subjugation and poverty can erode the spirit so deeply.

A prisoner is herded to the rear. Hands stretched over his head, he wears a close-fitting black tunic. More than anyone Germanicus has seen, this captive has the high-bridged nose and determined jaw of a Roman. But the crowd pelts him with small stones and insults. Without shame, the man blubbers and wails.

A small lorry bounces up the road. It carries four men, two seated abreast. They are pleased with their welcome. They wave and make jokes to each other. Next to the operator sits a striking-looking man with a nose and cunning eyes that compensate for a weak chin. Although he slouches in the same lackluster uniform his infantrymen wear, he is every bit the commander. The quality shimmers from him like summer heat. He covers his head with something that looks like a lungweed pouch turned upside down. It has three stars on it. So does the placard affixed to the lorry's front.

The commander motions for the operator to slow down. He smiles at a boy of ten. *"Campidolgio?"* he asks. *"Dov'é Campidolgio? Capisci?"*

The husky little boy nods enthusiastically. *"Sì, Generale* Clark. *Mi segua!"*

He skips ahead of the lorry.

It is not until they are out of sight that Germanicus realizes who the boy was. It was he. It was Germanicus Agricola.

The sky is growing pink with dusk. "I must gather up another dream," he mutters. "It is not easy to be dead without a dream."

CHAPTER XI

GERMANICUS LOOKED UP into the faces of Scilla and Rolf. "Where am I?" he croaked.

Scilla was shaking. "Never have I seen something like this."

Rolf was dumb with shock.

"What place is this?"

"Agri Dagi, of course. We're still in Pluto's Villa—for the moment. Here is your sword, sir."

"Not Rome?" Then Germanicus shook his head as if shrugging off his own question. "What is that sound?" He saw that both men were clutching their *pili*.

"The Scandian Renegades. They're skiing in a circle around us. They've been doing it for hours."

Rolf growled and started to raise his weapon in exasperation when Scilla batted the muzzle down. "One shot, centurion, and we never leave this mountain."

"Help me up," Germanicus said. "Why are you two gawking at me?"

"Procurator!" Scilla's mouth hung open. "A few minutes ago you stopped breathing. I felt no pulse. You were dead,

123

Germanicus, and now you're alive!"

The dawn was glorious. The panorama of frosted mountains filled him with joy. Silently he prayed to Jupiter for a moment, then turned to his men with a smile. "What gives with our Renegades?"

"You're happy right now, aren't you? Why?"

"All things are possible, Scilla, as long as you're still breathing." He patted the colonel's arm. "Why have the Scandians encircled us?"

"To jump us. This is their version of cat and mouse." Scilla's face was pasty with exhaustion. "Don't you recall what happened last night?"

"My mind's a fog."

"The bird that attacked you from the sky—"

The cheer drained out of Germanicus' eyes. "So that's what the bloody thing was."

"A white screech owl," Scilla said. "It dived for your chest, knocked you down, and flew off—more frightened than any of us."

A flare-up of laughter snagged their attention to Jann, who urged his confederates to ski faster as they tightened their noose around the Romans.

Rolf spat at the man and said hopefully to Germanicus, "He say foolishness, that one. It be a *good* omen from Minerva. The owl be her symbol, aye?"

"What did Jann say it meant?"

Scilla checked the bonds on their young barbarian prisoner, who watched the Scandians with loathing. Then the colonel handed Germanicus a *pilum* and began telling what had happened after the owl had come screaming out of the sky.

The Renegades had panicked and fled into the rocks while Scilla and Rolf were trying to revive Germanicus. But Jann soon rallied his friends and stood them before the Romans.

Sniggering, he said that a Valkyrie, or female servant of their god, Odin, had struck down the procurator. To each combat on the face of the earth, Odin sent a Valkyrie to wander among the warriors to decide who would die and who would triumph. Jann boasted that, during the ambush, one of these women had whispered in his ear that he would survive. So he danced atop the boulder without fear. Odin liked Jann's show of boldness, regarding it as a sign of respect, and ordered the Valkyrie to strike down Germanicus.

Jann was sure all the Romans were doomed. It was bad luck to go on to the Purple Village with men marked for death.

"That's when the real shouting match began," Scilla continued, his eyes following Jann as the Scandian made his orbit. "I argued that a Valkyrie was invisible except to those fated to die. They all grumbled yes—all but Jann, who smelled a trick. I lied I hadn't seen the thing and told them you hadn't either."

"True," Germanicus said. "I didn't."

"Jann—I told the beggars—was the only one of our number who had seen the Valkyrie. So it was he who was going to die. This really sent him into a fury. He howled that he had *heard*, not *seen*, the woman. This is when they began skiing around us."

"The bastard be wrong," Rolf said doggedly. "It be an owl—a sign of great wisdom."

Germanicus scooped up a handful of snow and nibbled at the moisture between chapped lips. "Omen or not, why would a bird behave that way?"

"This." Scilla clutched the Minerva-head pendant dangling outside Germanicus' suit. "It's been a hard winter with a lot of snow. The animals are hungry. The owl mistook these two emeralds for the eyes of a mouse. It hit your chest before it saw its mistake."

Rolf looked unconvinced but said nothing.

One of the Scandians hollered and fired his *pilum* three times.

"We've got to do something quickly, Germanicus," Scilla said.

"How greedy are they?"

"They'd rather loot than fornicate."

Germanicus smiled placidly. "Then have no fear. Discharge your *pili* when I give the order. And, Colonel—translate my words into Scandian so they don't miss a thing." Then he mounted a small promontory so he could be viewed by all. "Now, Scilla!"

The Scandians skidded to a halt, not understanding what the Roman shots meant, and gazed at Germanicus with a mixture of expectation and contempt.

"Good morning, my friends," he cheerfully began, "I think it is time you know the reason we make this dangerous journey to the Purple Village." Germanicus turned to confront Jann and found himself looking down the bore of a *pilum*. It was all he could do to keep the fear out of his voice. "If you kill me, Jann, you risk the wrath of Odin himself. Then it will not be known if I died because of his decree or your impatience."

Jann's eyes understood at once, but he did not break off his bead on the procurator. The seconds were endless as Scilla translated the warning in Scandian. Then the other renegades began urging Jann not to tempt Odin. With a grunt, he complied.

Germanicus could breathe again. "We go to the Purple Village to recover the greatest treasure the world has ever known."

As soon as Scilla had finished this much, the Scandians began making sidelong glances at each other.

"Over two thousand years ago, Alexander of Macedon sacked the city of Persepolis. He burned it, carried off its women, and most important of all, emptied the state treasury. The caravan he sent back toward Macedonia was two miles long. This train groaned under the weight of valuables you cannot imagine. Gold and silver in every conceivable form: talents, ingots, coins, even gold nails! And vases overflowing with gold dust. Glittering cups that had touched only the lips of Achaemenian kings. A mountain of jewelry pieces studded with precious stones. And grandest of all: an ibex of solid gold—life-size!"

The Scandians were listening to him without blinking. Germanicus hurried on. "Now, Alexander was afraid of brigands. So he deposited half the treasure in Ecbatana, which was fortified in those days against the likes of the Scandian Renegades." After the delay for translation came hoarse laughter. "Today these lovely little baubles are in the palace of the Emperor Fabius. I say 'baubles' because this shipment was made up of trinkets compared to what was on the manifest of the second great load.

"Informed by his spies that an ambush was waiting on the Royal Road, Alexander sent the second half north over these very ranges toward Lydia, where it would be put aboard ships that would sail on to Macedonia. This portion—which we have come to call the Persepolis Trove—never made it to the Lydian coast."

There was excited chatter among the Scandians when Scilla had filled them in. Jann was involved in two or three arguments at once and was rapidly losing patience.

Germanicus filled his lungs with tingling air—it was turning out to be a splendid morning. "Near Agri Dagi bandits fell upon the caravan and slew all who guarded it."

"How do you know this?" Jann cried.

"Because when I was a young tribune serving in these parts I found something."

"What, the treasure?"

"I'm afraid not. But I did stumble across a fascinating tidbit. This!" Germanicus produced a coin from his suit. "A *daric*—the coin minted by the Achaemenians prior to Alexander's conquest."

Scilla joined Germanicus on the promontory and took the coin. "This isn't a *daric*, sir," he whispered after examining it. "It's an Etruscan *fufluna*—any schoolboy would know that."

"Let's just hope Jann isn't any schoolboy." Germanicus held up his good luck charm. "You're all free to examine it."

"I shall." Jann rocked forward on his skis and seized the *fufluna* from Germanicus' hand. He flipped it over several times. He bit it with his eyetooth. But his mistake was that he took too long, for the others rushed up and grabbed it from him. Jabbering with feverish delight, they wrested it back and forth from each other until it fell from one man's trembling fingers and was lost in the snow. Frantic digging failed to turn it up.

"No matter," Germanicus said. "There are millions of others exactly like it up in the Purple Village." He was glad to see that Rolf had positioned himself behind the Scandians, ready to drop them should they bare their fangs again. Like a good centurion, he had even dragged along his prisoner charge.

Jann began barking at his pack, even going so far as to seize one of them by the scruff of the neck when the man dared to disagree.

"It looks as if a leader has emerged in our force 'of one mind,'" Germanicus said. "What's the gist of the bastard's argument?"

"He says this is a ruse, that we Romans will all be dead by the time the sun sets—he's harping on that right now. Oh, here's something about there being no treasure."

"Doesn't look like he's convincing anybody."

"Least of all himself."

"Then let's try this." Germanicus extended his arms. "Good fellows, I think I know why Jann has no interest in the Persepolis Trove."

The bickering subsided and all eyes fastened onto Scilla's lips as he translated.

"What good will this fantastic wealth do poor Jann when he is rotting in his grave? You see, there's a problem to his story. How did he know it was a Valkyrie who whispered to him unless he saw her?"

"It was a Valkyrie!" Jann exploded.

"How can you be certain, friend?"

"Because . . ." Flustered, the Scandian sputtered silent words, then roared, "It is you, swine, who will die!" This time his own men restrained him.

"Let Odin decide."

"What?" There was a quick spasm at the corner of Jann's mouth.

Scilla quickly broadcast Germanicus' offer, and the other Renegades agreed for Jann, who looked upon them with contempt.

Germanicus said, "We shall trade off taking the point position. Let the powerful god Odin decide which of us is to return to Valhalla with the Valkyrie and which is to heap himself in riches."

Finally Jann relented with a smirk. "I will take the lead first." And he skied off with a savage yank on his poles.

Germanicus rested by putting his arm around Scilla. "Tell the others all will receive a share of the trove equal to mine."

Scilla grinned. "The gods favor you, old man."

"Don't tempt them. It's just been a lucky hour."

"Where are your beaver tails?"

"Kindling, thanks to barbarian *pili.*"

"You know, Germanicus, all you've really done is delay the inevitable."

Germanicus laughed. "You have just described successful living in a nutshell."

CHAPTER XII

IT WAS LIKE walking on the icy roof of the world. Germanicus was thankful for the brimmed kepi and smoked glasses Scilla had given him. The sun beat down on his head through the thin air and made the snow blaze in a wall of excruciating white. Below, in every direction, was a gray froth of storm that blotted out the view of the Agri Dagi garrison Germanicus had enjoyed just an hour before.

He now gave care to his footing. It was a long way to nowhere.

The imperial party had spent the morning traversing the col that bridged the western volcanic ridges to the great mountain, Jann and Germanicus exchanging the perilous vanguard every hour, the returning man smiling as if to say, "See, I told you it wouldn't be me!"

He was preparing to turn back and be spelled by Jann when a pebble skipped across his path. His gaze followed its dotted trail up the slope to an outcropping of the same kind of stone that jutted from the drifts. This fortress-sized chunk of lava had been deeply curdled as it cooled in primordial times, now affording a sniper excellent hiding places.

Gasping for breath, Germanicus went prone and raised his *pilum*. "Just keep in mind," he mumbled to Odin, "I was the one who *didn't* see your damned Valkyrie."

Suddenly a dark face materialized in the midst of the carob-colored rock. The tribesman glared at Germanicus. Then, with a haughty flick of the chin, he vanished again.

Germanicus crept back toward the rest of the patrol.

"I don't know what this means," he said to Scilla. "There's a man in those rocks up ahead. He could have had himself a procurator. But instead of felling me, he showed his head."

Jann grinned, his teeth like alabaster in comparison to his heavily tanned skin. "The wrappie knows a dead man when he sees one."

"Get forward," Scilla ordered him.

Before slipping away, Jann sneered at Germanicus. "Savor this hour. It will be your last."

Scilla stooped on his haunches and began filling his canteen with ice. "This confuses me too. Why haven't we been ambushed again?"

"For some reason, he's changed his tactics against us."

"He?"

"Our big *zaim*. Why try to overrun us in Pluto's Villa where we could use the ground in our favor, then let us stroll up the side of Agri Dagi, where his men can pick us off at their leisure?" Germanicus bit his lower lip. "Call for the centurion to bring us the prisoner."

For a second time Scilla's terse interrogation had no effect on the barbarian youth. He stared off into the blue void and squeezed his lips shut. "It's no good," the colonel finally said. "This one won't talk."

"Not about anything he figures we can use. Ask him about his *zaim*."

The black eyes sparkled to life. The boy spoke rapidly, fervently. His self-assurance and regal bearing were not lost on Germanicus.

Scilla smirked. "The lad boasts his leader is the mightiest fellow in the world. He will kill us all with a single prayer—when he is ready. He will destroy Rome and build a minaret from the rubble of the Forum."

Germanicus' ethereal experience during the night came to mind. He winced. "What a lovely thought."

"We're on to something here."

"How's that?"

"If you recall, in this dialect, 'father' and 'leader' can be the same word. When the boy refers to 'him,' he uses the familiar form. There's a damned fine chance we've got the big man's son."

Despite his long absence from the district Germanicus was tempted to speak directly to the boy in the musical mountain tongue, but he also knew it was a good moment to play the imperious Roman. He stuck to Latin. "Tell him his father tosses his warriors away like chaff but is a miser with his own flesh and blood."

When Scilla finished, the boy scowled at Germanicus.

"Tell him his father hides away his son, then throws the sons of others against the Roman *pili*."

That was all the prisoner would take. He clenched his bound fists and let go with a flash flood of words.

"Well, well," Scilla said over the torrent of invective. "The procurator's color has just won the chariot race! Our boy's father is indeed the greatest *zaim* of all. He says his father has sacrificed all his sons but him to their god in holy wars. He regrets he was captured before he could join in the ambush— and die. But he is glad he cut off Hagg's arm. And gladder yet the man died of the wound. Now he will have an infidel slave in paradise." The colonel frowned. "At the moment, he's making unkind references to my birthmark."

Germanicus plucked the *jamadani* off the youth's head and stuffed it up his own sleeve. The boy shook out his matted black hair, then snarled at the indignity of Germanicus' act. Scilla slapped his cheek to silence him.

"Centurion!" Germanicus cried.

"Aye!" Rolf slogged up to them.

"Hand me your *pilum*." Germanicus cut the sling off the weapon with his short sword, tied one end of the leather strap to the muzzle and the other around the youth's neck, then carefully gave the piece back to the centurion. "Do you know what this is?"

Expressionless, Rolf nodded. "'The dead man's trigger.' A Hibernian trick."

"That's where I learned it."

"How does it work?" Scilla asked. "I never came across it."

"A good sniper can kill you before you can do the same to your hostage. But this device insures a dead captive if any of his comrades tries to drop you. As you fall away, your finger stays around the trigger. The *pilum*'s muzzle remains fastened to his neck. It discharges."

"Do you want me to tell him this, sir?"

"Look at his eyes, Scilla—he knows." Germanicus took off his wife's Minerva pendant and looped it over Rolf's head. "Hold this for me until we return, centurion. Our fortune rides on your shoulders."

"Aye."

"Take this boy back to the garrison. Let no one have charge of him but you. Tonight, send up a brace of green flares to let me know you made it. I believe this hostage will give you safe passage. Otherwise I wouldn't send you alone."

"That be no matter, sir." Rolf kissed the goddess' golden cheek, then dangled the pendant down inside his suit.

"And tell Colonel Crispa . . ." Germanicus felt their curious gazes burn on his face.

"Sir?"

"Tell her I depend on the loyalty she showed me that day long ago."

"What day be that, Procurator?" Rolf asked as if afraid he had misunderstood his instructions, or perhaps it was the uncertainty in Germanicus' voice that made him inquire.

"She'll know."

The youth began squawking, angry because his headgear had been confiscated.

"He definitely wants his *jamadani* back," Scilla said.

"That depends on the reasonableness of his father." Germanicus could hear the Scandians impatiently digging the tips of their ski poles into the ice. "Centurion—get on your way."

"Hail Fabius!"

"Hail Fabius."

Farther and farther up the northern slope of Agri Dagi they went, crisscrossing the dazzling snowfields. Their concentration grew as thin as the air; Germanicus and Scilla complained to each other of headaches that made them feel like their skulls were about to crack. When the Renegades skied down from time to time to report sightings of brazen tribesmen, Scilla shouted at the Scandians not to engage the barbarians unless attacked first. Then he would lean over as if the fibers of his muscles had been spun from lead, and with chest heaving, wait for his strength to return.

Germanicus could barely speak. "I went...to the top... Mount Olympus...once..." But he could not remember the point he had wished to make.

"Why are the bloody wraps backing off from us?"

"Our...hostage."

"I hope you're—"

A *pilum* crackled through the soughing of the wind. An echo warbled the sound from all four directions, so Germanicus briefly imagined Rolf and the *zaim*'s son were dead until Scilla dragged him down into the snow and gasped. "They got Jann!"

"You sure?"

"I saw him pitch over...."

"Why kill us...now?"

"Your centurion didn't make it."

"No, we would have heard...two shots...below." Germanicus peeked over a lip of ice. Unmoving, Jann lay on the slope a hundred yards ahead, his arm bent outward at the elbow. "Can you spot...sniper?"

"I see nothing but white."

"How about...the Scandians?"

"Staying low like us."

"Damn."

For an hour they lay on their bellies, icy moisture seeping through their clothing. Then Germanicus said, "Makes no difference if we go forward or backward, does it?"

"Except that it's always better to advance, Procurator."

Germanicus grinned. "Exactly."

Scilla rolled over on his back and considered the blue depths of the sky. "Just as true as a woman's eyes."

Germanicus added nothing.

"You must promise me something."

"Yes?"

"Return Crispa's love as best you can."

Germanicus raised an eyebrow. "Friend, there are... circumstances in my life."

"Given those circumstances, still love her." Scilla turned over again and stuffed his last three rounds into his *pilum*. "Tell me, old man, is it usual to die feeling unfulfilled?"

"Absolutely."

"That's a relief."

They struggled to their feet and leaned into the effort of reaching Jann's body. Their kepis flew off. Scilla soon outdistanced Germanicus, whose running slowed to trudging within a few feet. A hail of *pili* reports set fire to his heels for an instant, after which he slogged drunkenly to an exhausted halt, then resumed with the measured stride of a parade march. He slung his *pilum*. He drew his short sword with a loud scraping noise. The blade stood at attention from his fist.

On the upslope flank the Scandians were being slaughtered.

One cartwheeled to oblivion, leaving red blotches down the side of the mountain. Another genuflected on both knees. Gingerly he probed his chest with his fingers. Then his head began sagging, and he flopped forward.

Germanicus crashed into the snow near Scilla and Jann. Amazingly, the Scandian was still clinging to life after a round had pierced his rib cage and shattered his elbow, but he could not turn his head more than an inch in either direction. Blood trickled from the corner of his mouth in a continuous stream. His eyes bulged with agony. "No treasure?" he rasped.

"No treasure," Germanicus said.

"Hah!" Then Jann, bastard grandson of Old Balder, died.

The sun was low enough to cast long blue shadows across the drifts. Germanicus scanned the terrain ahead. It might have been a picture of the future. Melancholy. Featureless. Undulating toward a horizon smeared by the wind.

"Ready for the next hundred yards?"

Grave-faced, Scilla shook his head no.

"What is it?"

Grimacing, the colonel raised his arm, revealing a crimson circle that was radiating out from a small hole in his suit.

"Dear Jupiter." Germanicus ripped back the dirty white cloth and pressed the heel of his hand against Scilla's wound.

The colonel rolled his head back and forth as if to say it would do no good. In minutes the color seeped out of his skin, leaving it translucent like quartz marble. He began to look very sleepy, but as he grew closer to death, his fingers tugged at the flap of a small case he wore on his waist belt.

Germanicus helped him remove a coin. "Is this what you want?"

Scilla nodded, then opened his mouth.

"What?" Germanicus knew that many a legionary carried a coin to be deposited in his mouth upon death. It would be to pay Charon, the ferryman, who would transport the dead soul across the Styx. But he had never expected Scilla to honor the tradition. "Not so soon, Colonel. I need your help."

He could see it in the depths of the man's eyes, the question: What lies on the other side of this horror?

"I can't say, dear friend. Perhaps a personal underworld is tailored for each of us. Mine is a ghost city. May yours be Capri in the springtime. I just don't know."

Scilla smiled. Then he was gone.

Germanicus slipped the coin between the man's teeth.

A shadow fell over him. He glanced up. He reached for his sword but stopped.

"Quite wise, *pasa*," a remarkably ugly barbarian with a large, shapeless nose said in patrician Latin. "It would compromise my orders if I had to kill you."

"You speak . . . well."

"Thank you. As a child, I was made a hostage by Fabius to assure the good behavior of my father. I am Prince Sala."

"I am Germanicus Julius Agricola."

"I know, *pasa*. That is why you are alive and they . . ." he gestured at the lifeless imperial patrol scattered over the mountainside, his chalk-colored *haik* billowing in the gusts ". . . are dead. It is now one prisoner for one prisoner. Come, we go."

CHAPTER XIII

THE WOODEN DOOR slammed shut in his face. He blinked at it in the dim purplish light, then shuffled around on numb feet to inspect the chamber.

It was an old mosque. A niche in the south wall called the *mihrab* pointed toward the barbarian holy city. Opposite it loomed the *minibar*, or stone pulpit. His eyes followed the graceful columns up to the horseshoe arches that supported a parapeted balcony. Above this the structure mushroomed into a vault. The only source of brightness was a hole in the domed ceiling. He was looking for a passageway leading up to the balcony when . . .

The eerie wail of massed voices rose from beyond the door. Ordinarily, this would be the hour of the evening *salah*. But what he heard was no ordinary prayer. It was a demonic whine that threatened to pluck the fortitude out of his soul.

He hid his ears in his hands. His face was burned raw from the sun and wind. He licked lips.

A heap of clean straw beckoned from beneath the *mihrab*. Keeping his ears covered, he staggered across the mosaic floor and collapsed onto the prickly mattress. "If I don't mourn you, dear Scilla," he whispered deliriously, "it's only because the dead don't make it their business to mourn the dead." He was amazed by how much his own voice reminded him of his father's.

He dropped his hands from his ears. Silence. He slept.

Later—how much he did not know, except that smoky torches now glowed on the balcony—a taciturn middle-aged man brought him a meal as two guards with curved daggers on their heavy leather cummerbunds waited at the door. It was surprisingly hearty; goat meat, a squat loaf of bread, cheese, dried fruit, and tea with sugar.

Left alone, he wolfed it down, not bothering to muffle the greedy noises he made as he ate.

Suddenly the chamber was cast in green. He looked up. A cone of bright emerald light flowed down from the ceiling hole. The flares. Rolf had made it back to the garrison.

Briefly he felt like weeping.

Soon, the food swimming in his belly, the warm straw, the amber shimmering of the torches—all acted as a narcotic on him. There were muscle spasms in his legs, yet he saw them through half-closed eyelids rather than felt them. He slipped back into dreamless sleep.

He awoke feeling that something was about to happen. He had no idea what. The torches on the balcony were extinguished, and a single, unpulsing star showed the aperture in the dome.

Then, just when he was sinking into drowsiness again, came the unearthly wail from outside. He stopped his ears with his fingers.

His terror wound down into a long period of anxious rumination that wavered between nightmare and madness. He knew that most men are poor historians of their sleeping hours, but it seemed that this fitful dreaminess lasted most of the night. The straw flattened out under his endless tossing.

Breathing shallowly, he retraced his steps up the mountain, witnessed again the deaths of the Scandians and Scilla, and finally slogged into the Purple Village, the prisoner of Prince Sala, who made the indignity smart all the more because of his curt civility.

It was the most grimly haunting place he had ever seen— this village tucked in a gash on Agri Dagi's humped shoulder.

High livid cliffs loomed overhead, darkening the crooked lanes and rock dwellings with perpetual shadow. At the head of the chasm a glacier crested in waves of gritty ice. From its foot rumbled a milky stream that farther down the mountain became the Ahira River. Here and there the cataracts were spanned by rickety wood-and-rope bridges that groaned ominously underfoot.

Besides the tribesmen native to the district—who were tall, hard as iron, and fierce-looking—the village population was a hodgepodge of barbarians from every discontented clan in the province. Every rebel to have escaped a Roman prison, every legion turncoat, and every religious hothead in Anatolia seemed to be here. They jeered and beat their chests with their fists when they recognized the prize Prince Sala was bringing in.

He rolled on his side to banish from his mind these images that sickened his sleep.

He saw their rotten teeth bared in grins. Again he made the long walk down a tunnel of angry humanity. He smelled their awful breaths as they shouted in his face.

The torches were flickering again on the balcony.

He fancied that a dark figure was peering down over the parapet at him. But he convinced himself it was a trick of dreaming eyes and rolled over with a heavy sigh.

His memory wandered down long-sealed corridors and found Quinctius and Thascius, the young tribunes who had gone with him to the Purple Village to find the Persepolis Trove. He moaned in his sleep as they died again, each pinned to the ground by a gaggle of jabbering barbarians. And rising above the din—Quinctius' clear boyish voice, "Run for it, Germanicus! We're done for!"

Lying on his back in the latest of a thousand uncomfortable positions, he gazed upward. Two stiff figures now leaned over the parapet. He rubbed the grogginess out of his eyes. And bolted to his feet.

"You!" he cried. "You there!"

The forms—definitely human—did not stir. Their faces were masked by shadow, but no eyes sparkled from indentations that marked the sockets.

He was scanning the interior of the mosque when his attention fastened on something extraordinary. Where only air had been before, a balustraded staircase wound up to the balcony.

He touched the railing as if it might be made of vapor and pressed his boot against the lowermost step, fully expecting the slates to be immaterial. The bannister was solid. The stone steps held firm under his weight.

He began mounting the stairs.

"Jupiter," he whispered, as it all became evident.

At first, the horror was so outrageous he could not believe what he saw. He groped for the railing, coming close to tumbling down the flight. "Barbarian bastards!" he raved. "This is the kind of thing that brings our rule on your heads!"

It was a grisly parody of youthful insouciance: two mummified corpses draped over the parapet, turned toward each other as if in the midst of gossiping. Their bony frames were held upright by wire forms that twisted around their death-blackened limbs. Their lips had shrunk back from their mouths, exposing banks of bleached teeth. Both dead men were clad in the style of uniform worn by imperial tribunes twenty years earlier.

Germanicus sank to his knees and kneaded his hands together. "Their bloody *zaim* will pay dearly for this! I promise you that, my friends!"

CHAPTER XIV

"THIS IS THE last straw—this slap on Rome's cheek!" Marcellus fumed. "We must rescue the procurator at once!"

"Agreed—immediately." Poppaeus rested a fleshy hand on Rolf's shoulder. "You've done well to make it back alive with this hostage, centurion."

The German said nothing. He tightened his hold on the boy's arm.

"Turn over the lad to my praetorians, if you will. Then draw yourself some meat, drink, and rest. Enjoy my private stores."

"No, sir."

"I beg your pardon?"

"My orders be to keep personal charge of him. These be the procurator's own."

Poppaeus chuckled. "You're interpreting Germanicus' instructions too literally. It's well within the scope of his desires that I take command of the hostage."

"I think not."

"I order you."

Not a muscle moved in Rolf's ruddy cheeks. "I already be with orders, sir."

"Then consider this, centurion. Will you share a cell in our praetorian-manned stockade with the barbarian lad?"

"If I have my weapons, aye."

Poppaeus frowned, then graciously smiled, all within the same breath. "Of course. And we'll provide for your comfort."

"That be no matter."

"My dear fellow, that's the *only* thing that matters." Poppaeus was motioned aside by Marcellus. "What is it?"

"We've got to gain control of the prisoner—now!" the colonel whispered. "If this centurion hears Germanicus is slain, the oaf will cut the boy in two!"

"Worry is your weakness." Poppaeus wiggled his fingers in the air. "My praetorians will keep an eye on this stubborn fool."

"We shouldn't wait."

"Patience, Colonel—patience."

Marcellus' ears perked up. He saw the centurion quietly talking to Crispa, who had taken the news of Germanicus' capture all too hard for his liking. It disturbed him to see tears glistening in her eyes. "What's the difficulty here, centurion?"

"Nothing, sir."

Crispa turned away from Marcellus. His lips tightened. "Is there more information from Germanicus?"

Rolf glanced at Crispa, then back at the Parthian. "Only one thing."

"Out with it man."

"The procurator orders two green flares tonight—to let him know I be safe."

"Very well, I'll make the arrangements." Marcellus wanted a private word with Crispa, but suddenly he had a fresh problem. After silent minutes of staring at the colonel, the *zaim*'s son was coming close to recognizing him. In youthful naïveté, he might blurt this out, so Marcellus seized the opportunity to leave the underground atrium when Poppaeus tugged at his elbow.

"We'll put together a sham of a rescue guaranteed to fail," the fat man said. "I'll pick those officers and legionaries most likely to support our beloved procurator. I love the convenience of a good massacre."

"Did you hear the centurion and Crispa?" Marcellus said angrily.

"What?"

"Germanicus had a personal message for Crispa—I know it."

"A trifle, I'm sure."

"No, she's changed lately. Her heart isn't in this."

Poppaeus rolled his tongue to the side of his mouth and gently bit it. "What are you saying?"

"I'm not sure."

"You doubt her trustworthiness?"

Marcellus stopped walking. "I . . . don't know."

"You have to know."

The Parthian filled his sight with her. The lovely eyes, the white skin, the graceful shape of her arms—all these conspired with his lust to make him hesitate. "Give me time. There's something I must do first."

"I didn't like some of her comments at the luncheon yesterday." Poppaeus bit on a fingernail. "Perhaps there is something to your suspicions."

Marcellus glanced at her a second time. "I'm not ready to call them suspicions."

"She has a certain fondness for Germanicus, doesn't she?"

"He's been a grandfather to her. That's all."

"Well, that's not what I hear."

"You hear trash!" Marcellus shouted, making Crispa and Rolf look up from their solemn conversation on the opposite side of the chamber.

Poppaeus giggled. "It's your misfortune, Marcellus, not to know your own mind." Then, with a swish of his ermine cloak, he spun around and strolled away.

The night howled at Marcellus as he trudged across the parade ground. Sharp flecks of ice pelted his face. He felt nothing. At random intervals a giant searchtorch probed the mountainside with a needle of light. He failed to notice it, even when the torch was aimed skyward to reflect off the undersides of the clouds. In this eerie glow the garrison became a necropolis inhabited by ghost-legionaries with ashen visages. Marcellus indirectly perceived this image of the underworld; suddenly, he was afraid.

"Good evening, Colonel," the sentry outside the *ballista* bunker said. "Hail Fabius."

"Hail Fabius."

Inside, the legionaries who had been swapping stories around a brazier jolted to attention at the officer's entrance.

"As you were, men," he said. "Who's in charge here?" Marcellus was careful not to single out the dark-complexioned soldier before the man stepped forward and said, "I, sir, Corporal Mehmet."

"I bear orders from Poppaeus. Let's discuss them outside."

"We'll leave, sir," one of the legionaries offered.

"No need. Better two brave the cold than six," Marcellus said—he prided himself on his popularity with the troops. His courtesy was met with grateful approval, and the legionaries crowded around the warmth again.

"God is great," the Parthian corporal said as soon as Marcellus and he were out in the darkness.

"God is great. What news from Agri Dagi?"

Habit made the corporal look over his shoulder before speaking. "We have the procurator, and they have the son of our Holy One."

"I know. Tell me what happened to Scilla?"

"Wiped out. Just like the rest of the patrol."

"Excellent. Can you get word to Prince Sala before dawn?"

"Difficult. My sturdiest runner was killed yesterday by Scilla's infidels."

"Inshallah," Marcellus automatically intoned. "The need is urgent, or I wouldn't ask."

"Of course, *satrap.* I will do my best. Your message?"

"Tell Sala I appeal to the memory of those days we spent together as hostages of the demon Fabius. Ask him to recall the shame we can never purge from our hearts. Then he will know the time has come to kill Germanicus Agricola."

The whites of the corporal's eyes enlarged. "But what shall become of the son, Khalid?"

"Give Sala every assurance I have the boy safely in my hands."

"But do you, *satrap?*"

"Within minutes, yes."

The soldier frowned. "The message shall be delivered."

After leaving instructions with the man that two powerful *ballista* flares be readied, Marcellus strode off toward the praetorian stockade. It enraged him that Poppaeus confused his natural boldness for impetuousness. He would show that waddling pile of shit how a man took a hold of events. He reassured his hand with the feel of his sword hilt.

The tribune on duty at the stockade told him that Germanicus' centurion and the *zaim*'s son had just been locked away. Thanking him, Marcellus padded down the main passageway of the prison, his footfalls becoming softer as he approached the cell to which the tribune had directed him. He rounded a corner. And clenched his teeth.

Jabbering to Rolf through the talk-hole in the door was a praetorian guard. He was also a German. The men spoke heatedly to each other in their guttural tongue. The praetorian caught sight of the colonel on the border of his vision. "Hail Fabius! Sir, what be your pleasure?"

Marcellus tried to disarm any suspicion the man might have. "Just checking on our little ward. Please forgive my solicitude. But I *am* the procurator's adjutant."

"All be well here, sir," the praetorian said, sounding somewhat irritated by the interruption.

"Aye, Colonel," Rolf echoed with a grave tone that sent a twinge down Marcellus' spine.

He would wait until after the changing of the guard. Perhaps Poppaeus was right about patience. Marcellus withdrew.

The Parthian corporal's crew had finished loading the *ballista*. "Green, as ordered, sir," he said, his legionaries drawn up in a rank behind him.

"Fire when ready."

"Aye, sir."

Marcellus mounted the ladder that led to the roof of the bunker. A moment later the corporal joined him there, and they stared at the dusky hulk of Agri Dagi.

"May I ask the purpose of this, *satrap?*"

"Germanicus wanted a sign his prisoner was safely delivered." Marcellus chuckled, feeling good for the first time that day. "Let's give the old bastard some false hope. It makes for a doubly bitter death."

The *ballista* thundered twice. Two bright dots burned through the overcast. Then the night erupted into emerald.

CHAPTER XV

"COME, *PASA*," Prince Sala said, looking uglier than ever. "You will be seen now."

Germanicus huddled in the recess of the *mihrab*, knees drawn up under his chin. He stared at the vacant balcony.

"*Pasa?*"

"There is no stairway."

Sala raised an eyebrow. "What do you mean?"

"No Quinctius, no Thascius."

"*Pasa* did not rest well?"

He glowered at the prince. "No—not well."

"Please hurry. We are fortunate the Holy One has found the time to see you."

Germanicus thought the prince was leading him through the pebbly alleys toward the minaret of the new mosque until Sala announced, "This way, *pasa*," and directed him up a defile in the cliff wall. The natural corridor had been roofed in the style of an eastern bazaar, and small shops had been chiseled out of the volcanic stone. Walking behind Sala so swiftly, Germanicus saw the interiors of these establishments only in a blur, but nevertheless he caught whiffs of successive odors as he rushed up the steps: leather, tea, smoked meats, lungweed, and even perfumes strong enough to penetrate the morning chill.

The tribesmen no longer showered their rage on him. They gave him the same sullen glances he always encountered on the streets of Nova Antiochia. This business-as-usual attitude in the barbarians heartened him. He began to think in terms of a future again. His step livened, and he caught up with Sala.

"Where are we going?"

"He awaits you in the *tekke*," Sala answered without turning.

This, Germanicus recalled, would be some kind of monastery.

Just then their progress was blocked by two abutting doors. The alchemy of centuries had transformed the wood into silver. "Are these oak?" he asked the prince, trying to appear as nonchalant as his courage would allow.

"Gopher wood, *pasa*. They were cut from the ark that came to rest on this mountain after the great flood."

"Fascinating."

Sala detected the irony in his voice. "We are a quaint people, yes?"

Germanicus simply folded his hands behind him and politely smiled.

The doors of legendary wood creaked open. Deep shadows awaited him. Sala gestured for him to enter first.

Beside a marble font the prince instructed him to wash his hands, mouth, nostrils, and feet, then handed him two lengths of white cotton from a folded pile of these cloths. Germanicus tossed them back at him. "The Emperor Augustus made no people forswear their own religion for his. Are you any less liberal than he?"

Sala bowed obsequiously.

Germanicus stepped deeper into the entrance hallway of the *tekke*. It was cold and cheerless. Now, when only a few feet separated him from the source of his bedevilment, he was not sure he had done the right thing in coming to Agri Dagi. The presence within this forbidding place was very strong. To Germanicus' senses, it took the form of an irreconcilable resistance—two like magnetic poles being forced toward each other.

For the hundredth time he made sure the boy's *jamadani* was still rolled up inside his sleeve. A candle, the single source of light in the hall, puffed out on a traceless breeze. His eyelid began twitching.

From an adjoining chamber came the sound of flute and drum.

His hand groped for the sword that was no longer on his belt. Then he burst through an arched doorway. Heart fluttering, he waited for his eyes to adjust to the stronger light.

A man Germanicus guessed to be of his own age was dancing rhythmically to the music of the two unseen instruments. He had a luxuriant snowy beard. It hung down to his chest.

Germanicus thought that here was the most interesting-looking human being he had ever seen. Stately and well-proportioned, the dancer wore a coarse woolen habit that dangled in white folds down to his ankles. His moist, slightly amused eyes did not fail to notice who had entered the *tekke*, and his lips curled in a courtly smile of acknowledgment. The man seemed as relentlessly stirred by great purpose as the tides. Germanicus thought that here was a zealot cursed with the endless dissatisfaction of someone who takes his religion too seriously.

Holding a finger to his thick lips, Sala motioned for Germanicus to be seated.

Suddenly an old man, heretofore unnoticed, smacked his palms together. The dancer spun gracefully to a halt. Speaking the common Anatolian dialect that Germanicus understood with ease, the septuagenarian corrected the dancer about the position of his hands. The younger man took the criticism well, clearly showing affection for his critic, who was also bearded and garbed in wool. The only difference Germanicus could draw between the two men—other than age—was that the older's eyes were thoroughly amused. They had seen everything, even the worst, but still found the universe engrossing.

"Which is your *zaim?*" Germanicus asked Sala.

"He who dances," the prince whispered. "The other is his *shaykh*, or spiritual master."

"Why does your *zaim* dance when we are all on a war footing?"

"To cultivate an inner harmony."

The *zaim* looked up and dismissed the musicians, who were concealed behind a screen on the balcony. He took his *shaykh*'s hands in his and profusely thanked him. It bordered on worship.

But instead of accepting this show of gratitude, the old man said something that surprised Germanicus. He castigated the *zaim* with words Germanicus understood to mean, "A man is not truly a man as long as he is given over to temper—beware."

The *zaim* nodded reflectively.

It occurred to Germanicus that this was all an act to make him feel unimportant—the messenger boy of an infidel despot instead of the governor of a major province of the greatest empire on earth. He decided not to play along with them. Rising despite Sala's hushed protests, Germanicus squared off with the *zaim* and his *shaykh,* who seemed intrigued rather than intimidated by this stance.

Germanicus snapped the *jamadani* out of his sleeve. He let it hang limply from his fingertips.

For an instant the *zaim*'s expression was that of a father fearing the loss of his son. Then that strange indifference glossed over his eyes.

Sala began making apologies to the *zaim* for Germanicus' behavior.

Germanicus turned on him with the rage of an exhausted man. "Make no excuses for me!"

The prince blinked at him. He said no more.

Germanicus saw that the *shaykh* was carefully watching the *zaim,* who began speaking. When it became evident that Sala was sluggish in translating for him, the holy man barked at the prince, "Quickly, I speak no Latin!"—Germanicus caught that much of the mountain dialect and was gratified to see that his foe was capable of anger.

"The Holy One welcomes you to this sacred retreat," Sala began. "He begs to ask what you mean by presenting this worthless rag to him. He might have expected silk from a Roman."

"Tell him he knows precisely what I mean."

"The Holy One invokes your forgiveness, but he does not understand."

Germanicus met the gaze of the *zaim.* "Tell him his son's life is in our hands."

The man glanced askance at his *shaykh,* then laughed in a gentle and cultured way before speaking again.

"The Holy One says that is impossible," Sala said.

"He knows better than I that his son went down the mountain yesterday with my centurion."

"Oh, he does not doubt that fact, *pasa.*"

"Then why is it impossible?" Germanicus felt as if he were arguing with madmen.

The *zaim* spoke with deep conviction. Sala whispered, *"Inshallah,"* before translating, "Khalid's young life is not in your hands. It is not even in the Holy One's. Such matters are in the hands of God, who made man from a clot."

Germanicus let the headgear drop to the floor.

Sala continued. "The Holy One says that when his first son was killed his own faith was not strong enough, so he hated God. By the time his second son was crucified he was more receptive to the word of the Prophet, so he took comfort from God. Now he is farther along the hallowed path. He knows that he and all whom he loves are but a breath away from the perfect company of God. If he does not fear his own death, would it be fitting for him to fear for the lives of his children?"

Germanicus crushed the *jamadani* underfoot. "Tell him he lies."

Sala shook his head, "I will not do so."

"He understands how powerful the dread of death is. That's why he tried to haunt me with the bodies of my friends!"

The *zaim*, his *shaykh*, and Sala looked back and forth at each other as if Germanicus were out of his mind. His hands balled in fists, he glared at the barbarians, taking their surprise as just another ploy.

"The Holy One is baffled by what the procurator says."

Germanicus tried to hold still his eyelid. While no guards could be seen in the immediate area, he had the hopeless feeling that escape was impossible. "If your *zaim* has so little regard for his son's life, what concern does he have for the welfare of his people?"

The *zaim* listened intently to Sala, then conveyed with more acidity than Germanicus expected. "The people are precious to him like a child to his mother, like gold to a poor man, like truth to—"

"Tell him I don't believe this rubbish."

Sala was flabbergasted. "Be wary, Roman. You are in the presence of the holiest of men. Death is swift here."

"There are worse things than death."

The *zaim* insisted on a translation. When told, he had a new respect in his eyes for Germanicus. Stiff-backed, he eased down onto a rug beside the old man.

"The Holy One will listen for ten minutes," Sala said. "He does not limit your time as a discourtesy. Constraints sharpen a man's attention. This, he thinks, is the swiftest way for him to see what is in your heart, *pasa.*"

Germanicus paced back and forth, pondering. The *shaykh* smiled at him—not sardonically, but as if to say that the silence was well spent.

"If you sanction another *jhad* now, you do not realize the disservice you do to your own people...." Germanicus explained that Anatolia was part of a mighty and prosperous empire. The province shared in the benefits derived from the Great Artery, the engineering feats that brought water and energy to where there had been none, and—most important of all—the maintenance of order. "A host of capable men has brought justice and peace to the villages. The bloody feuds among the tribes have been ended. The rural highways are free of bandits. The frontier is securely closed to marauding armies. Would this be so if Roman power were removed?"

Sala relayed a question from the *zaim*. "How many men does your Emperor have under arms?"

"Ten million, and half that number again serving as auxiliaries."

"And territory, *pasa*—he wants to know how much."

"Over twenty million square miles stretching from Sarmatia to the Novo Provinces—an area of sixty times the size of Anatolia."

The *zaim* thought about this for a moment, then said, "I am reminded of the tale of the mouse and the crow..."

Listening to Sala, Germanicus folded his arms across his chest.

"The crow wanted to humble the little creature, so he snatched him off to see the greatest beast on land—the elephant. 'What do you say about this magnificent thing?' asked the crow of the mouse. And the tiny voice answered, 'There must not be much to him if he is so large!'"

The *shaykh* cackled.

Sala squeezed his lips shut to keep from laughing.

"The mouse is cocky because he's unable to accurately size up the elephant."

"Please explain, *pasa.*"

"He can't feel the tonnage of the giant beast with his eyes, so he's ignorant of its true weight. But if, in folly, he stumbles under the huge foot, it's too late to feel anything."

The *zaim* nodded to indicate the point was well made. Sala frowned. "The Holy One asks if the elephant intends to step on the mouse."

"That depends on the little creature, doesn't it?" Germanicus said. "If more attacks are made on Roman forces, if attempts are made to weaken or humiliate the Emperor's government here—then there is no alternative. And, judging from the experience of my own country, nothing does lasting damage to a country like a vengeful army."

"What can be expected, *pasa?*"

"In ancient times, Hannibal ravaged the south of Italia. He scorched the land. Poisoned the wells. Bullied the people into submission. This will be the bitter fruit of another *jhad.*"

The *zaim* rose, and pinching his chin hard with his fingers, stared up at the purple light filtering through the high windows. His *shaykh* appeared displeased. The *zaim*'s voice was agitated, and Sala had to speak rapidly to keep up with him. "He asks *pasa* how his countrymen liked the indignities visited upon them by the son of Hamilcar Barca?"

"They despised this oppression."

When he understood this, the *zaim* sniggered.

"The Holy One wants to know, then, why *pasa* cannot understand the indignation of the Anatolian people."

"Hannibal came to destroy. We come to build."

At last the *zaim* revealed a furious temper. His beard wagged as he shouted at Germanicus.

"The . . . the Holy One declares that you are building a godless world. He spits on Rome and all its corrupt minions."

"He neglects to mention our Emperor."

"The Holy One will begin this *jhad* by leveling the garrison at Agri Dagi. Then, one by one, all the Roman fortresses between here and the Aurelian walls will be put to the torch. When Rome is smashed, he will march to the palace and burn the body of the lecher Fabius, who will already be dead of—"

"Tell the Holy One he is a great fool."

Grimly Sala patted his dagger. "Is *pasa* prepared for the order that may follow this rashness?"

"Yes."

But before the prince could open his mouth the *shaykh* began talking to the *zaim*, who listened, brow wrinkled. Germanicus tried to catch as many of the old man's words as he could and, after a few moments, began to get the theme if not the particulars of this lecture in the mountain dialect.

The *shaykh* believed that everything discussed so far was unimportant. He warned the *zaim* not to become preoccupied with Roman power. No useful knowledge would come from this.

"With what should I concern myself?" the *zaim* apparently asked.

"This man standing here." The old man pointed his liver-spotted hand at Germanicus. He advised the *zaim* to find out what was in the marrow of the Roman's bones—that was the lesson to be sifted from this experience.

Respectfully the *zaim* protested. Germanicus was not sure what he was getting at, but it might have had something to do with *massing*. He did not know how tribesmen referred to the phenomenon but did catch the expression "brain-fire," which sent a chill through him.

"You are supremely gifted in this," the *shaykh* said in the more understandable Anatolian dialect. "But the stepping stones to wisdom sink beneath our feet as soon as they become obsessions."

From the minaret in the distance the *muezzin* summoned the villagers to the noon prayer. The *zaim* was visibly moved by the lilting voice. He sighed wistfully. *"Inshallah,"* he whispered finally, sadly troubled.

Germanicus guessed that here was a man in the throes of a private crisis. This circumstance provided both opportunity and danger, and his foreboding was not relieved when the *shaykh* said, "The difference between knowledge and obsession is that between molten and brittle glass. Now break all the glass you have let cool in the pot of a stubborn head!"

"How?" the *zaim* asked.

"With new ideas."

He shrugged as if to say, "What thoughts, master?"

"Is it possible God desires a Roman rule over us?"

"Ah!" the *zaim* cried as if he had been lanced.

A grin cleaved the old man's beard. "I hear glass breaking."

The *zaim* focused all his frustration on Germanicus and rattled off a string of incomprehensible oaths. His face took on the color of port wine.

"What was that?" Germanicus asked Sala.

"He says you are a camel driver for a whore-master."

"And the rest?"

"He tells his *shaykh* that, after all these years, this is the most difficult test. He fears he must disappoint his most beloved friend." Sala roughly seized Germanicus by the arm. "And he orders you out of his sight—immediately."

CHAPTER XVI

THE WAILING BEYOND the door of the old mosque seemed to go on and on forever. The sun bored down through the aperture in the dome and seared him with a pillar of light. He writhed back and forth over the straw, which was now so matted it no longer rustled under his body.

The terrifying symptoms had hit him with the first sound of the noon prayer—that eerie wail the barbarians concocted in their throats. His eyelids began to flutter. Then the hair stood up on the back of his neck and buzzed until he thought he would go mad. His knees buckled, followed by his legs going out from under him. And the next thing Germanicus knew he was atop the straw, groveling for his breath. His left shoulder started to tingle, and shortly thereafter, his left arm. The onslaught of pain in his chest sickened him. He would have vomited had he been able to gather enough air in his lungs.

What an indignity it was to die in waves, he thought—the mind bobbing up and down on swells of agony, knowing with dread that calm waters lay only across the dark edge of the horizon. These were the latitudes his wife, Virgilia, had to navigate each dwindling day. Germanicus cried out in pity for her. At the same time he lamented the cowardice that had kept him from telling Crispa how deeply he loved her.

"If you can come to your feet, do it now, man!" a familiar voice said in a plain Greek.

Germanicus opened his eyes. He followed the flowing woolen habit up to the sensitive, powerful face of the *zaim*. Suddenly there was breath again. The wailing died away. He staggered to his full height.

"You must forgive my unmindfulness, *pasa*," the holy man said gently. "But it did not occur to me that we both might get along in Greek, which I learned long ago to study Aristotle."

"It is your guile I must forgive. And my Greek no longer has oil in its hinges."

"Nonsense. You sing it. I merely speak it." The *zaim* rubbed his hands together and frowned. "Are you ill that you suffer so?"

"You know my malady."

The *zaim* stared at him for a moment. *"Pasa* blames me for something I do not know."

"In the name of good manners, wouldn't it be enough to put me to the sword? Why take my spirit apart in pieces?"

"Spirit apart . . . ?" He was slowly shaking his head in confusion when he suddenly froze. *"Inshallah,* is it possible you think . . . ?" He chuckled. "So that is why you are flailing yourself to death!"

Germanicus glared back at him.

"I fire an arrow at one infidel and strike another."

"What do you mean?"

"Enough has been said about this matter," the *zaim* said sternly. He began pacing in and around the balcony columns as if he were weaving a web. "Do you realize what hangs over the heads of you Romans in Anatolia?"

"I have some idea."

The *zaim* halted. "And?"

"We have overcome all the rebellions that have gone before. No matter how costly the campaign, we outlasted our enemies."

"But this revolt could cost you your command—every last man."

"I know."

"Then for what reason does *pasa* pit his forces against us? Why doesn't he leave and spare the lives of his soldiers?"

"I have my duty."

"If you understood the true nature of duty you would not serve an emperor like Fabius."

Germanicus examined his hands in the warm shaft of sunlight. "I've killed over fifty enemies of Rome with these. Had I fretted over the true nature of killing, how could I have lifted a finger against those men? But that is the purpose of duty. It suspends the need for contemplation in some things. That is why a legionary needs it."

"Will it also be your duty to execute my son?" the *zaim* asked.

"I don't want that. He's a brave lad. Proud and angry—like his father."

Involuntarily the holy man's eyes glistened. "Did he conduct himself without fear?"

"He showed none."

"Good." The *zaim* nodded fiercely. "He has inherited the courage of his brothers."

"The others—how did they die? Has it been during my procuratorship?"

"No, *pasa*. The first was slain after you first left our country— your Parthian mercenaries slew him for a brigand."

"Was he?"

"Fudail was a devout adherent to the prophet." The man's trembling hands pulled hard at the reigns of his rage. "The second was crucified by your predecessor."

"His crime?"

"There was no crime."

Germanicus cocked his face to the side. "How do you know when I first left Agri Dagi?"

"You have much fame here, *pasa*. Was it not you who bled us at the garrison?"

Germanicus said nothing.

"And—one year earlier—was it not you who crept up to this holy place?"

"That was a long time ago."

"Your poor comrades. I have always been curious—what did you hope to do with an army of three?"

"We were young and foolish."

"But why climb up here?"

"Because of a legend. We came to find the Persepolis Trove."

"The trove is no legend, *pasa*."

"It is the most insidious legend of all—honey laced with poison."

The *zaim* glowered at him. He hesitated a moment, then his face grew red with anger and he snapped, "Come, I will show you!"

Germanicus felt the thread that connected him to reality stretch closer to snapping with each stride he took. He was becoming wary that the *zaim*'s tactics were meant to confound him, so as they entered the grand new mosque he was determined to keep his wits about him.

This was not easy.

The gorgeously tiled floor was jammed with all the *zaims* of the province, who argued and gesticulated among themselves until they saw their supreme leader appear and raise his arms in greeting. "God is great!" he called out to them.

This triggered an ecstatic adulation of the man. Hands strained out to touch him. Doting old men, too frail to brave the crush of bodies, knelt down in his direction and busied their lips with prayers. The holy men were so absorbed by the sight of this *zaim* of *zaims* they had no hostility to spend on Germanicus, who followed the man through the crowd, tight-lipped, holding his head high.

"A word! A word!" he understood them to cry out to the *zaim*.

The man drew Germanicus to a halt. He smiled at his cheering lieutenants and spoke in the more common Anatolian dialect. "Soon we will close a noose around the neck of unholy Rome. Our power is at its fullest. God embraces our work as his own. A message has been received—the devil's dog has taken ill!"

"*Inshallah!*" The holy men cheered.

The thought sifted through Germanicus' anxiety that the *zaim* might be talking about the Emperor. But Fabius was as healthy as a young bull, and Germanicus displayed his doubt by smirking.

"Do not let your hearts waver for an instant!" Then, without any further demagoguery, the *zaim* led Germanicus out of the clamoring assembly and down a hallway to a small chamber where two spear-wielding sentries were posted. After prostrating themselves, they hurriedly rolled back an ornate carpet, revealing a silver ring anchored to the floor, then slowly lifted out a shaved stone three feet square.

The *zaim* took a torch from the wall and held it over the black hole. "After you, *pasa*."

The dark air was fetid and cold. Germanicus eased down the wooden ladder, listening to each groan the rungs made under his weight. He anticipated the bottom with every step but was disappointed time after time. He fought not to frighten himself by thinking he might never find the nadir of this hades. But finally his boot sole touched a hard surface, and he awaited the descent of the holy man, who streaked down with surprising agility.

"This, *pasa*, was a cave long before there was a village."

In the dancing shadows cast by the torch, Germanicus made out a long, snaking tunnel. The ground had been paved with volcanic blocks. They were smooth with ancient wear.

The *zaim* reduced his voice to a whisper as they padded deeper and deeper into the mountain. "Here bandits dwelled. See how the ceiling has been blackened by the smoke of their cooking fires."

"How did they get out? Not by that shaft we came down."

"Oh, no. The cave opened to the surface in those days. But the brigand who took the trove filled the portal with rocks to safeguard his riches. He was caught by Persian cavalry serving Alexander the Greek. He died rather than tell about this place."

Germanicus could glimpse no end to the underground passageway. "How was it rediscovered?"

"In the midst of a famine, the most blessed *shaykh* ibn Ghazali had a vision from God. He saw gold gleaming in the blackness. He told his people to dig down, and they found the cave. The coins in one jar were enough to buy a year's grain."

"I don't believe it," Germanicus said.

"Nor do you believe in God. But yours is not the final word on the matter. Here is the first of the treasure."

Confused, silent, Germanicus passed thousands of Roman *pili* stacked against the walls. It seemed as if there were a mile of the new weapons. "Did you bring me down here to try to intimidate me with your armory?"

The *zaim* smiled sedately.

"Were all these captured from us?" Germanicus asked.

"Bought from you—through secret sources."

"The traitorous bastards—who!"

"Romans without your sense of duty."

"Where did the money come from?"

"Why, the Persepolis Trove, *pasa*—as I have been trying to tell you. It has sustained our village through the centuries. And the last remaining piece of it will buy us victory over you." He directed Germanicus aside into a spacious vug that had been a huge bubble when Agri Dagi was molten. The object within took away the procurator's breath. "Here is that which you do not believe."

Germanicus floated around the man-size winged ibex as if he were moving in a dream. It was made entirely of gold. He stroked the glimmering horns with his fingers and stared into the ruby eyes. For an instant the fever that had drawn his young comrades and him up the slopes of Agri Dagi was rekindled—and once again he understood the passion of greed. "It's beautiful."

"It is an idol made by infidels to honor a false god. Such a thing cannot have beauty."

"The Emperor would ransom a legion to possess this."

"It will be melted down into bricks soon."

"That's barbaric."

The *zaim* smiled. "Yes. And we barbarians shall pay for mercenaries to join us in the *jhad* against you."

Germanicus sank down onto the electrum pedestal of the priceless statue. "Do you really understand the kind of world you are trying to create?"

"One governed according to the words of the Prophet."

"An angry globe of child tribes, each jabbering unintelligibly to the others, each inventing new terrors to frighten off the others, each cutting its own throat in the end."

"Ah," the *zaim* said, reflectively stroking his white beard. "I see what lies at the marrow of your duty, *pasa*. You believe that we are children. Rome comes to us as a mother."

This was so central to Germanicus' view of the universe, he was genuinely surprised the holy man was giving it the attention ordinarily reserved for a new and confounding idea. "Of course."

"And we cannot rule ourselves."

Germanicus firmly met the man's gaze. "No, you don't have the tools at this time. When you acquire them you shall be our equals in the administration of the Empire."

"Rule comes from God, *pasa*, not tools."

"In the name of Mars, what power do you really have?"

"Must you feel it again to know?" A concentration so hard came into the *zaim*'s face, his eyes lost their human animation and the brown tones of his skin became underscored with fiery red. In a pulsing rhythm the man emanated a force Germanicus likened to *ballista* shock waves, each buffeting him with an insistent fury.

His eyelids twitched. The nerves of his left shoulder were jangled again. He began fighting for his breath. "Do you think . . . *this* . . . will be enough to rule Anatolia?"

"Do not belittle what you do not understand."

Grinding his teeth together so savagely that flakes off them were floating in the bottom of his mouth, Germanicus twisted down to the stone floor, then reached up for a leg of the ibex, trying with all his might to pull himself to his feet again. "You . . . you are not the only one."

Poppaeus stood shivering on the parade ground in an afternoon snow flurry. He was eager to crawl back into his warm underground nest. He cut short the send-off for the rescue force by interrupting the officer who was briefing the legionaries he would lead to doom. "I don't think we have to put too fine a point on it, centurion. The procurator has been taken by the barbarians. Get him back. Be on your way!"

"Aye, sir, hail Fabius! Century advance!"

The hundred men marched off toward Agri Dagi with downcast glances and stooped backs. Every man knew why he had been picked. In this way or that, each had earned the distrust of Poppaeus or one of his lackeys. Now they would die. It was an implaccable military fact—a cohort, let alone a century, could never make it alive to the Purple Village. So this was the ultimate bad luck of a legionary who had not learned the essential art of fawning. Don't complain, it does no good; don't complain, it does no good—their boots drummed on the crackling ice.

Poppaeus hurried Crispa and Marcellus before him up the windswept flights of stairs. He was positively cheerful, prattling all the blustery way despite the momentary discomfort of the cold. He had good reason. A coded message had arrived from Rome this morning with the routine dispatches. Fabius was complaining of breathing difficulty and severe indigestion. Bless Pamphile and her avocation as an herbalist.

He leered at the creamy nape of Crispa's neck and lusted

to feel it with his lips. But this desire would not prevent him from poisoning her as soon as they were back in his chambers. With his praetorians holding their *pili* at the ready, Poppaeus was certain he could make Marcellus see reason. He judged the colonel to be a man who would soon forget the loss of his Nordic mistress—especially when a *satrapy* was to be had.

Affably he patted the Parthian's shoulder.

Marcellus was startled out of a troubled silence. "What is it?"

"Easy, my friend. Tension is the worst enemy of an ambitious man."

The colonel scowled and burrowed deeper in his cloak. His eyes were rimmed with red, and his stomach was rumbling with hot juices. He had not nabbed a minute's sleep during the night. As chance would have it, most of the praetorians on duty or just loitering around the stockade were Germans, and all were friendly to Germanicus' centurion, Rolf, who—as it turned out—had been a damnable praetorian himself at one time. Marcellus didn't trust a one of the lot, so he had not been able to gain control of Khalid's safety. Poppaeus' indifference to this problem infuriated him: "Dear Colonel, the boy is locked away in my personal prison. If that does not amount to total control, what does?"

"We have put a wolf in his cage with him!"

"The centurion is just as eager to protect the lad as we are."

"Until he hears Germanicus is dead."

"We can intercept any such word."

"I can tell you, Poppaeus, legionaries can pass a rumor through a mile of marble!"

Now Marcellus scarcely noticed their passage from daylight to the dank netherworld of Poppaeus' headquarters. He regretted sending premature word of Khalid's security to Sala. And, under the weight of this depression that enveloped him like a blanket soaked in blood, he cursed his own stupidity for not going directly over to the *zaim*'s camp, as Sala had suggested when they met at the Purple Village last September to discuss the *massing* against the Emperor and the revolt to follow the report of Fabius' weakening. But at the time Marcellus had thought he would be more valuable to the cause inside the Roman machine. Besides, he reveled in the dream of killing Germanicus with his own hands. Had he followed the prince's advice, at this moment he could be enjoying the sight of the procurator squirming at the Holy One's feet—and would have been spared all this intrigue. His was a straightforward and admittedly impulsive nature not suited for dabbling in the devious arts. How he hated a crooked trail!

But more than anything else he was sorry that the events of the last week were digging a gulf between Crispa and him. At first light that morning, when his fears had been their keenest, he had tried to take her in his arms, but she had nudged him away.

As they entered the *vestibulum*, each silently engrossed with his private worries, Marcellus bumped his hand against hers a few times, inviting her to join palms with him. She stepped farther away from him and kept looking straight ahead. He wanted to see her dead at that moment.

It was horrible—and the precognition became harder for Crispa to bear as it drew closer to reality. Germanicus was about to experience more pain than a man can endure—she knew this as surely as she was on the verge of going mad from terror for him.

But who was going to do this awful thing to him?

Marcellus tried to take her hand, and she would have snapped at the fool had she not feared breaking the fragile connection she had formed with this distant scene.

Darkness—Germanicus was somewhere underground as she was. A single torch flickered in her brain.

The beard—again that extraordinarily beautiful white beard.

She wrestled with the picture, straining to squeeze some meaning out of it, but something more urgent began to blot out the vision. There was immediate danger for herself. She floated down like a moth onto one of the silken couches in the infamous chamber. A snake slid off into the shadows. It disturbed her that all these trappings of evil were beginning to seem commonplace.

"Wine, my dear?" Poppaeus asked.

A slave held a tray before her.

One of the three silver cups on it was empty.

"No," she answered, "I prefer vinegar."

"Very well," Poppaeus said congenially. "You shall have some."

"From my own stores—it's from Scandian apples."

"The finest, I'm sure." Still, Poppaeus showed nothing but a compulsion to please her every whim. "Fetch her canteen."

This was rushed to her from the chamber in which she had fitfully slept. The slave filled the cup from it, and the vessel was halfway to her mouth when it struck her odd that her needs had been so perfectly anticipated.

Why was an empty cup placed on the tray—precisely what she would require if she chose to drink her own vinegar?

Crispa glared at Poppaeus, then spilled the liquid onto the floor.

The huge man laughed uproariously.

But at that instant she fully perceived how Germanicus was being threatened.

"No!" she cried. "Fabius, yes! Germanicus, no!" Running out into the vestibulum with Marcellus shouting behind her, she made her way to Poppaeus' cascade of red-lighted waters. There, her ears filled with the roaring flood, she gathered her energies and concentrated on the vision of the white beard. Then she vowed to show the man with that beard the power of her love.

The *zaim* clapped his hands to his ears. Shouting in anguish, he turned his eyes on Germanicus. They were tremulous with tears. He clutched the folds of his robe in his fists. "You . . . ?"

Whatever its source, Germanicus was thankful for the unexpected relief from his own agony. He muscled himself up to his feet by grasping the legs and wings of the gold ibex. He watched the *zaim* grow more and more dazed under the blows of his invisible torturer, and the holy man started to totter on the balls of his feet.

Then it all stopped.

Both men crouched with their hands on their knees, chests crashing in and out.

The *zaim* looked utterly amazed. He could not shut his mouth. *"You* have the power!"

Germanicus struggled to hide the puzzlement he felt. He did not say a word.

"You . . . an infidel."

"Yes," he said guardedly.

"It is not possible."

"Why not?"

"This power issues from God."

"Then your God wills me to have it."

"No! This is . . . is not acceptable." Then the *zaim* spun

around so swiftly that the torch flame roared, and he began walking deeper into the mountain as if to sort out his confusion in privacy.

Germanicus leaned against the wall and watched the torch become as small as a firefly. He knew he had to press the advantage handed to him by this mysterious turn of events. The *zaim* should not be given the opportunity to recover his balance. Somehow Germanicus empathized with him. Without warning, a void had ballooned inside the holy man, one as achingly empty as that which Germanicus had felt while drifting down the streets of an alien Rome.

Germanicus' instincts told him that it was time to make gentle blows with wooden swords. He followed the receding flame.

When Germanicus was a few paces behind him, the *zaim* pivoted wildly but was caught off guard by the smile on the procurator's torchlit face. He stared but said nothing.

Still smiling, Germanicus looked around. Niches had been hewn out of the black stone. "I sense that this place is holy."

The *zaim* thought for a long moment. When he spoke, his anger had melted into weariness. "You are in the Tomb of the *Shaykhim*. Many of our famous . . . teachers sleep within this place. As I shall one day." He lit up one of the cavities. There, an ancient corpse was laid out in repose, so insubstantial that a sneeze could have reduced it to dust. Despite the work of the natural mummification of the tissues in the dry, cold air, the face had a striking serenity to it, an apprehension of mankind that took everything into account but still found reason for a quiet joy.

"Who was this man?"

"The *shaykh* Sanai," the *zaim* said as if warmly remembering a friend.

"When did he live?"

"Eight hundred years ago." He lightly stroked the woolen habit now brittle with age. "He loved songs and poetry. Like the prophet, Sanai took pleasure in the company of women: 'Oh, a star glitters in the garden pool,/And I share the night with the blossom of the moon . . .'"

The men lapsed into silence as they studied the shell of the long-dead holy man. Germanicus was convinced that, at this moment, the *zaim* shared his jumbled sense of futility and longing. It did not seem possible to have an enemy in such a state of mind.

"And here lies the *shaykh* Hasan," the *zaim* half whispered, continuing down the line of the dead. "There was no poetry in him, for verse was not his path to enlightenment."

The dessicated countenance was stern and unyielding. "What did he teach?"

"That all of history has already been written by the hand of God."

"Then what effect has man to change events?"

"Like flesh itself, his effect is temporal. He can briefly divert the waters, but God will always return the river to the channel he has cut for it."

"It is Hasan, then, who gave authority to your expression, *inshallah*."

"Ah," the *zaim* said with sudden cheer. "You have suggested an excellent subject for meditation, *pasa*."

The men walked side by side with the pensive grace old mentors of long association fall into when strolling together. "Thus, whether or not there is a *jhad*," Germanicus said, "the result has already been written."

"Hasan might say that is so."

Uneasily they exchanged glances.

Germanicus raised his chin at the last niche. It was more recessed than the others, and he could not see its occupant. "Who rests here?"

"The great teacher Isa ibn Maryam." The *zaim* lowered the torch into space.

"But there's no one here," Germanicus said.

The holy man burst into laughter. "That is one side of a bitter controversy, *pasa*."

A piece of ivory-colored cloth was hung from the ceiling. Well over twelve feet long, it stirred at Germanicus' approach as if it had a life of its own. "What is this?"

"The death shroud of Isa ibn Maryam."

The *zaim* shone the flame through the back of the cloth. Slowly an apparition appeared in the fibers of the material— it was the imprint of a man, and although it was vague, Germanicus could easily distinguish stout, patrician features on the face and points of ancient Roman armor on the chest. Germanicus frowned with confusion. "If this is the shroud of a *shaykh,* why does it bear the image of a Roman?"

"A Roman procurator—see the insignia yourself. And to answer your question—well, *inshallah,* God willed it so."

"What is the impression made of—oil or charcoal?"

"Our scholars believe the image to have been formed by the heat of great light."

Germanicus slowly shook his head. "And where is Isa's corpse?"

"That requires more of an explanation. Still, there is no one answer to satisfy all men."

"Tell me," Germanicus insisted.

There in the vacant tomb Germanicus listened to a tale that both fascinated and disturbed him. He could not believe his ears and thought, from time to time, that the *zaim* was reading his mind to find information with which he could fabricate a baffling coincidence, for here was the same story Demetrius related from the Sibyl at Alexandria!

"Isa preached in Judea, where the simplicity of his truths attracted many followers."

"Was he a Jew?"

"Yes, *pasa,* like Abraham and many of our holiest prophets. The wrongdoers plotted against him, and he was dragged before the Roman *pasa* to answer for his teachings. He was found blameless and let go. Whereupon Isa was forsaken by those who had loved him. He wandered to this mountain and spent the last years of his life in the company of other saints."

"I've heard this before—but the man was called Joshua Bar Joseph."

"They are one and the same. His father was Joseph and his mother Maryam."

"But what became of his body?" Germanicus fixed on the lips in the midst of the white beard and barely breathed for fear of missing a word.

"Herein lie the arguments, *pasa . . .*" After Isa died in his sleep, his body was borne to this tomb, the *zaim* explained. It was bound in the linen cloth with a mixture of myrrh and aloes—as was the Jewish custom. "Then Isa was left to crumble to dust, as all men surely must. . . ." Yet when attendants, whose lineal descendants were still guarding the entrance to the tomb, inspected the niche months later, the shroud had been cast aside and the body was missing. Germanicus grasped from the *zaim* that there were two divisive opinions about the dis-

appearance of Isa ibn Maryam's remains. One camp said that
the body had been stolen by the agents of those who had taken
issue with the great teacher. The other—quite the minority,
the *zaim* was quick to point out—declared that Isa himself had
given answer when he prophesied: "I will be sent forth by God
to a new country where no thing moves by wheel and no tax
is levied. There I will be condemned by the one who released
me and then magnified by him in the company of young
princess."

"What is your opinion?" Germanicus asked.

The *zaim* held the torch behind the shroud again, silently
comparing the face of the apparition to Germanicus'. What he
saw seemed to unsettle him for a moment. "It is written that
Isa said of himself, 'I am sent forth to you by God to confirm
the Torah already revealed and to give news of an apostle that
will come after me whose name is Ahmed—the Praised One.'"

"Then tell me of this 'news.'"

"With profound pleasure, *pasa*, but first let us leave this
darkness to walk in the light."

As they moved back up the length of the tunnel, Germanicus
began to understand that this new man with stimulated eyes
did not want another *jhad*. He wanted to fill his hours with
talk of philosophy and ancient holy men. And even more—to
come to grips with his own secret anger. But he, too, had his
duty.

CHAPTER XVII

As EVENING THICKENED the purple sky, Germanicus and the *zaim* craned their necks to watch the spectacle high on the clifftop above them. A wavering dot of hot orange touched two cone-shaped piles of wood on the lip of the precipice. Fed by the night winds, the flames grew and grew until a pair of long banners snaked along the mountainside with sparkling tails. Nothing was said—not even among the barbarian warriors— for the half hour the pyres raged. Then the embers throbbed like red clusters of stars and scudded along the surface of the snow before blinking out.

"Thank you," Germanicus said.

"Let us go. It is nearly prayer time."

Germanicus had been gratified when the *zaim* granted his request to have the bodies of Thascius and Quinctius cremated, and to see to it that Scilla and the Renegades were recovered from the slopes for the same purpose. This amounted to a confession that those grisly relics of his young friends did indeed exist. So Germanicus' faith in his own sanity was restored, even if the holy man made no apology for the atrocity.

Later Prince Sala whispered that the *zaim*'s father had commissioned an Egyptian pilgrim to mummify the tribunes. "For what purpose?" Germanicus asked, his face hard.

"So that we, too, might have hostages."

A proper funeral for Scilla did much to assuage Germanicus' grief and guilt for the loss of his former adjutant. And the Scandians—regardless of their infamous behavior—had died in the service of Rome.

The only distinction he asked to be made between the Romans and the Renegades was that two pyres be built and that they be separated by at least fifty feet to prevent the accidental intermingling of the ashes. This request amused the *zaim*, who commented, "To assure that, *pasa*, I would have to split the world."

Germanicus found himself chuckling at his own parochialism, but he would not allow a single pile for all the bodies. "You did not know these northerners."

"On the contrary, we knew them all too well."

As they continued their way down the icy path, Germanicus became entranced by the sight of the village. Penetrating the dusk, lamplight twinkled from a hundred windows. It fell across the amethyst lanes in square carpets of gold. With ponderous majesty, a gigantic moon rose behind the minaret of the new mosque, which came to life with the haunting song of the *muezzin*. It all amounted to a consolation that made death seem insignificant.

"Tell me," Germanicus said, breaking the spell before it could ensnare him, making him want never to leave this place. "When was the mosque you are keeping me in abandoned?"

"Two years ago."

"Was money from the Persepolis Trove used to build the new one?"

"Yes."

"Why was it built?"

The *zaim*'s eyes blazed with anger once again. "How can you pretend not to know?"

"I don't pretend anything."

The holy man curled a tuft of his beard around his finger. "It was because of the edict."

"Whose?"

"Yours!" His shout echoed up the chasm.

"To order what?"

The *zaim* sighed in exasperation. "To place an idol of your Emperor in each of the mosques of Anatolia."

Germanicus was slack-jawed. "Not only would such an edict be against my better judgment, it's against Roman law!"

"Then you deny it?"

"Completely!" Germanicus paced back and forth in front of the moon. "From where was this madness issued?"

"The garrison here."

"Poppaeus," Germanicus hissed. "The fat son of a whore. So this is the fire that has been sweeping across the province!"

"Hearing what has happened here, all the holy ones are afraid other indignities against the Prophet are sure to follow."

"But the old mosque—"

"One holy one—I will not honor his name by speaking it— hoped to put Roman gold in his palm by desecrating our worship place with a statue of Fabius. He has been put to death, but his blood proved too weak to cleanse the mosque."

"Damn!" Germanicus fumed. "I swear on the head of the god Augustus that Mother Rome tolerates the religions of all her children. This wickedness is the work of one man who shall pay for it with his life!"

"Your wrath comes too late, *pasa*," the *zaim* said sadly. "It is simple to put out the fire when it is a coal—but hard when the flames are taller than yourself."

"Then you believe me?"

"I do. But I also know that man can be no more honest than what he understands honesty to be."

Minutes later Germanicus was left again in his mosque-prison, and the *zaim* departed looking preoccupied, saying only that he would try. He did not specify what.

The wailing commenced.

Germanicus braced himself.

But nothing happened, and he slowly unwound. His spirits were soon dampened by a fog of rumination. What if Poppaeus were blameless and this was all a barbarian ruse to make Germanicus distrust his commanders? What better way to weaken the garrison at Agri Dagi than to unleash an avenging procurator on the people who manned it day in and day out? The *zaim* was no doubt capable of deviousness. But a lifetime of dealing with sly men told Germanicus otherwise in this case.

He knew that Poppaeus was a tireless plotter. In fact, the man had been exiled in his youth for his role in a conspiracy and was pardoned finally only at the insistence of the Empress, who favored the unabashed voluptuary.

But a good governor does not condemn a man simply because he finds him distasteful.

Over the next half hour Germanicus stepped on each individual tile a dozen times in his unceasing tours across the floor. He twisted and kneaded the events of the past week in his mind like a washerwoman squeezing the water out of her laundry. Then he paused mid-step.

"No."

His hand softly touched the place over his heart.

"Dear Jupiter, not that."

He pressed his lips together so no sound might escape. Nevertheless, he finally had to bow his head and cry out, "Not that!"

The door banged open, and the *zaim* returned, face flushed, robe swirling in the wake of his haste.

Germanicus turned away from him.

"*Pasa*, you cannot wipe out centuries of enmity with an instant of goodwill. But I have prevailed upon the other *zaims* to hear your words. They will do so now."

"Who among my staff has sided with Poppaeus?"

"I know nothing of Roman affairs," the *zaim* answered curtly. "All my true allies are on this mountain."

"What is a true ally?"

"One I need not buy. Shall we go?"

The night was a riot of stars. Germanicus filled his lungs with the cold air and was tantalized by the smell of woodsmoke—until he realized that this wisp hanging around the minaret might well bear the earthly components of Scilla and his other friends. It was as sobering as the chill to think that, despite all his craft and cunning, a man wound up like this—a whiff of bittersweet smoke. Then, how useless human ingenuity was in the face of death!

Whereas the darkness was pure, the blazing hall of the new mosque reeked of the closely packed bodies it harbored. A cry of rage erupted as Germanicus entered, and the gust of fetid breaths hit him like a slap. He noticed Sala glaring at him and beckoned the prince to approach.

"Yes, *pasa?*"

"I should like one of those garments now."

Sala made a big show of civility, even going so far as to

bow, but his hatred was clear. "Of course, *pasa.*"

The *zaim* waved his hands to quiet the holy men. Their feeling for him did not seem quite as adoring as before. This made Germanicus believe that some kind of argument had taken place while he waited in the old mosque.

"In the name of God, the compassionate, the merciful," the *zaim* began in a strong, noble voice. "Blessed be he who has revealed Al-Furgan to his servant, that he may warn mankind; the lord of the heavens and the . . ."

The more fervent listeners punctuated the *zaim*'s phrases by jabbing the air with their curved daggers. The old *shaykh,* who had been surveying this scene with droll eyes, suddenly regarded Sala's taking of the pilgrim cloths to Germanicus with deadly seriousness. It was as if he had been waiting all his life for such a thing to occur, and shock rippled across his features. He gaped at Germanicus.

" . . . the unbelievers serve, besides him, other gods which can create nothing and were themselves created," the *zaim* continued, "idols which can neither help nor harm themselves, and which have no power over life or death, or the raising of the d—"

The old man rushed to the *zaim* and whispered in his ear. The younger man did not draw a breath, even though his eyes swelled as the *shaykh* pressed some fantastic message on him. "No!" he cried aloud once, and the old man scolded him by seizing him by the shoulders. Finally the *zaim*'s gaze swiveled toward Germanicus and his fine voice became a hoarse croak, *"Inshallah."*

Germanicus took the cloths from a sneering Sala. "Thank you."

"My pleasure, *pasa.*"

All that could be heard in the cavernous hall was the chafing of woolen robes.

The *zaim* came to Germanicus' side as if his feet were frozen. He, in turn, took the cloths from the Roman. "Remove the bloody rag you wear, *pasa,* and cast away your old life."

Germanicus stepped out of the mountain uniform and threw it aside.

"God is great!" the crowd intoned.

The *zaim* wrapped one cloth around Germanicus' waist and draped the other over his left shoulder. Then he stood back. The picture of the devoutly garbed procurator appeared to disgust him. "The most blessed *shaykh* has had a vision."

"Yes?"

"I cannot tell you of what it consists, *pasa*. Perhaps years hence you shall know. But this is not the time."

Germanicus glanced uneasily around the mosque. He had not anticipated anything like this. But he would be careful not to botch the chance it gave him. He patted himself on the back for thinking of the garment. Such shows of reverence had served him well in other encounters with tribesmen. Still, something disconcerted him: The moment was moving him.

"The unbelievers," the *zaim* now said in a hush, "have chosen other gods to help them. But in the end—" His face assumed a strange, twisted shape, and he could not finish.

"But in the end," the aged *shaykh* sang out in a voice as clear as a *muezzin*'s, "they will renounce their worship and turn against them!"

These words flashed through the holy men like lightning. All were too stunned to respond with another intonation. Germanicus fancied that the air smelled sulphurous—like in the lull after a thunderclap. He felt the *zaim*'s hand nudge him forward, and he knew it was the moment for him to speak. He faced a wall of ardent gazes. "Today, I heard for the first time a story of Isa ibn Maryam. I heard it from the lips of your Holy One. It is about the day evildoers tried to trick the great teacher into preaching sedition against Mother Rome. He was asked if it was right to pay taxes to Caesar. And Isa requested the evildoers to show him that with which they paid the tax. They handed him a coin. And he asked whose likeness was on it. They answered, 'Caesar's, of course.' Then he said, 'Give Caesar what is his, and God what is his.'"

Germanicus put his hands on his hips. "*That* is the agreement we have. And I will not be the first to break it. Now, Marcus Aurelius—perhaps the wisest of our Emperors—said, 'Everything that happens is as normal and expected as the spring rose or the summer fruit; this is true of sickness, death, slander, intrigue, and all the other things that delight or trouble foolish men...'"

The old *shaykh* milked the tip of his beard with his fist and chortled in agreement.

"And I am remiss because I have been caught unawares by what I should have expected from a foolish man. An evildoer— a Roman—has been making intrigue to give what is God's to

Caesar. Fabius himself would agree that such a thing is wrong!"

The excited murmuring grew louder as those who had trouble understanding Germanicus' thick Latin accent got benefit of a translation from their Romanized neighbors.

"It is the law, my friends, that no likeness of Caesar, of any member of the house of Jupiter, of Isis, or of any governor shall be put in a place of worship without the consent of the people who practice their religion there. And the spirit of this law comes from the days of Augustus!

"As long as I am procurator of Anatolia, I stake the honor of my family on the guarantee that no likeness whatsoever shall be housed in any mosque. All Romans shall—"

"This is not enough!" came a shrill cry from the crowd. Prince Sala lunged out of their midst.

"Why?"

"Because you are Germanicus. A just man. But he who orders you to come and go is a whoremonger!" Sala turned and addressed the *zaims*. "I know. As a boy, I was forced to dwell in the palace of he whom God will drag down by the scalp to the fire of hell. And if we are now stealing up to peace without our sandals on so God will not hear us—I declare I make no peace with evil!"

"As your God witnesses—you make peace with honorable men."

Sala tapped the blunt end of his nose with his forefinger. "A moment please, *pasa*. So you bow down to Him who decked the lower heavens with the constellations?"

"I . . . respect him."

Once more robes began rustling.

"Do you submit to Him who made men from clots of blood?"

Germanicus was silent. The hall exploded into a din of curses and shouts.

The progress he had won was punctured by the lofting of a hundred glittering swords and daggers. The promise of peace, so buoyant a minute before, now deflated around his ears. His heart pumped molten lead as he watched the *zaim* frantically mingle among his people—obviously the politician trying to call in old favors, but the holy man quickly got the drift of sentiment and returned to Germanicus' side with loathing in his eyes for the Roman. He found it hard to quell the tumult, "Believers! I have heard . . . believers!"

The old *shaykh* dolefully shook his head at Germanicus.

Then he strode from the assembly.

"I have heard Sala with my heart," the *zaim* shouted. "And I will weigh his counsel." Suddenly, with rough hands, he ripped the cloths off Germanicus, who glowered at him while enduring this rude jostling. "This infidel must leave our new holy place before it too is profaned!"

Fists pummeled Germanicus toward the entrance, and in a smarting daze he was pushed out into the night. Sala was the most vicious of his tormentors. The mask of politeness had now slipped from his face, and he leered at Germanicus. "You did not really think it would be so easy, did you?" And moments later as he shoved Germanicus down onto the straw of the old mosque, he hissed, "You do not remember me. I was just one of those little brown marmots scurrying around the back chambers of Fabius' palace. But I remember you, Germanicus Julius Agricola. You were the best of them. So I despised you the most."

Germanicus snapped a blade of straw in two.

"And now, *pasa,* we shall release you to a more wretched death than we could ever devise."

"What do you mean?"

"Khalid is safe, and—"

"Enough!" The *zaim* stood at the door. "Leave us."

The prince struggled to compose himself. "As you command, Holy One." Then he rushed outside, his teeth set in a shark's grin.

The *zaim* set the latch against intruders. He exhaled. His forehead and cheeks were awash in sweat. "It is written: 'Let no man mock another man, who may perhaps be better than himself.'"

"Then why do you mock me?"

"Truly, I do not." He sighed once more. "This is to save your life."

"Why do you bother? I'm your enemy."

"I ask myself that question—for I look at you and my heart fills with hate. But I am not free to share what the *shaykh* has revealed to me in this hour. Should I do so, you might try to divert what must come to pass. And the wrath of God would be on my head."

"What did Sala mean, that your son is safe?"

"Sala does not have the whole truth. But we have no time left. Come quickly."

They parted at the base of the Purple Village. The full moon glittered on the snow and made the cloud cover below glow with an eerie luminescence. A brisk wind tugged at the tails of the warm woolen habit the *zaim* had given Germanicus.

"This is yours, *pasa.*"

He took back his sword and sheathed it. "Tell me—do you know what I mean by *massing?*"

The *zaim* nodded gravely.

"If not me, who are you *massing* against?"

"Against evil, *pasa.*"

Germanicus briefly thought of his sword. But radiant eyes of the holy man stayed him. Quite simply, he did not know what to do. And violence seemed a poor substitute for insight. "About your son—"

"Say no more. He is in the hands of the most compassionate one. Do not test my faith any further."

"We can still have peace."

"And say nothing of the peace!" He kicked a spray of ice at Germanicus. "Had you submitted to God there would be no *jhad.*"

"Then it is written that there must be a *jhad?*"

The *zaim* hesitated. "There will be . . . a fight. And great changes will come in a single hour. Now depart away!"

Germanicus started down the mountain.

CHAPTER XVIII

THE MUFFLED FOOTFALLS of a large number of men rumbled up the canyons on Agri Dagi at the lowest audible pitch. It was like the first faint sound of an earthquake.

Germanicus, who for three hours had been sliding down the long, unbroken snowfields on the soles of his boots after sneaking through Pluto's Villa, skidded to a halt. He crawled down onto his belly to keep his silhouette out of the thin light of dawn. And listened.

He sensed the approach of advance scouts and drew his sword. There was no concealment where he huddled.

A line of helmets appeared over the frozen hump of a ridge. Legionaries!

Germanicus wrestled out of the barbarian robe. He flopped over on his back. Something had stirred upslope. Then he spied a scout slogging along to outflank him. The legionary went prone and took aim with his *pilum*.

"Stop!" Germanicus cried.

A crack ended the uneasy stillness, and a little fountain of white puffed up near his elbow.

"Stop, man!" He stood up so his Roman undergarb might be recognized.

More *pili* coughed into action. A centurion began deploying the main body of men along the ridge. These legionaries raced with more desperation than the sighting of one possible tribesman warranted.

Germanicus pitched down flat against the snow again. He waited for a lull in the shooting. Perhaps there would be none. He feared that Crispa had already been murdered, and he feared what it meant if she were still alive. Germanicus ground his teeth. And waited.

Finally the pelting noises around him became fewer and fewer. Then they stopped altogether.

He raised his head. "I am Germanicus Agricola!"

"What?" a distant voice asked.

"I am your procurator!"

He had always felt that he was reasonably popular. But it raised his eyebrow how vigorously these legionaries cheered his name. "What is your mission?" he asked the centurion, who looked like a capable sort.

"To rescue you, sir."

"That amounts to a death sentence. This mountain is impregnable."

"Aye." The officer was seething.

"Whose orders?"

"Poppaeus'. And no lots were drawn for this nasty job, Procurator. Every man here was handpicked."

"Why?"

Wariness made the man hold his tongue while he thought. "The answer to that question might ring like mutiny, sir."

"My own suspicions give you immunity. Go on."

"Poppaeus culled what he thinks were his rotten apples. Truth is, we're twice as loyal to a soldier like Colonel Scilla than to a cowardly bag of dung like this commander." His eyes scanned the heights beyond Germanicus. "Did Scilla . . . ?"

"No, he didn't . . . he didn't."

"He was the best officer in the garrison."

"Has Agri Dagi been attacked?"

"Not yet."

"Then we shall be first to do it."

The centurion's mouth fell open. "Sir?"

There, crouching in the snow, the two men took stock of their situation. The centurion was sure all the legionaries would be loyal to Germanicus. It was Poppaeus' praetorians who would be the problem, although the German guards were steadfast in their devotion to Fabius—if that would be a factor.

"It will, I think," Germanicus said. "What defense assignments do the praetorians have?"

"Other than Poppaeus' den and the stockade, the westernmost *ballista* bunker. It's the kingpin, so the fat bastard trusts only his own bullies to man it."

"That's where we breach the ring."

"Do we need to, Procurator?"

"If this century marches up to the garrison in formation, Poppaeus will welcome us home with his *ballistae*. Now, let me talk to the men."

Not a single legionary slouched or leaned on his *pilum* as the ranks heard Germanicus out.

"Your centurion tells me you left yesterday afternoon. What took you so long to come this far?"

Uneasily, the men glared at one another.

"You hurt my feelings. . . ."

Someone giggled—mostly from the tension.

"I'll keep it short, lads. There's a mutiny in the works. And Poppaeus is the traitor behind it. Will you help me win back the Agri Dagi garrison for our Emperor?"

"Hail Fabius!" they boomed.

"Listen, I haven't gone mad from the altitude, but I want everyone to fan out across the mountain. Kill a rabbit for me. Be careful not to bleed it."

A few of the younger legionaries began to snigger.

"That's it, go ahead, lads," Germanicus said with a grin. "There's nothing like a good laugh—especially when it's on the likes of Poppaeus."

The men whistled and hooted with glee.

"Don't be afraid to use your *pili* on our little hunt. It's all part of the plan. And we'll do a lot more firing within the half hour. Now find me a rabbit!"

The century spread out over the slopes. The legionaries bawled to one another wherever they crossed small animal tracks, screaming advice to which no one listened—like schoolboys on an outing. Some chattered and squealed in what they insisted were perfect imitations of wounded does of the species. A corporal jiggled the muzzle of his *pilum* inside a burrow. "This does the trick each time," he muttered. And— lo and behold—out popped a hare in winter coat. The burly man dived at his prey, missed it, and came up with a mouthful of snow.

This was enough for another legionary to bang away at the darting target. But all he accomplished was to crease the helmet of a soldier across from him, who growled, "Damn you, Licinius, be careful!"

Choking on their laughter, the men began hailing a fellow they affectionately called "the Hawk." "Here's our deadliest sniper," the centurion said to Germanicus.

One quick shot and it was over.

Germanicus accepted the game with flourish. "That's worth a fortnight of wine and women in Ephesus—at my expense, Hawk."

"I thank the procurator."

"Now, lads, let's make a battle that Poppaeus will hear from under his couch!"

The legionaries threw themselves into the stratagem with fervor. They discharged their *pili* into the air until the centurion had to caution them against wasting all their ammunition. As the uproar finally petered out, the centurion sent red flare after flare aloft, beseeching help he knew would never be sent.

Then there was silence. It was made deeper by the realization that, had Germanicus not come down the mountain, this feigned massacre would have been for real.

"Who are the six best hand-to-hand boys among you?" When the men had shoved their choices forward, Germanicus slit the hare's throat with his sword and doused these legionaries with the blood. They made a battered-looking crew. "Now, Romans, this is what we do . . ."

They waited on the heights above the garrison until the wind pressed the clouds down onto the pass. The scene became thick with chilly fog, as was all too common in the shadow of Agri Dagi on a winter afternoon.

Germanicus felt sure he had chosen the right man to crack the praetorian bunker. A natural ham with the features of a hound, he relished his role as a blood-splattered survivor, limping home with a tale of horror on his lips. Minutes after he was sent on his way, two more "wounded" were dispatched across the frozen pasture, and then one more, and finally the last pair, one riding on his comrade's back—a credible string of beaten legionaries.

While these men held the attention of the sentries on the wall, a force of ten scouts crept through the mists, keeping to a broken spur of lava that flowed down half the distance to the targeted bunker.

"Halt!"

Germanicus bit his lips. The praetorian guard was challenging the first man to straggle up. The words of the legionary's reply were too faint, but Germanicus could catch his tone of voice—which was piteous—and knew all was well when the praetorian laughed cruelly. The guard was about to unroll the ladder when his tribune came sauntering out of the bunker. The officer was either itching to give someone a hard time or had an inkling of trouble, for he apparently ordered the gathering group of legionaries to tie their *pili* to a rope, which was hoisted up in advance.

"I hope our lads like to use knives," Germanicus said to the centurion beside him.

"They *love* steel."

One by one the legionaries clambered up the ladder on what appeared to be their last strength. Then they followed the tribune into the bunker.

The praetorian sentry continued his tour along the wall.

Germanicus and the centurion traded anxious gazes.

"How many guards make up a *ballista* crew here?"

"Anywhere from five to eight, Procurator. It depends on how fat the duty roster is."

"Why is a tribune instead of a corporal in charge?"

"These praetorians trust no one—least of all themselves."

The sentry kept pacing back and forth. A patch of sunlight skimmed over him and down the valley like a bright scarf carried on the wind. He looked lost in daydreams as he marked time.

"It's taking too long," the centurion whispered.

"Men grapple to the last breath when it's for their lives."

Then the dog-faced legionary rushed out of the bunker and slit the praetorian's throat. He dumped the body over the wall and waved for the ten scouts to scramble up.

Reaching the top, these men raced to the other bunkers to urge the legionary crews not to rake their comrades coming in off the slopes. Soon more ladders were flipped over the side, and Germanicus whistled with relief. He and the centurion got up and began walking toward the garrison.

CHAPTER XIX

IT DID NOT take much to turn the legionaries against the praetorians. The cause of the legionaries' anger was more than the common rivalry between two different military units. The centurion told Germanicus that for months Poppaeus had been using the guards to bully the rank-and-file soldiers. And, unbeknown to anyone outside the garrison, Poppaeus had gone so far as to decimate the cohort, killing one out of every ten men after he caught wind of a mutiny rumor he himself may have started. The executions were reported to Nova Antiochia as losses in action.

After the wall was surmounted the backlash against Poppaeus gathered more steam than Germanicus had expected. The hated guards unlucky enough to be caught outside the underground complex withdrew to the praetorium, which was an annex of the stockade. From the windows of this stout building they began laying down fields of fire. Germanicus was prepared to talk them into surrender, but the legionary sappers beat him to the punch. Using their familiarity with the grounds, a pair of these demolition specialists crept up on the barracks from a blind side, chucked a satchel through an open window, then bolted for safety with satisfied grins on their faces.

"Mars, I hope we don't have to kill every last one of them—they *are* Fabius' own," Germanicus said, getting ready to plug his ears with his fingers.

"These bastards belong to Poppaeus," the centurion answered.

The windows of the praetorium shattered and belched licks of orange flame. Tiles spun off the roof into the overcast sky as a roar bounced from mountain to mountain.

"Good work, nevertheless." Germanicus began jogging forward. "Cut the wires, centurion. No messages are to go out until I know everyone who's involved in this."

The centurion noticed that Germanicus was veering off from him. "Where are you going, sir?"

"I'll lead these men to the stockade. You gather others and seal off the entrance to Poppaeus' headquarters."

"That'll trap the rat in his hole!"

Minutes later, taking sporadic rounds from the stockade, Germanicus and the five legionaries hunkered down behind a statue of the Emperor. "You in there!" Germanicus shouted. "We come in the name of Fabius!"

The *pili* fire stopped. Then Rolf's hearty voice came through a barred window. "Procurator?"

"Rolf?"

"Aye, sir!"

"Who's in there with you?"

"Praetorians what be loyal to the Emperor."

"Tell them I am Fabius' kinsman. Tell them I fight the traitor Poppaeus." Germanicus waited for Rolf's reply. He could hear fierce whispering inside the building. It was punctuated by hot-tempered cries that were stifled by protests in German. Then a *pilum* boomed within the walls. And an ugly calm followed. "Rolf, what gives in there?"

"All here be convinced now, sir!"

The praetorians on duty in the stockade were Germans to the man—all except the corporal who lay on the floor with a bloody divot in his forehead. "Hail Kaiser!" they blared.

"Hail Fabius!" Germanicus said.

Rolf smacked his fist into his palm as if to say that things

were finally looking up. "There be damn funny happenings
here, Germanicus."

"I know. How's your prisoner?"

"No trouble."

Germanicus smiled at the boy and said in Anatolian, "Your
father is well, Khalid."

He turned away without replying.

"Where is Crispa, Rolf?"

"Last I hear—underground."

"And Marcellus?"

The centurion frowned. "The same." He looked as if he
wanted to say something but was afraid to come out with it.

"Where are my staff officers?"

"I hear they be prisoners on your rail-galley."

"Very well, stay here with Khalid."

"I want to mix it up, sir."

"There'll be plenty of time for that."

Dutifully Rolf nodded yes, although he was clearly miserable. "I return this to you now." He handed over the Minerva
pendant.

"Thank you." Germanicus slipped it around his neck. "I'll
send for you shortly."

Outside, the legionaries had just launched an assault on the
mouth of the tunnel. But Poppaeus' praetorians beat them back
with thick, rapid fire, and the bodies of at least a dozen men
were left in a heap before the portal.

Germanicus kept the German praetorians close to him so
they would not be slain by the now furious legionaries. These
guards began calling to their comrades inside the tunnel—but
with no effect.

"Shall we try another entry, Procurator?"

"No, we'll need every man we've got when the barbarians
come down off Agri Dagi." Germanicus took a moment to
quiet a legionary and one of the German guards, who had started
quarreling, then shouted, "Praetorians!"

"Who speaks there?" came an uncertain reply from the black
opening.

Good, Germanicus thought, *at least the surviving guards
are confused by the turn of events.* "I am Germanicus Agricola!
And I fight to preserve the honor of the Emperor Fabius."

"As we do, Germanicus."

"No, you serve his enemy without knowing it. Poppaeus is

a traitor to the Emperor. That makes him your foe as well, for are you not sworn before the gods to defend the first citizen of Rome?"

"We are."

Nothing more was said for several moments. Germanicus tried not to think of Crispa. His heart sank as soon as he did— and he needed all the vigor he could muster. "What is your answer in there? Do you want to die serving the cause of treason?"

"What guarantees do we have, Germanicus?"

"My word."

Silence.

"Throw down your weapons and come out. Renew your vow to Fabius. Then take up arms again in the service of Rome and the gods."

"What of Poppaeus?"

"He must answer for his crimes. There is no alternative."

The wind howled in advance of another bank of frozen fog. "We are coming out, Procurator."

As a disciplined unit—and Germanicus admired them for that much—thirty praetorians came marching out of the darkness. They were led by a rawboned centurion who had done their bidding. He saluted Germanicus. "Hail Fabius! I surrender to your—"

Suddenly a legionary plunged his sword into the centurion's chest. This ignited a fray in which praetorians tried to wrest *pili* from the legionaries encircling them.

"Stop!" Germanicus screamed.

Miraculously, with the urging of a few level-headed salts on both sides, the scuffling came to a halt, replaced by a truce as thin as an eggshell. The praetorian down on the ice squirmed to a final stillness, the sword still jutting from his rib cage.

"You two," Germanicus ordered the guards restraining the murderer, who had a defiant air of fatalism about him. "He has forfeited his life for compromising my honor! Kill him!"

The sword was yanked out of the dead centurion and planted in the legionary before Germanicus could draw another breath.

"This," Germanicus said, trembling with rage, "will be the fate of those who break my word!" But then he had another concern.

Marcellus stood blinking in the stronger light outside the

portal. "Procurator," he said with a voice full of tension, "what kind of madness is going on?"

"You tell me, Colonel." Germanicus' face was emotionless.

"The last I knew we were awaiting a positive result to your rescue mission."

"You have one."

"Thank the gods." Despite the blast of cold air that met him outside, Marcellus' skin was pearled with sweat. His grin was as mirthless as a skeleton's. "Hail . . . Hail Germanicus!"

"Hail Germanicus!" the combined legionaries and praetorians roared.

"Where is Poppaeus?" Germanicus demanded.

"I don't know. I was dining in private when I heard *pili* and—"

"Where is Crispa?"

"I'm not sure, sir."

Germanicus gritted his teeth. He did not break off his glaring at Marcellus. The Parthian, in turn, watched the procurator with the fearful concentration of a hamstrung antelope awaiting the approach of a lion.

"These are your orders," Germanicus said at last.

"Sir!"

"Take this message to Poppaeus—"

"Directly."

"He is doomed whatever the case. His conduct out here has been an outrage. But this choice is his—does he want the notoriety of a public trial or will he commit suicide and save the reputation of his famous family?"

"Is that all?" Marcellus stammered slightly.

"Yes."

"Sir, he still may have praetorian fanatics guarding his person."

Now Germanicus knew that Marcellus had just left Poppaeus' company and had not been "dining in private," which—in the first place—was unthinkable for a man of any sociability. It was the colonel's use of the word "still" that tipped Germanicus off. "Carry a message to Poppaeus—not a sword. He'll hear you out—believe me."

"Of course, sir." Marcellus backed into the tunnel, saluting Germanicus all the way. Then his hollow-sounding footfalls slapped down the *vestibulum* tiles.

"Centurion," Germanicus said to the officer of the mission Poppaeus would have destroyed, "where are the people of my staff?"

"Held prisoner aboard your rail-galley—I just heard from a *decurion*. Their guard is light and prepared to surrender."

"Go win their freedom. Then send my physician, Epizelus, to me."

"Aye, sir."

Snow began falling again. Germanicus borrowed a cloak from a legionary. As time dragged on his shoulders slouched, and he looked older than his years. He presented such a figure of inconsolable sadness to the throng of soldiers that no one dared speak to him.

Staring down the black tunnel, he bitterly rued the fact that there was so little time to learn what he had to know. Poppaeus would never open a vein. He would opt for a trial and hope Pamphile's influence would save him—as it had once before. And what crime had he done? Could it not be construed to be a reverent act to order the Emperor's likeness displayed in conspicuous places? Likewise, he had no doubt that Marcellus would be utterly ruthless if backed into a corner. Germanicus had decided to let the two vipers tangle with each other first, then he would deal with the survivor. He was betting on Marcellus, perhaps with his own life.

"No!" Poppaeus screeched pathetically, protecting his throat with his pudgy hands. "Don't be a fool! Germanicus has exceeded his authority, can't you see?" He staggered backward, upsetting a brazier. "We have him! The self-righteous bastard will be forced to take a red bath!"

He overturned a couch in a feeble attempt to block Marcellus' deadly advance. "Please! Think of what you do!"

"I have thought too much. And acted too little," the Parthian said in a monotone.

Yes, Germanicus said to himself, this test was for Marcellus as well, who—like many a barbarian now in service—had gone from Roman hostage to Roman officer.

Finally the Parthian could be heard racing back toward the wan daylight. He burst out, drenched with blood. It took him a long moment before he could speak to Germanicus. "Poppaeus killed himself. Then his guards . . . they attacked me."

"And you won?"

"I slew them . . . both of them."

"Did Poppaeus make any confession?"

"Confession?"

"Did he name any other conspirators?"

"No . . . no, he listened to your message in silence, sir, then cut his own throat."

"You did well, Colonel."

"Aye, sir. Thank you."

"A barbarian attack could hit us at any moment. See to it these troops are deployed along the wall. Put all the *ballistae* in readiness. When this is done, report back to me."

"At once, sir."

Then Germanicus dashed into the tunnel at the head of a detachment twenty strong.

He discovered Poppaeus' most loyal praetorians slaughtered, one atop the other, at the entrance to their commander's unholy atrium. Their faces wore insipid expressions—as if they found something agreeable in the odor of composting roses and acrid incense that seeped from the darkened hall. The hilts of their swords lay across their open palms, but there was nothing to indicate that the men had been clenching them at the instant of their deaths. No—Germanicus decided, tapping his lip with his forefinger, these praetorians had been butchered out of the blue. Someone they trusted had strolled up and chopped them down as if they were cornstalks. "Leave them where they lie," Germanicus commanded. "Touch nothing you find."

Poppaeus' mountainous corpse was half wrapped in a silk curtain that had been pulled down off its mooring. Reeling in the throes of death, he had obviously fought to keep on his feet by clutching the material. Indeed, his throat had been sliced, as Marcellus had reported. A knife lay on the floor nearby. He had not lived long after receiving the wound— there was little blood.

Germanicus felt a tap on his shoulder, and the next thing he knew Epizelus was shining a torch in his eyes and ordering him to yawn.

"For Jupiter's sake, leave me be!"

The physician scowled. "A couple days without my care— and you're a basket case."

"Please." Gently Germanicus pushed him away. "Just give me something to keep me standing."

"A crutch then?"

"Epizelus, hurry!"

The urgency in Germanicus' raspy voice cut short any objection the Greek might have had. With deft fingers he took from his bag the pint of vinegar he stocked to slake his chief patient's thirst and stirred a white powder into it. "Drink."

In seconds Germanicus felt new energy throbbing through his arteries. "Why won't you ever tell me what this marvelous stuff is?"

"It enabled Alexander to conquer the world. It also killed him at thirty-three. That's why." He began rubbing an ointment into Germanicus' chapped skin.

"Listen to me carefully, Epizelus—go over this scene with your keen eye."

"What is the proposition this time? Another *massing?*"

"I hate to think who might have to bear the brunt of this *massing* business. But, no—the immediate task is to find out if Poppaeus took his own life. Can it be done?"

"Here we go again."

"Let me know as soon as possible."

"Why are these things never at my leisure?"

"You gave it up when you took your oa—"

They were interrupted by shouting out in the *vestibulum*. Then Crispa was jostled into Germanicus' presence by two legionaries, who enjoyed manhandling her.

Germanicus had to check a protective surge of temper. "What is this?"

"She was hiding beside the underground spring, sir," one of the soldiers said.

"I was not hiding."

It pained him to hear how listless she sounded. And the dark crescents under her eyes were those of a courtesan, languid from a long night of venality. This was not the girl who had been as fresh as a sprig of grass in Hibernia. "Unhand the colonel."

Even though the legionaries tramped out and Epizelus was busy questioning Poppaeus' servants, who had been peeking out from the back chambers like moles, Germanicus wanted a more private place. He led her out into the *vestibulum*. She trained her eyes on the distant fleck of daylight as if she expected an inquest.

"I have terrible news," Germanicus said at last.

She nodded—the gesture said she already knew.

"We've both lost a true friend."

The emphasis he put on "true" sent a shudder through her. Tears began rinsing the hardness from her eyes. "Scilla..."

"Yes."

They walked without speaking for a while.

"Before he died, Scilla demanded something of me."

She shook her head. She had no idea what this meant.

"He was quite insistent about it. You know how he was when some conviction took hold of him." Germanicus listened to the soles of his boots striking the obsidian tiles before continuing. "He told me to love you as best I can. And I will not disappoint Scilla." It surprised him how stiff and embarrassed his words rang.

But she rushed to him and buried her sobs in the warm space between his neck and shoulder. He enfolded her with his arms. It should have been the sweetest moment of his life. But it was not. It was acid.

Marcellus came bounding back toward them. He was not visibly angry at this show of Crispa's and Germanicus' affection for each other. In fact, he almost smiled with relief before reporting that the garrison defenses were in readiness. "And I've sent patrols out along the ridges, sir."

"Excellent." Germanicus recalled again what that melancholy Caesar, Marcus Aurelius, had written so long ago beside the black waters of the Danuvius. "...Everything that happens is as normal and expected as the spring rose..." And Germanicus vowed not to agonize over what must be done. Indifference began seeping through his emotions like ether. He feared the lifting of this effect. "Where are the tragedians, Marcellus?"

"Still aboard your rail-galley, I believe, sir." Without letting go of Crispa, Germanicus enveloped Marcellus with his free arm and led the two colonels forward, prattling all the while like some jolly uncle who has had too much to drink.

Crispa and Marcellus were eager to shake their nettlesome tension off, and despite their surprise at Germanicus' gregariousness, they soon found themselves being drawn into his mood. He described the entertainments planned for the evening. "Let's enjoy a play. We should take our pleasure while we can. Who knows what will happen tomorrow?"

It was fortunate for him that they could not clearly see his

expression in the shadowy tunnel. His face was screwed into
a grimace as he talked on and on. His mind had risen above
his empty sentences and a sad mental voice repeated again and
again. "...cunning...we suckled it from the teat of a she-
wolf...cunning..."

CHAPTER XX

"IT'S TURNED OUT better than if we'd planned it," Marcellus whispered to Crispa across the narrow space between their couches. The couple had stopped unconsciously twisting their hands around their cups the moment Germanicus had excused himself from Poppaeus' atrium, his bladder apparently calling with some urgency. "Have you ever seen the old fart drink like this before?"

"No," Crispa said.

"He's buggy with relief, isn't he? Thinks he came out of a mutiny without so much as a scratch."

"You poor fool." Crispa gulped her wine. Then she looked at Marcellus. The once flashing stream of her affection had now gone completely stagnant. "You just don't know. No one knows."

"Oh, yes, I do." Marcellus would not let her spoil his good mood. "Germanicus has sealed off the garrison, so we can't get a message to Pamphile right now. But when she hears Poppaeus is dead, who will she depend on to govern this new kingdom? Me—dammit."

"And what of your Great *Zaim?* What will he rule?"

"He'll be no problem. In the next few hours I'm going to save his son's life."

"You don't know . . . only I know . . ."

Marcellus' couch turned into a bed of needles under him. "I'm dying for news from Rome. Is Fabius still sinking?" He paused, then forced a smile. "Crispa, my dear—I'd like an answer to something."

She wiped her lips, beginning with the back of her hand and finishing halfway up her bare forearm.

"My darling, you think of the Emperor as I do . . ."

"He is Rome's offal," she said.

"Are you *massing* against him?"

Crispa began blinking as if she were confused. "The Sibyl said, 'Two young hearts and a flame this cause shall ensnare . . .'"

"Yes, yes, but are you following my suggestion? Are you actually *massing* against Fabius?"

Crispa would say nothing more.

Germanicus moved at double time. In the space of five minutes he sent to the stockade for Rolf and Khalid, took an emetic to rid himself of the quarts of wine he had been guzzling, and after the potion had produced its effect, set off to find Demetrius and his tragedians.

"Ah, Procurator," the actor cooed in a back chamber, surrounded by his fellows, who were in various stages of costume dress. "What a relief to see you safe. Your exploits make it necessary for the gods to give Virgil a second life!"

"Listen carefully. Can you do the play you described to me on the rail-galley?"

"If you wish."

"I do." Then, seizing Demetrius by the wrists, Germanicus rattled off a string of instructions so baffling the old actor tried to interrupt but was cut short by the fierce impatience in the procurator's eyes. "Is there a bit of treason in this work?"

Demetrius beamed. "Why, a most poignant betrayal right before—"

"Then do this . . ."

A moment later, Germanicus raced from the chamber, leaving the tragedian to shake his head. Demetrius sighed, then ordered the girlish Sicilian to cover his cheeks with white lead.

"No one in this bloody Empire seems to understand that you can't fiddle with art like you can a hairstyle!" He tossed a flaxen wig at the boy. "Here, pull this down around the only inviolate cavities you have!"

Germanicus was delayed by Charicles, his aged servant, who was having a hard time balancing a single cup of wine on a tray. "Germanicus—"

"I'll take this, old friend."

"I've never seen you so... silly, Germanicus."

"I have never felt less silly. How are you?"

"Disgusted!"

Germanicus smiled with one corner of his mouth. "With me?"

"Aye, but not as much as with that harlot slave girl of Poppaeus'! Do you know what she just did?"

"I tremble to ask—"

"She offered me her wretched favors for a cask of wine! Why, *I* wouldn't even have relations with me—whatever the price. Germanicus, it's up to you. She has to be disciplined. What kind of house is this where—?"

"I'll handle it at the earliest opportunity." Germanicus slipped around him and swept back into the atrium, taking care to appear unsteady on his feet. He smiled warmly at Crispa and Marcellus. "I'd forgotten what both a pleasure and a nuisance wine can be."

Marcellus sniggered. But Crispa, who at first had seemed to welcome Germanicus' buoyant spirits as a pardon, now languished with her chin buried in the couch rugs.

"Sir," Marcellus said airily, "tell us about the Great *Zaim*."

"He revealed things to me I would have never imagined."

"Did you two talk of peace?"

Germanicus noisily inhaled the musty air within his cup. "Two old sailors don't talk about their times in port. They tell each other of the stormy seas they've crossed." Then he grinned. "Come, toast the Emperor's health with me." That Crispa and Marcellus stiffened was not lost on Germanicus. "To Fabius— may he live forever!"

"*Ave* Fabius!" Marcellus downed big quaffs of wine, but Crispa did not budge.

"What is it, dear girl?" Germanicus asked. "Won't you drink to our beloved Emperor?"

"I've had enough."

The bite in her voice smarted him. "Very well. We all should know when we've had enough. Ah, here comes my worthy centurion!" Rolf led Khalid into the hall. "And my great enemy's son!" Germanicus saluted with his cup hand, slopping wine across the floor. "Well, enemy or friend—my guest nevertheless. Take a couch. Rolf, you relax between the good Colonel Marcellus and Khalid. Khalid's your name, isn't it?"

The boy snarled in the mountain dialect to which Germanicus' ears were now attuned, "Soon my people will come. I know that hour will be my last. If you honor me as a guest, let me enjoy those moments unprofaned by the stink of Roman company."

"Take a couch!" Germanicus hollered. He held the flat of his hand up to his forehead. "I've had it up to here with barbarian insolence!" Tramping around the brazier, his pupils glowing like the coals, he worked himself into a fury. "And you're quite right—should your father break the peace, I'll cut you down like a sapling! That is the law!"

Marcellus started to squirm on his couch.

"Colonel!" Germanicus barked at him.

"Sir!" Marcellus snapped to attention in a single bound.

"As soon as the first *pilum* is fired, you strike this pup's head from his shoulders!"

"Aye, Procurator," Marcellus mumbled.

"Why do you stand as you do?"

"Sir?"

"You keep turning your back to this barbarian."

"I was not aware—"

"Look him in the eye, dammit. Let him know you're serious. That's the trouble with the world today. No one thinks Rome is serious."

Slowly Marcellus rotated toward the boy. Again sweat erupted on his face. Glowering from his couch, Khalid suddenly changed his expression from one of loathing to one of hope. Quickly he smeared the contemptuous frown back on his lips—but it was too late to have escaped Germanicus' notice.

Germanicus let it pass. The rage in his voice of a moment before melted into mawkishness. "But it doesn't have to come to that, you know. There is no love like a father's for his favorite son. None in the world."

Marcus Junius, his staff tribune, whisked in, anxiously rat-

tling his sword in his scabbard for attention. Germanicus drew
him toward a corner of the atrium. "Report, tribune."

"The wrapheadies, sir, they've hit one of our patrols."

"How strong is their force?"

"A hundred or more. Funny thing is—they broke off right
away. But they still gave us a couple of casualties."

"Call in our patrols."

"Is this it then, sir?"

Germanicus nodded soberly. "Within the hour—I'm sure."

"Can we be reinforced?"

"This is already the fattest garrison in the province, lad. Go
back to the wall. Make sure that all is in readiness."

"Hail Fabius!"

Germanicus spun around on squeaking heels and spread his
arms to encompass the entire party. "Let's not have any more
quarrelsome talk. Marcellus, you are hereby appointed master
of the drinking." Germanicus was referring to the old drinking
law enacted in Augustus' day to combat alcoholism. Each host
was required to pick a levelheaded sort to regulate consumption
during the evening.

"What guidelines will you have, sir?"

"Mix the wine with sea water—but no person leaves here
with clear eyes!"

Marcellus laughed uproariously and began ordering the slaves
to haul out a full aluminum *amphora*.

Gently rocking back and forth on his heels, Germanicus
smiled at Crispa. "We have laws for everything. Order is our
passion." She implored him with her aquamarine eyes. But he
didn't dare ask himself what might ease her pain.

"Everyone! Drain a glass!" Marcellus merrily shouted.

"Procurator?" Demetrius asked, poking his head out of the
split in two curtains hung at one end of the atrium.

"Ah, here are my tragedians. Are you ready?"

"We'll begin at your command. May we ask for your pardon
beforehand?"

"Do you mean to insult me?"

"Oh no, good Procurator. It's just that what delights one
soul might slur another."

Germanicus waved him on with good-natured impatience.
"You have my pardon. Now on with the play." He flopped
down on a couch and held up his cup for it to be filled. "Give

me my cheer!" he shouted as if he were in a wineshop.

"You once took all your cheer from vinegar and comradeship," Crispa said softly.

"'Men who won't touch a drop get from the gods nothing but evil days'—Horace."

Crispa poured a stream of wine into the brazier. Sour-smelling steam curled up around her face. "Poor, simple Horace," she said. "He never walked the higher paths of life."

"In that he showed excellent sense." Germanicus hoisted his drink as if to salute her wit, but in secret he nearly choked on her remark. He knew well what was happening. The territory each of them stood on was splitting apart, exposing a chasm no amount of yearning could close again. Even his unspoken desires were unraveling. They lay strewn across the floor like uncoiled springs—a quiet intellectual retirement in the company of good books, a rustic villa in the country, and Crispa. Gone forever. Germanicus drunkenly licked his lips and sang out, startling everyone with an unexpected recitation.

> *"To bring yourself to be happy*
> *Acquire the following blessings:*
> *A nice inherited income,*
> *A kindly farm with a kitchen,*
> *No business worries or lawsuits,*
> *Good health, a gentleman's muscles,*
> *A wise simplicity, friendships,*
> *A plain but generous table,*
> *Your evening sober but jolly,*
> *Your bed amusing but modest,*
> *And nights that pass in a moment;*
> *To be yourself without envy,*
> *To fear not death, nor to wish it."*

Marcellus clapped as if his life depended on it. But Crispa scrutinized Germanicus with what he had hoped never to see in her eyes—disappointment.

"Was that Horace, sir?" Marcellus asked.

"Oh, no—"

Then the lights in the atrium flickered out—all but the reddish glow of the brazier by which dark figures could be seen darting forward across the hall. Germanicus had his sword half drawn before a pillar of white fire splashed down upon the form of Demetrius, who—as always—projected a magnificent presence. On the faint periphery of this light the other tragedians waited in their places like obedient children. Demetrius finally spoke in a voice deep and rich enough to make Jupiter envious:

> *"The Prophetess of Ptolemy's town*
> *Reknits the fabric of the ages,*
> *To tell of the divine so renown*
> *In Tacitus he has no pages.*

> *"In Judea of Herod the Son ..."*

Germanicus turned his eyes on Marcellus and Crispa. There was a frustrated air about them—the entertainment was already grating on their nerves. Germanicus was thinking: *I don't want to see this happen: I need my bloody illusions about her.* For the first time he actually drank to fortify his spirits.

Joshua Bar Joseph made his entrance. Here was no ordinary prophet, cheeks swelled with bombast. There was a melancholy amusement to his expression like that of the aged *shaykh* Germanicus had met in the Purple Village. Joshua spoke. His lean words plucked at Germanicus' dogged loneliness on all its strings. Longings for the survival of his dead son's spirit came to life—and made his eyes burn.

But there were tawdry moments when Demetrius' treatment of the tale showed like marionette strings. To answer whether it was fitting to serve both Caesar and God—which the *zaim's* Isa ibn Maryam had juggled so deftly without dropping either piety or common sense—this Joshua pilfered from Virgil, "'Tiberius' art is this, to impose the custom of peace, to spare the humbled and wear down the proud!'"

Germanicus frowned at Demetrius, who shrugged. Plagiarism was an old Roman custom.

Epizelus crept in. Marcellus tracked him on his straight path to Germanicus' couch like a hawk following a mouse. The physician knelt beside Germanicus and whispered, "You were right."

Germanicus chortled as if he had been told a bawdy joke, then said out of the corner of his mouth, "Tell me everything you know. But laugh first."

The Greek caught Germanicus' meaning and giggled convincingly. "The strike of the cut is all wrong. Poppaeus couldn't have done it to himself. Besides, the knife was in his right hand."

"So?"

"His slaves all agree on one thing—he was left-handed."

"What about his guards?"

"What about them?"

"Did they die before or after Poppaeus?"

"I would say before."

"Why?"

"Poppaeus' face was splattered with blood," Epizelus said. "I couldn't figure how it flowed upward from his throat wound, so I tested it. Wasn't his. Came from one of his praetorians."

"How does this tell you they were killed first?"

"When Poppaeus' body came to rest, it was on its side, turned away from the guards. He had to be standing toward the mortally wounded men to have his face splattered with their blood."

"Very well. Find my tribune, young Marcus. Have him contact my brother, Manlius, in Rome. I want to know how the Emperor fares. As soon as this is done, order him to break off the line again. Let no one sneak out a message—report the names of those who try."

"Aye, Procurator." The physician withdrew. Again Marcellus' predatory eyes followed him.

Demetrius thundered:

"And Judas of this scruffy command..."

An actor who bore himself with leonine pride stormed out into the focus. He greatly resembled Marcellus. But this was wasted on the imitated man. It was Crispa who regarded Germanicus with suspicion before turning back to the play.

Judas, a follower, embraced and kissed Joshua. Two Hebrew priests watched knowingly from the background. In short order two raffish legionaries and an effeminate centurion marched in to drag Joshua away.

Marcellus began rubbing his chin with a nervous finger. He snorted as if to laugh but then froze during the long moments Germanicus glared at him. Then the colonel turned his attention back to the play with deadly concentration. He put down his cup. He was no longer interested in being master of the drinking.

"To Pilate of the Glorious Realm..."

The model Demetrius had chosen for the Judean procurator was no mystery even to Germanicus. Chuckling to show everyone that no offense was taken, he said, "Only a whale could have a heavier jaw!" But when the laughter had died around his ears, Germanicus sank into silence, his fist pressed heavily into his cheek. He could see that this fellow governor had a sick heart. How well he himself knew its cause—the nauseating sway a man of authority feels between punishment and compassion.

Sighing a windstorm, the ancient procurator called for the crowd to choose for Joshua or a local bandit to go free. They cried out in the bandit's favor. Before another argument could be shouted, a cross was borne into the atrium on Joshua's shoulder. And he was crucified.

"This is really too much," Marcellus said, trying to turn a choking reflex into a giggle.

The tortured corpse was taken down to a trilling of flutes. Ceremoniously the body was wrapped in linen and deposited in a papier-mâché tomb. A stone was rolled across the portal.

"A concubine of Magdalene birth..."

As the light dimmed around Demetrius, the Sicilian "courtesan" pranced out on her toes, sweating from under the flaxen wig. It was the same color as Crispa's hair. Arms flailing in the air, "she" began pining with all the agonized abandon of a fresh widow. Crispa winced as she watched, but then quickly hid the lower half of her face behind her cup. Her eyes were dripping with rage. She refused to look at Germanicus.

Judas, the traitor, crept out of the shadows. He took the courtesan in his arms and varnished kisses on her neck. She returned his passion, and the two intertwined like serpents.

This made Crispa and Marcellus eye each other and then Germanicus, who did nothing to unruffle the moment. He impaled them on his gaze. Disgust bent down his mouth.

"The harlot and the traitor to Zeus ..."

Demetrius said these words with less conviction, showing his resentment that Germanicus had tinkered with his master-work, and the action grew a bit creaky as the actors accustomed themselves to the new plot. But soon they fell into the spirit of things, and the Judean lovers were busily converting the people of Rome to their strange sect.

Not that the willowy courtesan's argument for peace among men was spurious. She said that her god had lovingly invested in human affairs—unlike the members of the house of Jupiter, who had always been preoccupied with their own adventures. Her call to devotion rang in Roman hearts. Legionaries threw down their weapons. Gladiators strolled out of the arena arm in arm. The vestal virgins switched allegiance to Joshua Bar Joseph, retaining only the costume of the old faith. All but Constantine were convinced. This amused Germanicus, who had been regaled since youth by tales of this gruff, martial Emperor.

He caught Rolf's eye and winked that trouble might be coming in short order. The centurion nodded. No sooner had Germanicus done this than the courtesan pressed her fingertips to her temples in an obvious gesture of *massing* and went into a terrible concentration. In the background Constantine began shaking so violently his armor rattled. Then he collapsed and died.

Crispa and Marcellus turned to granite. Their fear crackled around their heads like electricity.

Demetrius now spoke in a hush:

> *"And pitched among its marble bones,*
> *A city less than half the old ..."*

"Enemies to Rome," Germanicus whispered. But he might have screamed it for the effect it had on the dinner party. The seconds pounded away in silence. He turned his head and looked at the couple like a bull stirring to rage. But his eyes did not see them. He saw the desolate Rome he had drifted through in that strange dream on the mountain. Enemies to Rome—these vicious young people he had trusted and loved would strike down their Emperor and bring an ignoble death to the most glorious city in the world. "Enemies to Rome."

Marcus Junius tramped in. His face was feverish and he could barely speak through the urgency of his message. "Procurator!"

"Report," Germanicus growled.

"The Emperor Fabius is near death!"

Germanicus recoiled as he saw out of the corner of his eye that Marcellus was lunging toward him. He reeled back and out of the path of the Parthian's shining knife blade. It was the young tribune who took the brunt of it. Caught in the belly, he fell without a sound, his features twisted like a wrung towel. Rolf was off his couch in an instant. He swung at the colonel with his short sword, missed, and swung savagely again. Marcellus stumbled backward, his face all teeth and eyes. He was distracted by the wordless, agonized way Crispa was crying.

The tragedians fluttered out of the atrium like flushed partridges—Demetrius scurrying them before him. They left a trail of cheap jewelry and gaudy vestments across the floor.

His back pressed against the wall, Marcellus watched two German praetorians and then a third rush in to hold him at bay. Rolf closed in for the kill. His forearms were knotty with tension.

"Wait!" Marcellus shouted. All his hope dribbled out of his face through a grim smile. "By my own hand!"

Rolf was not prepared to grant this last wish and was still moving toward the colonel when Germanicus said, "No, Rolf—as he would have it."

Trembling grotesquely, Marcellus turned toward Germanicus. He tapped his chest. "All I have to do, old man, is imagine this heart to be yours—and it becomes easy. For Parthia!" Then with wild swiftness, he jerked the knife through his sternum. He collapsed. But his eyes still had life.

Crispa flailed past the praetorians and rushed to him. She held up his head—he was rapidly growing too weak to do it himself. His once-brown cheeks were now the same color as her fingers. She could not help herself from stroking his hair, although she knew Germanicus was watching like a madman beset with hallucinations.

Marcellus was washing away all the contempt she had recently felt for him—with his blood. He struggled to lift his face to hers but could not do it.

Crispa wept for her former lover and the fact she could not hide her feeling for Marcellus from Germanicus.

"I . . . must have missed . . . the heart," Marcellus said deliriously. "Strike again . . . for me."

"I can't!"

"Yes, my love, I know," he said with a smile. Then he faded into death as comfortably as a child falling asleep in his mother's arms.

Two young officers shouted from the *vestibulum* at the same time, blurring each other's message.

"What be your report?" Rolf asked, firmly holding Khalid in case the boy had been inspired by Marcellus to make his own attempt on Germanicus' life.

"The barbarians are coming down off the mountain! They'll soon be in *ballistae* range!"

"Orders, Procurator?" Rolf said.

But Germanicus' attention was fixed on Marcellus' corpse. He spoke without expression. "By this act, his family may retain their estate. He has a mother, I know."

"His estate?" Crispa cried. "How can you think that his estate matters at this time!"

Germanicus said nothing. He was filled with guilt for all the times he had betrayed Virgilia in his heart. His Roman wife would have never asked such a question. And now loneliness enveloped him like drizzle—he did not know this half-barbarian girl, nor did she know him. His black mood was compounded by a strange lust that fed on the sight before him—a woman who had betrayed him made vulnerable by swift defeat. He did not like himself for coming close to relishing this sensation, so he returned to duty once again to salvage his own precious dignity. "The *ballistae* may fire when the tribesmen are close enough. But caution the centurions to keep an eye on the ground where no *ballistae* are aimed."

"Hail Fabius!" The young officers sprinted back toward the wall.

Then Germanicus drew close to Rolf and felt a bit more encouraged simply by standing beside the centurion, for vigor and righteous anger throbbed in waves around the loyal German. "Turn Khalid over to the other praetorians for return to the stockade. The barbarian fools—his life is forfeit. I'll need you on the wall."

"And her?" Rolf glared at Crispa, who was now stroking Marcellus' black hair with her fingers.

"Yes—she must go to the stockade as well."

"Germanicus!" the centurion hissed. "She must go to her death!"

"I must wait a little longer. How else then could I be sure that I didn't . . . do this thing to her just because she loved a traitor."

Then Rolf said something that abashed Germanicus, who had not expected such words from such a rough and simple man. "Maybe you never be sure."

Outside, the *ballistae* began booming. Germanicus tramped toward this warring thunder. He nearly paused beside the body of young Marcus Junius—but dared not.

CHAPTER XXI

BEFORE GERMANICUS WAS even out of Poppaeus' underground complex he had filled his head with prayers. To Mars: that he might win what could prove to be the bloodiest battle of his career. To Vulcan: that Roman technology and discipline would stand up to barbarian fervor. To Minerva: that Crispa might be found blameless in this quagmire of intrigue. And finally to Jupiter: strangely enough, that the *zaim*—Germanicus' enemy—might survive this struggle to invest the remainder of his years in contemplation. This was the only desire Germanicus held for himself, as well, now that all else seemed in tatters.

"Hail Germanicus!"

He raised his arm to acknowledge the salute of legionaries. Then he strode directly to the wall and surveyed the scene.

Mauled by the first salvos of *ballistae*, the barbarian forces had withdrawn—but only a short distance to be out of range of the artillery. Illuminated by Roman flares, which exploded overhead with martial regularity, the tribesmen were drawn up like hoplites in neat phalanxes. There must have been at least five thousand of them.

"Well, they've learned something from the west," Germanicus muttered.

"Procurator!" Rolf rushed to his side.

"We've got a fight on our hands this time, centurion." Germanicus pointed at the dozens of barbarians left slaughtered by the *ballistae*. "Their *zaim* wouldn't do this for the hell of it."

"Ja, he means us to keep looking forward from the wall."

"Exactly."

Quickly Germanicus took stock of his forces. The garrison was manned by two cohorts, or about eleven hundred legionaries. But through his excesses Poppaeus had pruned this force to nine hundred fighting men and women. This loss was now felt all the more keenly because the majority of those slain had been *principes*—veterans thirty years of age or older. Germanicus had brought with him on the rail-galley a full maniple, or two hundred Romans, but these were staff personnel whose only calluses were on their index fingers from scratching out orders. Then there was the century of praetorians, now reduced by a quarter for their part in Poppaeus' infamy.

The guards had not been deployed along the wall but were instead held in reserve. Their ranks on the parade ground were silent. They were feeling the shame the day had heaped on them. Their Emperor was near death while they had been dancing on strings held by a traitor. "Lads," Germanicus said, "it's been a dark hour for the lot of us. I, too, have heard the rumors: The man who keeps us all in wine and meat is on his deathbed. Well, to tell the truth, I don't know. But if by chance he is a bit under the weather—what better to cheer him than to hear of the valor of his beloved praetorians?"

"Aye!" they shouted back as a single man.

"Will you follow me?"

"Aye!"

"Centurion, turn them around."

There was much confusion with this order. Perhaps they expected to be killed in punishment for their association with Poppaeus. A lesser commander than Germanicus would have slain every tenth man of their number just for drill.

But Germanicus had a far different aim in mind.

For no sooner did Rolf relay the order than the *ballistae*

began hammering away at the renewed advance of the barbarian host.

It was baffling to the praetorians—to be implored to do battle then commanded to turn tail and march out of harm's way. "The wall," a man in the stamping mass said, and the cry was soon taken up. "The wall! The wall!" It was not disobedience on their part so much as the fear that they were being refused the opportunity to redeem their honor.

"Hail Fabius!" Rolf growled above their voices. There must have been something reassuring in his tone, for their chant died away. And their boots crackled over the ice-sheathed paving stones.

There was nothing to be seen on the churlish heights behind the garrison, but some of the praetorians must have been nipped by Germanicus' apprehension as they marched nearer and nearer the base of the cliffs, because they craned their necks to look up—and a few even covered their bared throats with their hands as they scanned upward.

"I feel more with each step we take," Germanicus said to Rolf.

"Aye."

The rock face descended into a shallow ravine, the garrison side of which the Romans had reinforced with a rampart surmounted by a parapet of birch logs. The handful of sentries posted along this breastwork looked back in surprise to see the arrival of such a formidable body of troops to reinforce them. Time and again they had been reassured that theirs was such a comfortable stretch of the perimeter no *ballistae* were necessary to strengthen it. It had become the place to send legionaries who had grown too portly or could not see well in the pitchy mountain night. Germanicus had no doubt that the *zaim* knew this and a thousand other details about the imperial enclave.

The minutes hung off Germanicus' back like a hair shirt, and he began picking at his hunch with skepticism. While the cliff remained calm the garrison behind him was cast into flame and smoke as the legionaries got down to the business of repelling the barbarians. When the Romans started discharging their *pili*, Germanicus knew that the tribesmen had rushed right up to the muzzles of the *ballistae*. He was at the point of ordering the praetorians to the wall when there came from above the sound of a rock being dislodged. It clattered into the ravine.

"Easy, lads," he whispered, "it won't be long now."

Nor was it. Within the minute, *pili* on the heights showered metal down on the heads of the praetorians, who scrambled for cover as best they could. True to their rigorous training, they did not return fire, for there was nothing to aim at.

Germanicus peeked over the lip of the parapet in time to see hundreds of ropes uncoil down the length of the precipice, then wiggle as tribesmen eased themselves toward the bottom.

He seized a corporal by the cloak and shouted, "Go back for a Greek firer!"

The other praetorians were picking off the descending tribesmen in twos and threes—but it was not enough. The sheer numbers of men coming down the mountain were alarming, and it was not long before dozens were standing with their feet flat on the ground, unslinging their weapons.

Stilicho had been a praetorian half of his forty years, so he did not give much attention to the prisoner screaming for his attention down the stockade hall. He had closed his ears to much worse while guarding Fabius' own person. Besides—leaning on the window sill, a hot mug of vinegar in his hand, he had a cozy ringside seat on the battle and was not about to miss a thing.

Young Rufinius came trotting down the hall with echoing footfalls. "Centurion!"

"Aye, what does the Scandian harlot want now?"

"She demands writing materials."

Stilicho spat vinegar on the stone floor. "Tell her to plant a kiss on my pubis."

"She won't shut up."

"Then beat the bitch!" A blast of *ballistae* lighted up the old praetorian's grim and pitted face. "I don't know her part in this farce, but I do know that some of our best boys died today because of her and that Parthian cocksman of hers. The Emperor may never see fit to pardon us."

While Rufinius had the tender face of a boy, a certain cruelty shone through from the underlying bones. And his mouth became sly whenever it was not smiling. "I think we should grant the colonel's request."

"What?"

"In order to save our own lives—perhaps."

Stilicho squinted against a distant flash of Greek fire. "Speak, dandy. There's a bit of the fox in you. I'll admit that much."

"You and I know damned well there's been a plot against the Emperor."

"Aye, and it's been beached on a mighty hard rock—Germanicus Agricola, that's who."

"Well, let's do our bit and help weed out the conspirators."

"How then?"

"Let Colonel Crispa write all night if she wants to. Don't you see? She's trying to get in touch with the chaps in Rome who are behind the plot. Whatever she scribbles—and whoever she names—we hand over to the praetorian prefect. And he saves our skins because we saved his bloody honor, right?"

Stilicho smiled with a blunt finger held against his lips. "Do it."

Rufinius strolled back to Crispa's cell like a child sucking on tart candy. He rolled back the iron door as if the hinges were made of glass and lingered at the threshold, one foot balanced on its toe behind the heel of the other. "Colonel?" he called gently into the darkness.

Despite the carnage the praetorians were inflicting on them, the barbarians kept pouring down off the heights, driven down by the gravity of their zeal. The Romans picked them off the face of the cliff until a great pile of corpses rose up to the rim of the ravine, but more tribesmen climbed down, staggered over their dead comrades, to grapple with the guardsmen on the parapet.

Rolf rushed to wherever the line was weakest—shouting encouragement and fending off attackers with his short sword whenever a man needed the opportunity to reload his *pilum*.

At last the praetorian runner returned with a Greek firer strapped to his back, and the Romans clambered down off the rampart, hotly pursued by the barbarians. The firer nozzle flicked a short blue tongue of flame at the enemy, then spewed an orange festoon thirty feet long up and down the parapet. Those tribesmen unlucky enough to be caught in its sweep were instantly transformed into ghastly figures from the underworld, spinning wildly in robes of fire.

But then white sparks chipped up the pavement around the praetorian on the firer, and Germanicus realized that the guardsman was the target of every sniper crouching on the heights.

All at once the man was struck, wheeled around as he fell,

and poured horrible death on a dozen or more of his comrades. He vanished forever at the heart of an explosion.

Germanicus shielded his face against the heat with his hands. The smell of his own singed hair offended his nostrils.

Now it was useless trying to hold the barbarians at a point inside the rampart. There was nothing but parade ground in their path—a smooth highway on which to overwhelm the praetorians. Germanicus shouted, "Back to the stairs!" and the Romans found their feet. They did not flee in headlong panic. Instead they ran in calm urgency toward a new position they might hold. They scrambled up a flight of steps and fanned out across the top of a stone terrace to once again face the tribesmen, who were screaming at their heels.

The eight-foot height was enough to stall the momentum of the barbarians. Their swarms clogged the base of the stairs but were quickly met mid-flight by a score of praetorians stubbornly determined to halt their advance.

Reluctantly Germanicus dispatched a runner to bring reinforcements from the main wall. Beset with their own difficulties, these legionaries were fending off the *zaim*'s frontal attack. Awaiting their arrival, he raced back and forth along the edge of the terrace, joining the praetorians in the scuffle wherever the barbarians threatened to climb into their laps. The pace of the fighting grew too madcap to allow for the reloading of *pili*, and the air became spangled with flashing blades. Clawed fingers groped for eyes. Men bared their canine teeth and growled.

"Hold your ground!" Germanicus cried at the top of his lungs.

Inch by inch the praetorians were forced to the top of the stairs, leaving half their number to be trampled underfoot by the barbarians. The guardsmen had done their best. But it was not good enough, and their shame at this became headlong rage. A corporal, stunned by a head wound, sat at Germanicus' feet. Grinning viciously, he looked up and said, "It's like trying to kill a whale with a bloody toothpick!"

"Yes, lad, but one toothpick in just the right place . . ."

The man struggled to his feet. He picked tufts of his own hair off his uniform as if they were lint. "Very well, Germanicus Agricola. Tell Fabius of this." Then he pitched himself down the stairs, bowing over the foremost barbarians and gaining a precious yard for his fellows before the life was hacked out of him.

Germanicus leaned slightly toward the drop-off, but Rolf's hand immediately seized him, then roughly shook him. "We be in need of nothing as much as our procurator right now!" he cried before adding his sword to the weary line.

"Yes," Germanicus whispered after him, "a good death tempts our sorrows."

At last he heard the brassy encouragement of trumpets. Two maniples came clattering in all their gear across the parade ground. They deployed among the haggard guardsmen, then visibly stunned the barbarians with heavy fusillade.

Germanicus spied Prince Sala standing in the eye of the enemy hurricane, directing warriors this way and that with sharp gestures and quick juts of his chin. The renewed bark of Roman fire did not seem to discourage him, but he appeared to be sensing the downswing in barbarian fortunes. Although his heroic charges had breached the ring of the Roman garrison, there was still strong resistance to be overcome. The ugly man was not so foolish as to ignore his losses. The bodies of his men were piling up. The living had to advance over a labyrinth of the dead. He did the only sensible thing. He called for a retreat to the rampart they had just surmounted, hoping to regain the spirit that had brought them this far before exhaustion set in.

The widening distance between the two forces reduced the battle to a bickering of *pili*. To the west Germanicus heard detonations and knew at once the thick rumbling came from the Great Artery, which the barbarians were blasting apart at a dozen locations. But that was now a secondary concern. The garrison came first. He sorely missed the presence of a few sand-galleys, but the craft had always been considered unsuitable for the rugged Agri Dagi district. He would have to hang on with what he had, and that meant not giving thought to that which he wished he had.

Rolf tapped him on the shoulder. "There be a message for your ears alone, sir."

"Where?"

"Aboard your rail-galley."

The ferret-faced wireless operator insisted on sealing the door before he would make his report. Still, he was upset that Rolf was permitted to remain at Germanicus' side.

"It's all right," Germanicus said. "I trust this centurion with my life."

"I fear your life's at stake, Procurator—so I trust no one." He hesitated, and his eyes grew watery.

"Speak," Germanicus commanded.

In a breathless voice the operator recounted how the Nova Antiochia relay station had tried to break in on the silence at Agri Dagi. "To no avail, sir," the operator said. "I would not disobey your orders. But the beggars were using your *personal* code. They said the message came directly from your brother, Manlius, in Rome."

"Go on." Germanicus began tapping his foot on the floor. Years ago he had given Manlius his code to be used in cases of extreme peril.

"That's all, sir. I did not answer but sent for you."

"Answer." Germanicus wrapped himself in his cloak. He found it hard to swallow. Dammit—but he was seconds away from finally knowing.

The man screwed a receptor into his ear and keyed the wireless that was as large as a chariot. "Nova Antiochia, proceed with your communication." He listened. Then his eyes bulged as if he had been squeezed around the guts. He could not look at Germanicus when he spoke. "The message is not directly from Manlius. Your brother, sir, is dead."

"What be this?" Rolf growled, glancing around the wireless chamber as if conspirators might materialize at any moment.

Germanicus had turned to marble.

"The message comes from Manlius' slave, Leo..."

"Leo," Germanicus said like a stroke victim who has suddenly spoken for the first time in years.

"The Emperor—all those loyal to him—poisoned. It was thus that your brother died."

"How be the Emperor?" Rolf asked.

The operator repeated the question, then waited for the reply. "He struggles valiantly for his life."

"Who be the villain what...?"

"Pamphile—his own wife. She has been put to the sword. Her servants tortured for information."

"Leo," Germanicus repeated.

"Manlius learned terrible news before he died. Poppaeus at Agri Dagi will assassinate Germanicus. Many will help him.

The Parthian Marcellus. And a female colonel. Pamphile's slave who revealed this did not know the name of the officer."

"She!" Rolf bawled before he could help it.

Germanicus hoisted a shaking hand as if to halt the spinning of the earth. "I want a list of all female colonels under . . . under my command . . ."

"There be only one woman colonel in all of Anatolia!" Rolf said.

"I want a thorough list. Let's . . . let's throw in tribunes as well. Yes, tribunes. How many have we? And centurions. I know of at least a dozen females of that rank in my command. Some of them have to be suspect . . ." He fought for breath. "We shall get to the bottom of this, my lads."

"I think it be ordered," Rolf said in a murmur.

"Ordered . . . what ordered?"

"Colonel Crispa must answer. The *Emperor,* sir!"

Germanicus stared off as if he had not heard a word. "I'm quite serious about this list. I want no one omitted. None is unimpeachable . . . I mean that."

"Even if it be that I die for it later, Germanicus, I know your answer. Stop me before I go to the stockade—if that be right."

Chest heaving, Germanicus tried to speak but could not.

"Hail Fabius!" Then the centurion bolted out of the chamber.

The iron door moaned open. The light from the hall fell on the floor in a trapezoid of amber. Germanicus' centurion stood at the ready. The tip of his sword had the cold gleam of a distant star.

Crispa sprang up from her cot. "I must see him—talk to him."

"That cannot be, daughter."

The languid swirl of empathy in his voice terrified her more than anything else about his presence. She began pacing from corner to corner on silent cat's feet. "You don't understand. I know what's coming for me. I can bear it. But only if I can speak to him first—touch his face one more time."

"Aye," Rolf said in a hush, "but *he* cannot bear that."

Suddenly she stopped. Her eyes became hot with temper. "Is that why you've come in his place?"

"Aye. Will it be by your own hand?"

She folded her arms across her chest. "What would the centurion recommend?"

He took out his knife, hefted it once in the air so the hilt was facing her. "This be the Roman way."

"I am not a Roman."

Respect softened his grave expression. "I give you a minute, daughter."

"Centurion—"

"*Ja?*"

"Will you please shut the door? The moon has just risen. I want to enjoy it."

When this was done, she turned away from him and knelt toward the high window in the cell. The moonlight flowed down on her. Her hair glistened. She smiled.

There was nothing left to be done. It was time to don acceptance like a downy cloak. The Sibyl had given her fair warning: There would be no last-minute rescue. So Crispa put the unfinished business of this world out of her head—even the letter she had handed over to the young praetorian guarding her. These things no longer mattered.

But the moon—what a final joy it was.

Taking a deep breath, she prepared to plunge her spirit through the window and into the fathomless night. She felt it rising as if of its own accord. In minutes would come that sublime sailing over the Pontus Euxinus and the forests of Dacia to that small Scandian graveyard with its rickety headmarkers.

She was nearly through the window when she heard, from behind, her own voice say with gentle music in it, "Now, centurion."

Rolf found Germanicus in the procuratorial storeroom aboard the rail-galley, squatting on the deck in the darkness, trying to smother himself in a huge quaff of wine that left him choking when he finally came up for air. Germanicus' face bobbed slightly as he studied the form towering over him. "Where is your sword, centurion?"

"I broke that one."

"Why?"

"I broke that one, sir."

Germanicus drifted off into his thoughts like a man wading into a swamp.

"The wrapheads press us. More and more come down off the mountain."

"Yes."

"Your brother must be avenged."

"All are avenged. All. No more . . . avenging . . . is required."

"Then there be the duties of your office, sir!"

"Yes."

"Ach!" The centurion's fingers opened the spigot on the cask and an icy stream of wine splashed over Germanicus' face.

"What insolence!" Germanicus cried, sputtering.

Rolf's cheeks were slick with moisture. It was astonishing—like the first rain in centuries flowing over desert granite. "It be a tenth of what you show me."

Germanicus advanced to strike the man. But, with fist reared, he halted and suddenly seized Rolf by his oxlike shoulders. "This is too much for me. Don't you understand? I despair!"

"That be lucky for you."

"Lucky?!"

"Aye. What worse than to die with a belly full of hope?"

Germanicus seemed to cough once, but it was not a cough. A grim laugh was trying to push past his sorrow. "Are . . . are the barbarians forming beyond the throw of our *ballistae* again?"

"No, sir." The light came back to Rolf's eyes. "They be coming down the mountain behind us."

"Then let's get the lads away from the main wall. Have them face the right direction, what? Help me out of my cloak. It's wet. It will freeze in the night chill."

"Aye, Procurator."

CHAPTER XXII

WITH NO REGARD for their individual survival, the barbarians hurled themselves at the terrace. Squad after squad was decimated trying to clamber up the stairs and breach the Roman line, although the failure of each preceding attempt did nothing to deter the one that followed. The dead heaped up, forming a crude ramp that smoldered after each scorching by Greek fire.

Rolf had shouted so long in Germanicus' behalf his voice was reduced to a rasp. Like the legionaries he directed, the centurion had begun to stagger from exhaustion. His arms hung at his sides until he could marshal the strength to lift them to fight again for a few frantic seconds.

At five the moon collapsed behind the western ranges. Within minutes, unexplainably, the Roman defense gave at the center. It was as if the tenuous morale of the legionaries had depended on that heavenly light. "No, no, lads!" Germanicus bellowed, seizing men by the tunics with his free hand as they squirmed past him. "On the way back, you'll pay for these steps in twice the blood!" He himself could not fall back with his legionaries, although a mass of tribesmen pressed right up to the point of his short sword.

"Look behind you, sir!" a tribune said, grabbing him by the forearm to get his attention.

Germanicus could not believe it. On their own accord, the legionaries were forming into a line across the parade ground. It consisted of segments with fronts of about twenty men, six men deep, and was well over two hundred yards in length.

"That's the way, boys! Now stagger it a bit!"

The centurions and the veteran legionaries—those with gray flecked in their stubble—knew immediately what Germanicus wanted; they began bawling at their troops so that in short order the various segments of the line were staggered, with men of the second and third ranks protecting intervals in the line to their front. They faced the enemy in a kind of checkerboard pattern. It was the classical quincunx formation. It moved Germanicus that his men were so devoted to discipline that they halted in the midst of a flight to voluntarily execute what he himself was about to order. "Thank you, thank you," he croaked, although no one could hear.

Germanicus fell in among them. Their breaths were hot. Hands reached out to touch him as if for luck.

The sight before them must have confused the barbarians. They slowed their pace. Where before they had tried to hammer their vanguard through the narrowest wedge in the imperial line, they were now presented with a dozen or more tempting gaps. But why? The question twisted their dark faces. They soon knew the reason.

"Come forward for your breakfast, wrappies!" a salty voice mocked them from the ranks.

The barbarians discovered that those indentations that had seemed so inviting moments before were nothing more than traps bristling with Roman weaponry. The recessed part of the line blazed with a continuous array of *pili* fire, for upon emptying their pieces the foremost legionaries would turn back to reload and allow those waiting behind them to step up to discharge their *pili,* and then those behind them—until it occurred to those tribesmen not cut down on the spot that this polished mechanism would never stop visiting death upon them. To add to the carnage, the legionaries on the sides of the adjoining unit flicked at them with their swords and knives.

Then Germanicus felt a thrill. It began as a visceral fluttering and quickly crackled to the hairs on the back of his neck. The line had taken a step forward.

This gave the Romans what they had needed all along—a little breathing space. A smoky gulf yawned open between the two forces.

The barbarians were most deadly when they were united in a rash advance. But when bogged down by hesitation, they tended to cluster like quail, skittering in tight circles, clucking at one another, waiting for someone to give them direction.

On command, the legionaries staggered their formation anew—fresh segments surging forward to relieve their neighboring comrades.

A drum declared a tempo.

The Romans began pressing the barbarians, whose leaders became visibly desperate. The *zaim*'s lieutenants elbowed their way to the front. They cajoled and goaded their men to stand fast. "Paradise! Paradise!"—Germanicus could hear them shouting above the roar. And the most agitated of their number was Prince Sala. He raised his arms to the dark heavens and wailed a prayer. He yanked at his beard with his hands. But as his rage gusted him up and down the barbarian line, he came upon a cadre of tribesmen as fanatical as himself. These men wept and implored him for a chance to attack again. Ecstatically they joined Sala in one last charge against the Roman *pili*.

The legionaries around Germanicus did not cringe at the approach of this final wave. He heard Rolf say with satisfaction, "This be their last drop of spit."

The barbarians smashed through the first rank of legionaries, their blades whirling and sparking wherever they struck Roman steel. Germanicus felt himself being reeled backward. But at the same time the legionaries behind him were pushing forward to close with the enemy and end this eternal night.

Germanicus' lips itched with laughter.

He had no control over the direction he would take. This tide of human bodies flicked him about as if he were a cork. He finally let go. It had its way with him.

The side of his face was buzzing. The sensation was strong and peculiar. There was no real pain. Instead there was a powerful odor in his nostrils and mouth. It was as if someone had whipped him in the face with a bouquet of mint. He had the strange picture in his mind of blood being poured onto a white gown. "Ah," he said to himself in a small, sad voice.

"Now I understand." It became very quiet. There seemed to be no promise that anything might follow. The world had ground to a complacent halt. He thought he heard his mother singing. But it proved to be a man's high-pitched death scream. Then the darkness became a bass throbbing that pulsed in the marrow of his bones. This was pleasant. The darkness. And if this was what Jupiter willed, so be it. His expectations had trickled away. He really wanted nothing more. It was enough. The darkness.

CHAPTER XXIII

"I GOT TO have an answer right now," the praetorian centurion Stilicho said in a crusty voice outside the procuratorial car. His echo seemed to gain—not lose—volume as it rolled down the length of the subterranean station. "There's a mob of lads outside the stockade. I need orders. If Germanicus can no longer speak, who will then?"

The lanky tribune tried to shush him. This officer had the face of a sheep. Attached to the garrison engineers, he had always found comfort in his insignificance. But fate had jostled him onto the rostrum. Labienus was the highest ranking Agri Dagi officer to survive the night. "A bit of patience, centurion. Germanicus' doctor has . . ."

He stopped. A hefty dollop of blood had plummeted from the stone ceiling and splattered around their shins. Warmed by the sun, it had worked its way down through the cracks between the paving blocks of the parade ground above.

"Besides," Labienus continued, "I have no authorization to execute this prisoner."

"Make your own, tribune." Another drop of red splashed

at their feet. Stilicho's eyes rolled upward to indicate the yet
unburied human wreckage a few yards over their heads. "That
number-one wrappie knew damned well what would happen
to his son if he hit us. It's time to give him his dose."

"There's no doubt the law must be satisfied. But still, I
have no authorization. Wait until the procurator recovers his
senses."

"What if he don't? Germanicus could spend the rest of his
days as quiet as a cabbage. I seen it so with legionaries what
had less a head wound." The air rumbled out of Stilicho's
nostrils in a noisy snort. "What's the word, tribune?"

The engineer rolled his bottom lip between his teeth. "Let
me put the question to him one more time."

Stilicho gestured for the man to lead the way. Through the
morning calm, a cross being hammered together could be heard.

Germanicus sat in a slump at the foot of his bed, arms dangling
into his lap. The silk sheets were red with his blood; they were
rippled like some crimson tide on which Epizelus had fretted
to keep his procurator's life afloat. Germanicus stared over his
shoulder at this sea, his eyes listless, slight snores escaping his
mouth. A sutured cut showed through a shaved patch on the
side of his head.

From the corner came a gentle *grist-grist-grist* noise as
Epizelus reduced some material to powder with mortar and
pestle.

"Procurator..." the tribune whispered.

Epizelus rebuked the intruders with his gaze but said nothing. He too was exhausted.

"Sir, there is a matter...we beg your attention..."

Germanicus did not stir.

"The men, sir—they've learned the *zaim*'s son is locked
up in our stockade...."

"It's their morale what worries me, Procurator," Stilicho
butted in. "There ain't enough officers among us to carry a
basket with four handles. And what's to consider? This here
execution is a perfectly right thing to do...."

Germanicus tried to steady his vision against the sight, but the
figure he saw shimmered and rippled in the unearthly light as
if the air had become some murky liquid disturbed by eddies.

He reached out his hand to touch it, but the thing floated in retreat exactly as far as Germanicus had extended his arm. "Who are you?"

The skin was like that of a drowned man Germanicus had seen washed ashore after a week of bobbing off Capri. It was utterly colorless. But the bald pate, sensitive lips, and weak feminine chin suggested an impression that went beyond the familiar; they advertised the famous. "Are you... Gaius Julius!"

The figure nodded with princely grace. It wore a smile that was undisturbed by passion.

Germanicus wanted to hide his face.

Before him was the man who had strode into the jackals' den of treachery and intrigue that was ancient Gaul—yet never lost his serene balance no matter how violently fate had howled at him. This past week in Agri Dagi would have been nothing more than a somewhat busy interlude between real campaigns to Gaius Julius Caesar. *How much less we are than our fore-fathers*, Germanicus thought, once again trying to touch the phantom, which again passively drifted back. "Speak to me, Caesar. Or am I so frail and humble I can't even hear the octave at which you speak?"

Caesar motioned for Germanicus to follow, but Germanicus shook his head no.

Then Caesar sailed through the bulkhead as if his pale body were a cloud.

"'It is easier to find men who will voluntarily risk death than men who will bear suffering patiently,'" Germanicus whispered, quoting from *The Conquest of Gaul,* hearing the schoolboy's voice that had once been his—but noting that there was no levity in it, no chipper pride in flawless recitation. The words had lost their virginity, and now the boy and the man were bound as one in a marriage of grief. Germanicus knew this was so, for he could no longer recall having ever been happy.

He longed to follow Caesar through that invisible rift into eternity.

Then he saw that he was not alone. Before him was a tribune he did not know, a praetorian centurion, and Epizelus.

• • •

"Look here, Procurator," Stilicho said as if he were addressing an old and feeble man. "If you object, give us a sign. A nod or a blink of the eye, yes? Otherwise, we take it that you want the wrappie crucified."

Germanicus did not move a muscle.

"Well, there you have it." Stilicho slapped the armor over his belly. "I'll pass on the procurator's order myself."

"No."

All eyes turned on Germanicus' mouth. The centurion's lower jaw hung halfway to his chest. "What is that, sir?"

"No."

The ceramic mortar slipped out of Epizelus' fingers and struck the deck.

Stilicho remembered himself and saluted. "But sir, the law demands—"

"The law needs no more flesh—not for a long time." Unsteadily, quickly offered an arm by Stilicho, Germanicus came to his feet. "How fares the Emperor?"

"No word, sir."

"Where is my centurion?"

"The German, sir?"

"Yes."

"On patrol. They've gone to take a look-see where the Great Artery's been blasted."

"Have our dead been cremated yet?"

"No, sir—there are so many."

Germanicus tested the side of his head and winced. "Colonel Crispa—I want . . ." He hesitated to keep his voice even. "Her ashes. Bring them to me after . . ."

When nothing more followed, Stilicho said quietly, "Very well, sir."

"It's time for me to get back to Nova Antiochia."

"Yes, sir, but the *zaim*'s boy—"

"Release the boy. Guarantee him safe conduct out of the garrison."

CHAPTER XXIV

IN THE EARLY afternoon Germanicus marched with his staff
and a century of legionaries down the maintenance trace that
ran beside the Great Artery. Overhead was a golden winter
sun. Its light flowed down like honey, making the mountain
country appear amber and warm. At first he thought that this
was melting the heaviness in his chest. But then he recalled
that Epizelus had given him a potion to relieve his persistent
melancholy and fortify him for the march.

A rail-galley was being dispatched from the Mus Station to
pick up the procuratorial party at a point west of the damage
the barbarians had done to the line during the night. From there
it was back to his headquarters for Germanicus.

Cradled in his arms, tapping his ceremonial armor with each
move he made, was a delicate urn of alabaster. Once, when
he thought no one was looking at him, he touched his lips to
the cool, smooth surface of the lid. When he glanced up, Rolf
was staring at him. The centurion abruptly quickened his pace
and soon joined the vanguard, dipping in and out of sight as
they slogged along the contours of the canyon.

"I know, my friend—I know," Germanicus said to him, although the German was far out of earshot by now.

Minutes later Germanicus saw Rolf and the other legionaries rear back in surprise. They sought cover in the snow, their *pili* at the ready.

"Support them," Germanicus called to the legionaries who formed his bodyguard. Reluctant to leave his side, they trotted down the trace and deployed among the weathered trestles above the vanguard.

"Is it an ambush?" Epizelus asked, hugging his bag of instruments and herbs as if the barbarians might snatch it from him any second.

Germanicus made no answer but to smile wanly.

Rolf came loping back up, slipping every few yards, using the stock of his *pilum* to keep from falling. "Procurator, a wrappie be standing below. He hold the imperial colors on a staff."

Germanicus understood this to be a sign of truce. "What does he propose?"

"A meeting 'tween you and a man from their *zaim.*"

Suddenly the light seemed hard, and the rocky slopes as treacherous as ever. Germanicus scanned for snipers, then resisted his own caution with a vengeance. "Tell him I come."

Epizelus fumed. "Use your head, man!"

"I am, good Greek. The danger is acceptable. I've taken a thousand risks to make war. Is it too much to take just one for the sake of peace?"

Germanicus' decision threw Rolf into fits. He argued so forcefully his sword rattled in its metal sheath. But in the end there was nothing for him to do but follow Germanicus up the slick mountainside to the promontory where it was agreed the parlay would be held. They halted. The two barbarians opposite them halted.

"This be madness," Rolf said as Germanicus stepped forward, still holding his precious urn.

"Yes, this be madness."

At the same instant a barbarian with regal bearing left the side of his bodyguard and moved resolutely toward Germanicus. The hood to his *haik* was snugged around his face so his features were half hidden. The two men continued to bear down

on each other until there was no more than an arm's length
between them.

The wind soughed as if it were making introductions.

Germanicus returned the gaze of the dark, intelligent eyes.
"It has been a bad night. Tell your *zaim* I want no more like
this one."

"He knew that from the beginning, *pasa*." The barbarian
opened the hood just enough to make his identity known. "But
the world is not ours to control. Even the exalted cannot move
the stars an inch—but that you shall find out."

Germanicus had a powerful, inexplicable urge to cry. For
the first time it seemed that there was majesty and not shame
in such an act. "It gives me joy that you live."

"I, too, rejoice."

"Do you think I could have killed Khalid? I lost a son."

"It is not for my son's release I rejoice," the *zaim* snapped
back at him, eyes now fiery.

"Why, then?"

"We are on the verge of a new world—and my son will
stand at your side as it is established. This is written."

"What does this mean?"

"You shall know soon enough, *pasa*. The knowledge was
not mine until my blessed *shaykh* told me that night in our
mosque. But it is possible to serve God in ignorance as well
as light." He reached out and gently stroked the urn. "What
do you carry?"

Germanicus tried to speak but his eyes loaded with tears.

"Might this be your heart, *pasa*?"

He nodded fiercely.

The *zaim* touched the side of the Roman's face. Intense heat
emanated from his palm. "Dispose of it. God demands obedience of us. Not a heart." Then he turned to leave.

"Wait," Germanicus rasped.

The *zaim* glowered back.

"What of the peace?"

"There will never be a peace. The word itself is but a Roman
dream, *pasa. Inshallah.*"

The haunting dusk of Agri Dagi—premature, yet so final it
could have passed for the disposition of the world—was elon-
gating the shadows cast by the members of the party when

Germanicus called a rest. Here a copse of stark birches hugged the Great Artery. He studied this lonely place for several minutes in silence, then called for one of the legionaries from the garrison.

"Sir?" The soldier had a bandaged ear. Being singled out unnerved him.

"Tell me—what is this place like in spring?"

"Just a bit of Anatolia, sir."

"Any grass?"

"Oh, yes, a nice little meadow to the right of the trees there. A brook there—but no deeper than my knife."

"And these birches—do they shimmer in the summer light?"

"I suppose they do, sir. I never noticed."

"Walk on," Germanicus said crossly. "All of you, get on your way."

When they were gone a short distance, he uncapped the urn. He ran his forefinger through the soft, dry ashes. He looked for some recognizable part of her in the dusty sheen that clung to his nail. Then he began sprinkling her remains over the snow. The blackened flakes of bone sank swiftly into the drift. Finally Germanicus broke the urn with his sword and scattered the pieces.

Rolf was patiently waiting for Germanicus when he marched out of the birches. They studied each other for a long moment.

"Be wary, Germanicus Agricola."

"What do you mean?"

"Come see."

They mounted a ridge that afforded a view of the broad valley below. In the last gilt light Germanicus could see an ornate rail-galley draped across the plain like a golden necklace. Its windows sparkled cheerfully. Somehow this deepened his sadness.

"That be Fabius'."

"I know," Germanicus said.

Rolf bruised the frozen ground with the toe of his boot. "There be a rumor..."

"Out with it."

"The Emperor be here."

"Off his deathbed—straight to Anatolia?"

"Aye, rage has given him new wings, the lads say. He come to kill all in this command. The innocent and the guilty together."

"What do you think of this rumor?"

"It be possible."

Germanicus gave the order. The century of legionaries and his own staff fell into marching order—but only four abreast so they presented as narrow as possible a target to the *ballistae* of the Emperor's rail-galley. Then they began stamping down a rolling slope that was scruffy with knee-high brush. "Hold your heads high, lads," Germanicus said. "You have fought well for his honor."

It was a long train of at least fifty cars, including two huge siege *ballistae* that swiveled toward the procuratorial party with alarming swiftness, although their muzzles remained elevated. The lights aboard blinked out, and at the same moment hundreds of praetorians began streaming out of the cars. Germanicus' experienced eye marked the strength of these polished professionals as a full cohort—six hundred men. It was the imperial household guard—Caesar's own.

Their officers divided them into two pincers that raced like spilled quicksilver on both flanks of Germanicus' modest force. "Keep heart—and your heads," Germanicus encouraged his people, although it personally disquieted him to watch this well-oiled praetorian machine encircling him. The gap was closed, and the legionaries within the circle took on the browbeaten look of prisoners.

"Look at what them guards do now!" a teenage legionary cried before he could check himself.

Indeed, it was baffling—each man of the praetorian perimeter turned his back on Germanicus' party, whose feelings went from terror to indignation. "Show us your butts, will you?"

"At ease," Germanicus growled.

"What be their game?" Rolf was trying to keep surveillance on every direction at once. His head snapped from side to side like a hawk's.

Germanicus pointed at a contingent of praetorians running briskly toward them from the rail-galley. "We'll know directly."

"Is that a senator with them?" a corporal asked in astonishment from the ranks.

"It is! It is!" someone else piped up. "I see purple on his toga!"

"Does all Rome want our blood?"

Germanicus faced his people. "It's me they want. Not you.

Throw down your weapons. I will not spill your blood in my behalf."

No one budged.

"Throw them down!" Germanicus raved. "Down!"

There was the clatter of *pili* and swords striking the rocky ground. An impudent Rolf stood away from the others, arms crossed over his chest. He still bore his weapons. He snorted once. His mustaches rippled from nostril to tip.

But Germanicus had no time to chastise him. The praetorian contingent arrived and arrayed itself in a line as neat as any he had ever seen at the Campus Martius. A colonel, as lean and elegant as an icicle, marched forward and saluted with precision. "Hail Caesar!"

"Hail Caesar!" Germanicus responded. "And how is he?"

Confusion flickered in the colonel's eyes for a moment. "Fabius is—dead, sir."

"Dead?"

"For more than twenty hours now, sir. It has been a state secret, but we sent a message to Agri Dagi this afternoon."

"I was already in the field." Germanicus closed his eyes and saw the man who had been the most powerful in the world in a more intimate light—his cousin, who had despised his growing paunch and laughed much too loudly at crude jokes. "Who is his successor?"

"Why, you—Germanicus Julius Agricola—as confirmed by the Senate and approved by the guard."

Germanicus' cheeks turned to white marble. "Is the royal family so destroyed?"

"I'm afraid it is, Caesar," the senator said. His name was Fortis, and Germanicus had always known him to be honorable, if not verbose. "A bloodbath that has sluiced the Julians down to their bedrock."

The colonel gestured toward the rail-galley. "We have come to guarantee your safe return to Rome. Caesar—"

Germanicus nearly jumped out of his skin as the massed praetorians, the survivors of Agri Dagi, and his own dazed staff cried in unison, "Hail Caesar!"

CHAPTER XXV

HOW WARM. How deliciously warm. How incongruously warm.

I must learn to enjoy things such as these with my entire spirit—this balmy Mediterranean morning, the towering cypress whipping its top in the breeze like a green coxcomb, the cool stone bench beneath me—and have no active regard for all the rest. I must be as imperturbable as poor Virgilia, who, three days before I arrived back in Rome, sank into a coma with no bottom to its dreamless depths.

Germanicus jerked up from his thoughts as boots scraped toward him across a marble path.

How quickly I forget my own firm resolutions!

Germanicus forced himself to continue his meditation of the Tellus Mater bas-relief on the Ara Pacis. But it was no good. The footfalls became louder and louder.

Then Palantinus, the praetorian prefect, rounded the cypress and saluted. He had given himself this name to crow that he was as firmly implanted in the Roman mainstream as the Palantine Hill. "Hail Caesar!"

"Good morning." *What a cobra of a man,* Germanicus

thought with revulsion—even down to his yellowish, reptilian eyes. But one needs a cobra for an ally when one lives in a pit of coiled vipers. And such a pit was Rome.

"Caesar, I must broach a delicate matter with you."

"Another recommendation for some aspirant to public office?"

"No sir—nothing like that." He perched a white envelope on his fingertips as if it were a dove. "It concerns—this."

"What is it?"

Palantinus hesitated before handing it over. "Two of my guards at Agri Dagi confiscated it. Their intentions were good. I ask you to recall that this was during the desperate hours of the conspiracy. They feared it might hold some clues to the identity of the traitors."

"Who wrote it?"

"Colonel Crispa. It was addressed to you."

Germanicus catapulted to his feet. It was as if he had been pricked by one of her hairpins. His eyes smarted and his hands trembled so terribly he could not read it. "Have you read . . . ?"

Palantinus was no fool to lie when he was expected to do just that. "I'm sorry, sir. I perused it for security concerns. I had no idea . . ." He purposely let his voice trail off.

"I count on your discretion."

Palantinus smacked his heels together. "It goes without saying, Caesar."

"Leave me."

With tremendous effort Germanicus steadied his grasp. This thin slip of paper had more magic in it than a mountain of talismans. It had the godly power to bring the dead back to life and let them speak once again. His head was filled with her scent, his ears with her voice:

My darling Germanicus,

As you read this, I'm already dead. Dead! How will I stand this temporary separation from you?

Two hours in the stockade have done something two days in Poppaeus' sewer could never do. They've cleared my head. How can I ever explain our last horrible minutes together? Poor Marcellus. I've had the misfortune of loving both the raven and the eagle, and although it must be expected that I'd feel the loss of either with equal pain, I've never lost the vision that tells me which soars higher in my heart.

I love you. Agri Dagi did not lessen that by one grain of crystal-hard passion.

Time! There's so little of it left for me! And so much to tell!

Last summer, I was summoned by the Sibyl at Ephesus, who had heard of my talents. She treated me like a daughter and said she'd entrust me with a great oracle— if I had the stomach to hear it. How foolish I was to have leaped at the chance. I could have feasted on the lotus blossom of hope all these months!

The oracle:

Germanicus Julius Agricola will become Caesar in the light of a full winter moon!

My heart raced with ecstasy—and faster yet when she declared you would leave a bigger mark on the world than Alexander or Augustus. Such fantastic things I know, Germanicus. And no time to tell you!

You will make a great conquest in the Novo Provinces and banish abomination from an island city. But more than that, my dearest Germanicus, your present sadness and solemn piety will serve you well. For the oracle insists that from a new Leonidas will spring greater gentleness in the universe—a quiet voice against depravity.

If ever during these past days I became cross with you it was only because I too am human and lost sight of this promise in a fog of depression. And for one black moment, I saw only your habits—not your splendid substance, which I worship with all my soul!

And if only you might find the tenderness to forgive me. From the beginning, it was ordained that each of us would play our part down to the last syllable. I despise the monster Fabius, but I have no better regard for his witch of an Empress. I did my part because I was born to do it. My only consolation will be your splendid reign to follow.

The *massing* was never against you. It nearly broke my heart when you fancied that you were the object of the world's fury. No, it was Fabius! Always Fabius! The barbarians you saw kneeling to the west were pointing toward Rome—not Nova Antiochia.

Did the *massing* work? Even if Fabius dies, only the gods will know for sure.

Germanicus, mankind yearns for freedom even more than bread and order—but I already know that it will be in the Novo Provinces that you will learn this—and from a woman with skin like copper. You'll come to love her. That I might fly over the huge sea and merge my soul with hers! For this love shall be consummated under a night as deep and cold as a mountain spring.

The guards are whispering down the hall. How I hate praetorians!

I've accepted every barb in the oracle but this—that my ashes must be left here in Anatolia. Please bear them to that place—I don't really know where, but it's where you've hidden your son's. Yes, I slipped that secret from your mind during these long years. Don't think I've constantly violated your privacy with my powers. That is not possible. It's only because you dwelled so often on the bitter loss. In truth, I will not be there, but it warms me now to think you will have a link with that which you once loved. There, in the shaded, salted air— wherever it is—I am assured of your occasional attention. And I will be happy.

I'm afraid I have no more time. I know whose feet are approaching, shuffling with reluctance.

Hail Caesar!

> With all my love, my love, my love
> Crispa

Germanicus looked up. A training century was marching past on the green before him. Sprinkled among the peach-faced boys were a few young women, some of whom seemed agonizingly lovely in the morning light, especially those with flaxen hair.

Caesar wept.